Pride of A Nameless Nation

Pride of A Nameless Nation

Where Love gets Muddied in Duty.

Daniel Mistir

Mistir's Messages

Published 2025
Printed in the United States of America
ISBN: 979-8-218-58288-3

Cover Design by Miguel Parisi
Interior Design by Daniel Mistir

For Information, address:
Mistir's Messages
Mistirsmessages@gmail.com
Los Angeles, CA

Dedicated to the oral storytellers who pass the lessons of life along, who make the best of time spent with people.

PREFACE

The events of this story take place in a fantastical and fictional world where five kingdoms rule the known world. Most of this story takes place in what is now Southern Europe, Northeast Africa, and Asia.

The period this story takes place would be around 10 A.D.

The story is split into vignettes, shifting POV constantly, but everything unfolding pertains to the protagonist, Prince Edjer. Shifts in time within the story correlate to *the Ceremony*, a peace accord in which five kingdoms will meet and hopefully come to a peace agreement.

Found family clashes with the fortitude of duty in this story. The main question posed throughout is: *Is a nation or country its people, or the land it sits on?*

Enjoy.

PROLOGUE

The Prince's dagger moved swiftly through the air. Sweat profusely ran down his face. He yelled with each ferocious and failing strike, wishing to land a blow while his screams overtook the quiet hall. He was filled with anger only a demon could hold.

Yet, she deflected each blow. The Queen was as formidable, as ferocious as her counterpart, the Prince.

But before long, the Prince's dagger sliced the Queen's skin. He slashed her back with his dagger repeatedly.

The Queen grimaced as she knelt.

She looked at him. Despite the Prince's anger, a line had been crossed. An awareness of the escalation stole the moment. They became still.

She no longer wished to simply defend her position, but instead attack the Prince.

Another witnessed the horrific events.

The King watched carefully. He was speechless, for he could not call his guards, or both his wife and brother, whom he loved dearly, would face death. Despite his crown, he was powerless in that moment. He knew not which side he wished to prevail. Either death would bring destruction. He wished only for the battle to end.

But the Prince was heartbroken. None could reason with his passion.

The fight took a turn. The Queen made a critical error and lost her sword. The Prince batted it away, prepared to kill her. His slight hesitation provided the Queen with a moment to remove a dagger from her thigh.

She struck the Prince's abdomen before looking into his empty eyes. Pain, that of a broken heart, stared back at her.

In her own gaze, The Prince found a mirrored agony.

The King turned silent watching their shared look. His wife's blade held still inside the Prince's flesh.

As she retracted her blade, fear took hold of The King. His brother, the Prince, still lived.

ONE

40 days until the Ceremony.

King Umid wishes his message to be read aloud to all our siblings:

Prince, I have never called him. Yet, he is your Prince, and as such, treat him according to his station when he returns.

He is a royal to our kingdom Perfuga, but to our enemies, he is the Prince of Death. The name is fascinating, but it is one he abhors as you know. The name is like morning haze over the seas, clouding the truth of the brewing waves below.

The name is menacing. I, like all of you, believe our brother deservedly earned it.

It is the reason I have chosen to end his exile. He is under the protection of the crown and will be given the full power of the title he once held. Prince Edjer shall make his return in less than a fortnight. He will be needed to protect our Ceremony.

I know no Prince of Death. Prince, I have never called him. When we were young, all of us refugees during the Great War, he was the first to acknowledge me, wiping blood from my face, clearing tears from my eyes. Edjer ripped his shirt, instructing a boy who had just lost his parents, he would always have ears to listen, he would be a brother for posterity.

I declare to you now, again, Prince Edjer's exile has come to an end. Many of you fear what that will mean. As his exile remains a secret, his return is due to the Ceremony's requirements.

We face a threat in our peace talks. Prince Edjer is one man I can trust to protect us.

Tomias, The Royal Scribe
To the Children, Ordered by King Umid

TWO

100 days until the Ceremony.

She was frozen, suspended in the air by lockets connected to the walls. Her thoughts lay as stagnant as her body.

An icy coolness seeped into the room. She hung near the back wall. Chains on her hands tore through her soft skin. She did not let the pain turn her face into anguish, nor did she fear the death that could follow a night's rest in her condition.

Soldiers bearing the green colors of their kingdom had done a number on her. The breeze in the room nipped at her deep wounds. Dried blood shrouded her back, cemented in the place where it once flowed.

She survived the lashes, denying her captors the satisfaction they desired. They neither knew of her deathly pain, nor the truth of the information they had recently attained. She remained as they found her, still.

A Silver Bear sigil sat alone on hunter green flags. Two flags were displayed on each side of the room, as well as a large one behind the hanging woman.

Two men, noblemen, princes, watched her without remorse. Her silence in the face of gorging pain spoke volumes of who hung in front of them. They waited for a sign.

One man, Semjaza, the leader, did not pester the woman as he watched her. He was as distinguished as a prince could be. His pristine, ivory white robes matched the milky complexion of his skin. His robes masked the scars of an aged warrior. He was focused, he knew what could be won with a victory against the woman. As she brought her head to her shoulder, he watched, angling his head with hers.

Lomotos, his brother, marveled at the woman's bravery. He was a burly man, tall, stained with confidence of a glorified warrior. His long, ponytailed hair was coupled with an untamed beard. He comfortably ate and drank in front of her, trying to break her through hunger.

She did not wither, as he ate and spoke inaudible words to her.

The woman, before the brutality, had once been a beauty to behold. She hung now, diminished, and broke down. Her dark skin was stained with acts of cruelty. She had hung for endless nights, above a fire from a pit brewing below, scorching her feet. Her feet had bubbled and broke out into the whitest of sores. Yet through the burns, she had persisted.

The men watching her sat on their golden cushions, eating, believing her surrender was near. She had been given time to think of her trials before the torture began again. They masked their urgency with a cemented table full of royal chalices, wine filled to the brim, a complete royal spread. Their prisoner was unaware of the timely manner in which the information was needed. She did not know about any Ceremony. This was a secret to be kept. If made aware of a time constraint, the two men knew her silence would never end.

The doors opened, and all, even the woman hanging, focused their gaze upon a regular visitor of the proceedings. The ruler of the Bear Kingdom, Azazel, walked in with his wife Liliah. They sat in silence for a moment before eying the hanging woman.

Finally, all the royals of the Bear Kingdom were present.

"Why continue, brother? We have what we seek," uttered Azazel.

Semjaza was focused watching the woman cook over the fire. "Do not overlook the need for confirmation, brother," replied Semjaza.

"Preparations have been made."

Semjaza chose not to respond to Azazel.

Liliah approached the woman, smiling. She was the architect of the woman's capture. Her attention to detail, her planning, had brought about destruction. As Liliah inched closer, the chains felt unbearable to the woman.

"My dear, time is neither an aid nor an ally. Speak to the information whispered to me, so these cautious men may sleep. You would find rest," inquired Liliah.

The woman looked down. She was speechless, but her piercing look spoke for her. Liliah turned away.

"My lady, you must know, not a soul lives that knows of your condition. Ghosts have no family," said Lomotos, stroking his beard.

Semjaza, as his kin circled the table of wine and refreshments, remained silent. He watched patiently. Threats and promises were useless. He respected the woman. He was angry that his citizenry, his people, lacked the resolve of the prisoner hung in front of him. His lands demanded a need for people with strength like the dangling woman. He deeply wished to restore his home to its lost prosperity.

There was a plan. His plan. The plot called for perfection, and to sit patiently for confirmation was an easy payment for the prize to come. Those who were to be killed and destroyed were but an obstacle. There were others, whose pain and torment were necessary for the Bear to achieve their goal. To the man in the robes, the dangling woman need not suffer, but she blocked the path to the people he wished to defeat.

"I can offer an alternative to pain." Semjaza spoke to her for the first time in days.

"You do not need to offer anything outside of pain to this woman," interjected Liliah.

Semjaza turned: "Cruelty is useless here. Diplomacy is required."

They all focused on Semjaza, dressed in distinguished white robes, the old attire of the Bear Kingdom's princes. King Azazel was a figurehead, and he, along with the rest in the room, knew his role.

Semjaza was the pride of the Bear, the keeper of power in both voice and standing in the Bear Kingdom, a sworn enemy of Perfuga.

"I will let one live once I capture what I desire, that is what I can offer. I will let one live." Prince Semjaza spoke with confidence.

The words pressed against the woman in the cool air. She was colder than ever before. She was more afraid than she had been when they had found her. Her breathing turned abnormal, as the thought of retribution returned to her. She betrayed her stoicism.

Her head gingerly rose to speak before falling. The sign was clear, a confirmation Semjaza had to settle for. He returned to his seat.

Tears trailed down her puffed, bloodied cheeks, knowing she had overplayed her hand.

"*Aghfar li,*" she whispered. *Forgive me.*

THREE

33 days until the ceremony.

"Children, please, let us conclude our lesson."

The children spoke all at once. Word spread worse than wildfire. They had seen him. Many dared to peek through the leaves, passing the message to their cohorts quickly, hoping for a glimpse of him.

"Class, *please?*" pleaded the Headmistress.

A boy in the back proudly raised his hand. He was the first to see it.

"Teacher, the Prince is here," whispered the boy.

Prince Edjer watched the class from under a tree, eyeing the children and Headmistress closely.

The class was held in the Perfugan palace. Lessons were always conducted in the hallways of an open courtyard, with a view of the Old Garden. A golden wall covered one side, where pearled poles, opposite the wall, formed an open frame to the gardens. The courtyard itself was encircled by hallways. It served as an attraction to traveling dignitaries, where the world could see the diverse and exuberant gardens. The peaceful serenity of the wildlife rivaled that of divine and sanctimonious times.

The students had been seated under the awnings for years, watching honorable guests and royals walk through.

Yet, they had never seen the Prince of Death.

The Royal Guards in the back of the class rarely intruded on the lessons. They were distinguished men, known for their stoic expressions. They, like soldiers of the king, wore black attire, with gold traced along the trim of their garments. In the middle of their robes was stitched a single sword dug into the sand, shaded in gold. They did not wish to deviate from their task, but they themselves wanted to obtain a look of the mysterious Prince Edjer, struggling to hold their impulse in check.

"Class, sit. You will be forced to recite if you continue to interrupt."

Headmistress Manissa tried to control her students. The bronze woman oversaw their education and welfare. She was slender, tall, with dark black hair, wavy, like silk. She, also, was Edjer's sister.

"Guards," she pleaded.

"Students!" shouted the guards. The students quickly sat and quieted down.

Prince Edjer hid behind the mirage of inverted tulips and irises. None could see him outright.

"Teacher, can we hear the story again, please?" asked the boy in the back. His mahogany palms came down after his question.

Manissa looked towards the garden, searching for the face of her lost brother.

"You all must recite on the morrow; do I have your word?" asked Headmistress Manissa.

They smiled, nodding. "Yes," replied the boy.

The students, together, shifted inwards, like an arrow, pointing at her.

"The inception of this school, that teaches you students, it is a known story."

Manissa wore a black dress. The cloth fell to her ankles and gripped her arms down to her wrist. She slowly knelt, creasing the seams.

"We were known as *The Children*. I, with forty others, none older than thirteen, were the first refugees ever allowed into Perfuga. We were watched closely. Our progress was important to politics. Perfugans debated the question: were we worth opening the borders?"

Edjer inched closer to the class. She dove deep into a tale he had not heard in years.

"We struggled as a collective. And if one struggled, all struggled. One did not eat unless others ate, one did not study unless others studied. Our first Headmistress was patient with us. She watched us every day from the garden as we learned what she wished for us."

The Children had traveled through deserts and wastelands destroyed by the old Great War between the kingdoms. Edjer, at the age of thirteen, had led children to Perfuga, a well-known land of peace back then. On arrival, he had pleaded for mercy and citizenship. The plea had forced Perfuga to open its borders to all refugees fleeing the war twenty-five years ago.

The decision had changed Perfuga's fortunes.

"Our journey began in an unknown land in the south and took years to complete. We began with seventy-six children. Only forty-one survived. All forty-one, we are brothers and sisters to one another. But to others, we are, *The Children*.

"The king and queen in those times could not bear a child. When they looked out of the palace window, they saw forty-one of us who would die for them. However, they could not afford a bloodbath with forty-one heirs. That is what we told ourselves when they chose to adopt Prince Edjer and King Umid," said the Headmistress, smiling, eyeing Edjer in the garden.

"When Perfuga took my two brothers as its princes, people were proud. The two became known throughout the kingdoms as the Two-Headed Beast.

"They were nearly the same age, twelve and thirteen, when we arrived. One was given the knowledge to rule, for the purpose of ending strife. The other, he was trained with the fortitude to endure, to destroy, to kill. But his role was to protect, to end all war."

Her last words lost the mystique of a talebearer. The heart's truth took hold: "Now with age and wisdom, they rule and fight to serve us. If you students would listen and study, you could rise in rank as they did," concluded the teacher.

A woman in the back clapped. Her intrusion surprised the students as well as the guards.

Queen Niobe wore the same dress as the Headmistress, but with gold bracelets, and a crown-like band in her hair. Her clear, golden skin matched the radiance of her sizable hazel eyes. Her dress was sleeveless, however, leaving her toned arms exposed, where the mark of a purple flower lay on her outer palm, the stem of the tattoo rising to the halfway point of her forearm. She watched with fallacious joy as the kids heard the famed story.

All rose at first sight of her.

"Please, children, be seated."

Niobe motioned towards the garden. She calmed her anxiety as she looked towards the garden, unafraid, dismissive: "He is ready for you."

Prince Edjer's ebony skin shined through the bright frame of his white robes, outlined in gold. The students watched his large, overstressed eyes avoid theirs. He motioned slowly towards the class before ascending atop steps that led inside the palace. Throughout his stride, he dropped his head low, in shame.

Edjer stopped once he reached Niobe. He refused to look at her.

"Niobe," he whispered and bowed, hiding his disdain.

"Edjer," replied Niobe. She then turned towards Manissa. "Apologies for the interruption, Manissa."

"Not a problem, *my Queen*."

The formality warned Niobe to an attitude from her Headmistress. Niobe smiled it off before trailing her palace guest.

Prince Edjer's steps were sluggish through the palace. He looked down, wishing not to see much of the home he grew up in.

Extravagant designs painted by the hands of children in previous classroom cohorts covered the first floor. It was the creativity of palace orphans. Murals of past kings, drawings of cities and kingdoms covered the palace in fluorescent paints.

The long hallway led to a staircase. There were doors between the murals leading to various quarters. The cooks prepared the meals on this level. The smell of boiled chicken and fresh bread infused the space. Housekeepers washed linens and stored amenities on the floor. They were quiet. Some peeked through to watch the Prince who once roamed the halls, a ghost now, walk the path to his brother's chambers. Few were brave enough to share pleasantries, bold enough to speak. Bravery was rewarded, graced with his uneasy smile.

As Niobe and Edjer made their way to the palace stairs, the walls dimmed in creation.

Niobe watched Edjer closely. She knew him, she had suffered with him. Niobe not only trained with Edjer, but she had also ventured hundreds of miles in the wilderness decades ago with him and the rest of *The Children*. Their bonds were forged.

Yet, she despised the way others worshipped him. She knew what Edjer represented.

"I was told to take you first to the council room."

"May I see my sisters?"

Her jaws clenched. They were on the steps, nearing the third floor of the behemoth. She ignored the question and moved forward. They were floors away from the top.

The tower housed the King. The chambers held the bed he and Niobe shared, while the floors below were left to traveling dignitaries. The healers and Headmistress shared the palace with the royals, while the orphan children lived in another building.

"He wishes you to first make your presence known to the Inner Council."

The Council Room had not changed since the years Edjer and his brother King Umid first snuck into the room as teens to prepare for their future. The room was designed to hold the close advisors to the king at a cement table, enormous enough to plan out campaigns and treaties. The table sat six, yet the smooth surface could hold the spread of a royal wedding. Silk coverings shrouded the chairs in the kingdom's regalia, the sigil of a sword dug deep in the sand.

A golden sword was stitched upon black silk on the chairs of advisors, whilst white silk was placed on the king's and Edjer's seat.

Members of the Inner Council looked up at Edjer's rugged face with mixed emotions. The room had a door in the back, past the table, which led to King Umid's chambers. Edjer needed first to get through the advisors before he could see his brother.

The first of the advisors, Alcaeus, sat nearest to the entrance. Edjer descended down three steps to match their ground, and after a few paces, he reached the table.

"Alcaeus."

"My Prince," said Alcaeus, in a pretentious manner. He rose as he spoke to Edjer.

Another advisor, seated across from Alcaeus, smiled at how Prince Edjer had grown.

"You smile as if I cannot smite you with my sword."

"The pupil must not forget the wit of his instructor," said the advisor, Myawi.

"Myawi, is your sword immune to rust?" replied Edjer. Edjer surprised himself, smiling, meeting Myawi's palm with his own. Edjer took his other hand, coupling his grip around his old mentor.

"I hear of a newcomer," said Myawi.

Edjer looked around. He did not wish to speak of the matter, but his respect of Myawi was too high to disregard the words. If Myawi felt safe to speak, he trusted him.

"We will welcome you; it has been some time for the both of us. He is on his last test."

They both smiled, reminiscing.

Near a window, sat an elderly man. He was not much older than Myawi or Alcaeus, but age had succumbed to grief. He sat near the window, his gaze plastered on the classroom below. The man watched as the students were dismissed. He had seen Edjer walk in but did not let his attention stray from the class.

Behind the seated man, was a large guard, similar in features to Edjer. He was a man of dark complexion. Scars could be seen on his arms from his sleeveless robes. He had no hair to accompany a face of focus. His piercing eyes stayed with the elderly man. He was the man's protector, a watcher of sorts.

"Demetrius." Edjer nodded to the guardian.

"Edjer," replied Demetrius, his brother, bowing his head. *The Children were everywhere in Perfuga.*

Edjer knelt. He eyed the old man, watching for a moment, seeing how the face of the stalwart was stained with a dry beard. The man's hair had yet to be washed, and a stench of the night's prior stupor stuck to the man.

"Uncle," said Edjer.

The old man, Edjer's uncle, turned. He had lost weight since Edjer had seen him last. Taking in his nephew, the man felt shame. He put his hand on Edjer's face.

"The prince returns," said Jabez. He was the brother of the king who had adopted Edjer and Umid.

"I have not seen you in some years, Uncle," replied Edjer.

"It is better you have not, the years have yet to show their kindness. Demetrius does what he can, but I am an ailment to his life."

"Do not speak like that, sire," interjected Demetrius.

Edjer and Demetrius shared a quick look, bringing a smile to Jabez's face. He tapped Edjer's shoulder, signaling him to go see Umid.

Edjer walked past them all, nodding to the scribe in the corner who took the notes for the royals. Tomias, the scribe, looked upon Edjer with reverence before nodding.

Following the exchanges, Edjer found himself in front of the chamber door. All watched for a glimpse of the initial reaction. In a kingdom built on rumors, many swirled as to the state of the once respected kinship between the brothers.

Once the door opened, Edjer walked through and shut it.

There was a desk by the chamber window, pressed against the back wall. The rugs in the room were black, with curtains shielding the bed, grayer now than the original white.

King Umid sat at his desk, cluttered with papers and amendments. He wrote in silence. His soft hands covered a scroll, the seal broken.

Edjer motioned past the bed to sit on a wooden chair. He waited for his brother in silence.

"There's a task I need done from you and your men."

As King Umid spoke, Edjer looked up. He noticed his brother's face had darkened. His eyes mirrored their uncle's. He smirked at how the soft white skin of both Jabez and Umid had wrinkled over the years.

"My soldiers are not prepared to negotiate a treaty with the Far East Empire."

Silence stole the room. These were the first words spoken between them in years.

"And your Royal Guards?" asked Edjer.

"They are ripe with anger. My Ceremony cannot be interrupted."

"Yes, *my king*."

King Umid stopped writing. His pen froze at Edjer's words, *my king*. He looked up to find his brother focused. Edjer's eyes were empty.

"A prince of the Far East Empire will meet you on a trading route tomorrow. It is less than a day's ride. I will have Tomias ride with you to obtain notes."

Edjer nodded at his orders, quiet.

Umid's impatience grew: "Your newcomer's coronation will have to wait."

Edjer's rigidness shook. An arrangement had been made to avoid disputes of this nature. "The boy is in his last test. If need be, our Uncle is of royal blood. He can honor the boy."

"I'll allow it," replied Umid.

Prince Edjer returned to calm. Umid watched as his brother's manner shifted.

"I'll demand a favor in return," continued Umid.

"– your message to me did not state a reason to end my exile."

Umid laid his pen down. He dropped the feather tip near a bowl of ink, next to his mountain of papers. "The Ceremony approaches. These peace accords with our enemies — Danger looms with every nearing day — I…" Umid stammered to find the right words.

"Do not waste our time," retorted Edjer.

"Which Edjer am I seeing in front of me? You have aged?"

"Your own eyes barely remain open."

"Tasks of a king — do not rest."

Umid and Edjer looked at one another. The love between the brothers had once been strong. Yet, it was malcontent in the king's eyes whereas Edjer held anger.

"A man walked into our borders and shared there was a threat to my Ceremony."

Edjer leaned forward: "Where was this man from?"

"I have yet to find my answers."

"What did he say?" asked Edjer.

"Simply what I have shared. There is a plot against my Ceremony," replied Umid.

"That is what forces you to call me back here?"

Umid rose from his chair. He walked towards his brewing fire. "The man has planted a seed in my mind. He believes there are traitors in my midst. That there are those who speak to my enemies... that there are those outside Perfuga who know you have been exiled."

There was a brief silence. Edjer cleared his throat: "Let me speak to the man."

"My Royal Guards will handle the prisoner–"

"–Your guards are fools!" declared Edjer.

"I have called you for one reason! Protect me! Protect Perfuga! If I fail to bring peace, I will fall! Do you understand!"

Edjer scoffed. They stared at one another, many old emotions returning in the look. Most remained unsaid.

Edjer stole from the silence, rising from his seat. He simply walked out the door.

Umid exhaled, unsure if the Prince of Death, his brother, would follow his orders.

FOUR

Tomias, the scribe, ferociously wrote. The agenda was full in preparation for the Ceremony.

King Umid watched all his advisors bicker over the tiniest of details: where the traveling royals would rest, the amount of food to be prepared, curfews. He watched Myawi, Alcaeus, Niobe and Jabez argue and compromise over issues that had nothing to do with his dilemma.

He signaled his advisors with a lackluster raise of his hand. All stopped speaking. It took a moment for his eyes to veer away from Edjer's empty seat.

"I have news," began Umid.

"There – a man has come to Perfuga with information. The man tells me I have traitors in my midst – Traitors who wish to attack Perfuga during our ceremony."

Niobe tightened. She did not know about this. She hid her anger at Umid's deception well.

Umid looked over to Myawi. As the spymaster, Myawi was privy to noise. Yet, he was stumped: "I have not heard anything, King Umid."

"It is true… I can feel it… in my heart, there is a fear that exists," doubled down Umid. The news discomforted the council.

Silence held the room hostage.

"What must be done, then?" inquired Niobe.

"We cannot cancel the Ceremony," said King Umid.

"I did not say we should," she replied. She wanted to, desperately.

"I have spent years planning and securing promises from four kings. Our enemies would deem us weak… so would our people."

Umid pleaded to his advisors more than giving an order.

"The governors report their cities are on the last of reserves. They cannot keep feeding those fleeing their lands coming to Perfuga," said Myawi.

Myawi attempted to reassure Umid. But Umid was beginning to feel regret.

"Mm – It is the reason I have brought Edjer here. He will secure Perfuga leading up to our Ceremony. Him and his men."

"No!" yelled Niobe. The whole council turned to her, in shock at her outburst.

Umid's jaw clenched as he looked at her. She relaxed, remembering where she was.

"It is a wise decision," said Jabez, speaking for the first time.

"I have no further information, but it is my duty to share with you a possible threat. Edjer has his orders…" Umid continued: "He will first meet with an emissary of the Far East Empire. We need their guarantee of attendance for the Ceremony. They have asked for him…"

Alcaeus, the voice of the senators in the council, raised his hand.

"Alcaeus?" said Umid.

"Senators from the Native Quarter are against the Ceremony. They are fearful of the deals to be made," shared Alcaeus.

"Umid, Alcaeus is afraid to tell you that you must call upon Edjer for this as well," shared Jabez.

Alcaeus groaned but quickly resigned any misgivings. It was true in fact.

King Umid looked at his uncle Jabez. His voice went low: "You know better than I, Edjer will not go on our behalf. He has not returned to the Quarter in years."

"It is not on our behalf. He will do it," said Jabez, confidently.

"Uncle, I leave that task to you. I ask that you relay the demands." Jabez nodded.

"Before adjourning, we have one topic of note. The Bear Kingdom." Myawi shuffled his papers to find one last note.

Finding his paper, he shared an inquiry: "King Azazel of the Bear wishes to travel with a legion of his royal guard. He does not feel safe without his men nearby if all the kingdoms will be in attendance."

Umid laughed: "The *fool* is embarrassed because he has taken too many losses… Send an emissary. The Bear Kingdom may travel with their guard, like the other royals. For the *fool*, I will permit a detachment, no more than 500 men. They are not to pass the last trading outpost, or our army will meet them."

Niobe scoffed, "Let us at least withdraw our own soldiers from the Far East Empire."

"No! We will not allow those disillusioned heathens to stall our work further!" replied Umid.

The council quieted.

"Yes, Sire." Myawi collected all his papers, ending the silence.

"Be discreet, Myawi. We cannot have the other kingdoms bringing their armies."

The meeting concluded, leaving Niobe and Umid to argue the decision to hide the mysterious man with information from her.

She had greatly detested ending Edjer's exile.

Many described the royal power given to Edjer as a decision to appease the people. Umid was the obvious choice to be king for the senators, but to the commoners and soldiers in Perfuga, Edjer was beloved. It is the reason Umid had to hide his decision to exile Edjer years ago.

Prince Edjer had his own unit of men called the Arms of the King. They were lethal fighters. And to the people, they were mythical warriors, vastly feared around the world.

Edjer and The Arms of the King were equipped with schooling and training as both royals and soldiers, to handle delicate conflicts requiring finality. The group was made up of the boys from *The Children*, the kingdom's first refugees, a legion of seventeen. At one time, this included Umid as well.

They were first trained by Jabez and Myawi.

The arts, history, espionage, the men were knowledgeable in all facets of life. They were separated from the military, given their own compound in the Native Quarter. Edjer maintained the integrity of the unit since being given the mantle of leader. The unit was his to dispatch and task while serving at the King's behest. While loyal to the King, the group was allowed autonomy upon which requests to honor.

Never had Edjer refused the King.

Yet, this Ceremony was altogether a different task. Umid had been in constant warfare with the four kingdoms around Perfuga since he became king: The Northerners, The Nation-States, The Bear, and The Far East kingdoms.

Umid created this ceremony of the five kingdoms to agree on a system for all the kingdoms to repay their debts to Perfuga. Perfuga had loaned money to the kingdoms over the years, but once Umid became king, the time had come to collect. Losing Edjer the last few years to exile meant Umid lost what the kingdoms feared most about Perfuga, the threat of death.

Regardless, Niobe vehemently argued against using Edjer over the course of the night. "His hold over you... it is still strong."

Umid avoided the truth, snickering before he spoke. "I need not describe the chance we have been given. This Ceremony can give us the peace Perfuga once knew. None of us can afford another Great War."

The threat of another, like the one they had survived, brought them to silence as they stopped to sleep for the night.

FIVE

32 days until the Ceremony.

Intuition warned Edjer of a coming danger. He sat in his tent, trapped in thought. He struggled to understand the call to return home.

The years had changed Umid and Edjer. Prince Edjer was trained to the highest degree possible. His route to royalty was unlike any in the kingdoms. All knew he venerated death. Death was his past, present and the future he was to live.

Edjer respected the act of war he was molded to end. He knew no desire but to act for survival. His own peace had long departed with the peace Perfuga once knew.

The candle in his tent began to flicker from the growing wind outside. Wax dripped beyond the plate designated to hold waste. He watched the excess fall into the grass beneath him.

The tent made up in width what it lacked in length. Stakes kept the contraption rigid, to hold in the eye of a brewing storm. The wind itself was a precursor to the coming rain. Edjer wore wool garments with blankets lying near him. Glass lamps, most unlit, were placed at the corners of his tent for warmth.

The fields around his tent were empty except for Umid's Royal Guards scattered all around him.

"Edjer." Men appeared from the darkness. His men opened the entryway.

"Cleanse yourselves before entering," ordered Edjer. Edjer was able to see puddles forming in the grass, the rain beginning its harsh fall.

His two lieutenants removed their muddied boots. They placed their wet overcoats on top of one another near the open crease.

The rain's dread increased as they conversed.

"Edjer, we spoke with the Far East delegates. Their men have stopped trading and declared the route blocked. It is set," said Habiel, a stoic Arabian man with glasses over his eyes.

"Good. Good. Any problems?"

Habiel hesitated. He expected Edjer to recognize his reservations.

"This seems easy. Edjer, we just fought them in a battle we did not trust the outcome of."

Habiel spoke freely. One could do so in the Arms of the King. He froze, thinking, "Can we trust Umid's intentions?"

"Habiel, be patient." Edjer wished to cool the tension.

The second lieutenant, Khalil, cleared his throat. Khalil resembled Edjer in look, a *Desert Man,* an African himself. His smooth dark complexion was matched with lengthy, kinky hair. He was eccentric, ungroomed, with a hoarse voice.

Khalil and Habiel eyed one another. They understood the weight of questioning Umid's allegiance.

Edjer found a darkness in Khalil's eyes. "Khalil, what did you see?"

Khalil tracked the water falling off the roof of the tent slowly, then moved his gaze back towards Edjer.

"The Far East… They did not protest the clearing of the routes. Edjer, you know the gold at stake in a single day of trading."

"All the kingdoms were told to slow trade for the Ceremony," added Edjer. He could see terror in their eyes. The lieutenants were dancing around something.

Khalil could not hold on any longer.

"I fear for your safety. Umid and Niobe are beyond our reach, but now, they are beyond the people's. They serve a purpose of their own. You have been away from the Capital. The people wish to see another ruler. You..." replied Khalil.

Silence. Edjer attempted to speak but stopped himself. "I – cannot... I will not..." whispered Edjer.

"The kingdom is not what it once was," added Habiel.

Edjer faced his men. "Umid does not forget what we have survived." Edjer froze in a moment of remembrance himself.

"...we cannot forget Umid trained with us. If he asks for my return, it must alarm us. It means he has lost the trust of those around him. If he asks us this, he wishes us to know how dire the kingdom has become."

Their silence worsened the truth. The conditions were intriguing. Who was playing a game with Perfuga? If traders were taken off the road, planning was involved.

The routes that spread to all the kingdoms were half a century old. The roads distributed culture, art, garments, and many unregulated prospects. Along these paths of commerce lay secrets these kingdoms, who in name were at peace, fought to obtain with spies. Any opportunist with a hold of critical information could trade for profit. Umid would not be foolish enough to ask them to be cleared.

The lieutenants shared news about The Arms of the King before quickly departing.

Hours into the night, alone, Edjer was trapped again. The cyclical nature of following orders, for the politicians and kings he fought for, took him away from his past. Moments alone, however, outside of the sanctuary of battle, his fears compounded. Memories as a child resurfaced.

When his eyes shut to sleep, a single vivid memory of the journey he and the rest of *The Children* had made decades ago returned.

Edjer and his kin had been once trapped on both sides. On one side were a curious squadron of Bear soldiers, and on another, a rocky mountain range they needed to get over. Umid had convinced Edjer they needed to get past the range to have a chance at survival.

The night before they made the trek, the best of *The Children* had snuck into the Bear soldiers' camp and slit the throats of their horses. The quiet endeavor had afforded them time as they began marching across a narrow passage in the scorching sun.

The crossing had struck fear in the young ones. The older leaders, Umid and Edjer, were both still twelve years old. But they had to hide their own fear.

That day's path had been difficult. Hundreds of meters high, slowly, *The Children* had crossed, shoulder to shoulder. Older ones led the front of the pack, while Umid and Edjer guided the rest from the rear. They were helpless as a few lost their footing and dropped to their death. Horrid screams of dying children had been deafening. Attempts to mute the wails had chipped away at their innocence.

Many times, Edjer's nightmares returned to the day of the crossing.

As one of the last to cross, he had grown scared himself. The impact of those who fell was loud in the soundless heat. Edjer vividly recalled the misstep of a sweet seven-year-old girl. He had carried her on his back for days. She had requested he carry her through the pass, but his refusal had cost her her life. Edjer did not want to tell her how afraid he had been.

The path had been tight. Rocks had pressed against them as they walked to the other side. Holding a child was not feasible. The young girl, Sevina, had begged Edjer to be held, bawling in tears as she made the walk. She had desperately wanted to cross on his back. She could not overcome her premonitions of falling.

Her soft hand had slipped off the dirt-stained rocks and she simply fell.

Five children had fallen that day. Overthinking and regret had led to Edjer's own misstep.

As Edjer began to fall, he had not screamed. The rocky edge had ripped into his flesh as he slipped. His robes had begun to stain with blood. The pain endured in the friction had saved him seconds for his brothers to react. For a moment, Edjer had looked down in silence, waiting, wishing, as his blood dripped to where Sevina lay. Umid had held his hand tight and would not let go. Habiel had grabbed his other hand, and with Demetrius, they had pulled Edjer up.

What Edjer had seen, *everything* he had seen that day, he could never forget.

Memories of the pilgrimage were the reasons Edjer, his lieutenants, were slaves to the Royal Guards' snores in the night, why following attempts for an heir, Niobe and Umid could hear the whispers in the palace.

———

The morning came on the eve of his eyes closing. Most days fed off similar sleep. Two Royal Guards came to fetch Edjer. In a combination of fear and awe, one decidedly spoke: "Prince, the — water to wash is at a brook nearby. Men are fetching it. Would you like us to bring some to you and your men?"

Edjer walked out before speaking, his uniform glaring in the sun: "Edjer... Edjer or General is what my men call me."

The second soldier snickered.

"We are not *your* soldiers. Our leaders call you, *Prince.*"

The first Guard was taken aback by his comrade's gumption. Umid's soldiers held various opinions of Edjer over the creation of a group separate from theirs. The resourcefulness of the Arms of the King made Edjer's unit either feared or disliked.

"As you wish," stated Edjer.

"Food will be distributed shortly. We will be eating near the tents with the provisions if you wish to join?" asked the first Guard.

Edjer turned his head to see the mirage of tents surrounding him in the middle.

"We will come to your cook," answered Edjer.

The second Guard did not appreciate the intrusion to come. He was the first to walk away.

The Royal Guards were leaders of the kingdom's campaigns, guiding armies to war, well trained and respected within the borders. Following Umid's ascension, they had become disgruntled soldiers missing the faces of their families.

Edjer empathized as he grabbed his brothers to go wash.

"The guards need to be educated," uttered Habiel.

It was no brook. In front of them, a small lake, trapped by terrain on all four sides. All its ends were visible. As they walked down, a backdrop of the greenest of trees lay beyond the waters. Habiel and Khalil marveled at the peace before they removed their garments and faded into the lake. Tomias found a small rock near the water to sit and watch. He had his writing materials with him.

Prince Edjer found himself looking at the reflection of the sky in the clear water. Even in Spring, the sun was a rare sight. Edjer began to move to his left, where Tomias sat. He looked at his feet in the deep grass, taking in the soft whistles of nature. The animals, the wind, Edjer knew of nature's dark side.

Tomias turned towards his brother. Tomias held an easy look to him, simple wool clothes with a commoner's approach to grooming, a shaved beard and plush mustache. His face was welcoming in its teething smile, hiding the remnants of a removed tongue.

"Habiel tells me you do not come to the Quarter," shared Edjer.

Tomias' smile faded. He moved his hands, sharing in the language his brothers and sisters had constructed to communicate with him.

"Umid would not want me near the compound."

Edjer sighed: "We are all brothers. All of us are tied."

"*I have access. I cannot damage that.*" Tomias avoided the dilemma.

Edjer followed in the voiceless language. Their language was only known by *The Children*. "*Your letters allow exiles to dream of home.*"

Edjer walked down to the water to wash his face before leaving for the camp.

The four returned to find tents packed away and horses carrying provisions. Twenty dispatched Royal Guards huddled around steaming black pots in the grass, eyeing down the outliers. Edjer led his brothers to the food.

The Guard from earlier, who spoke with awe, brought them four bowls of soup with bread and ale. The brothers refused the drink.

"They do not drink outside with outsiders," sounded off a Guard, loudly.

Edjer remained patient. He looked at the man as others laughed. The soldier rose to add to his bowl. It was the other disgruntled soldier who had fetched Edjer earlier.

"We are honored to dine with you," added the Royal Guard.

Edjer noted the sarcasm in the Guard's voice. He required silence from his men. The lieutenants did not look up, but Edjer sensed Tomias' shifts, the devilish look forming in the eyes.

"It is our pleasure," answered Edjer. He was confident he could deescalate.

"Posh fuckers," uttered the Royal Guard. Only half the men laughed.

Still, Edjer and his brothers were poised. The Royal Guard took his seat, chuckling at his own joke. Others in the camp began to sense the direction of conflict.

Soldiers who had fought with Edjer and his lieutenants remained silent. They knew.

"When will we enjoy the peace, the one we grew up with? You must know something, *Prince*," inquired the Guard.

The other Royal Guards shifted uncomfortably. The comments were true, but dangerous.

But Edjer did not see a problem. He nodded as he looked down. He ate, as did his unphased lieutenants. Tomias, however, played into the man's agenda, watching closely.

"*Prince,* you and your men have no words to speak?"

Every man in the camp, from cook to Tomias, was armed with at least a blade. They continued to eat, watching.

Edjer raised his head: "We are your guests. We serve one king."

"Yes, we do. But you are not guests. We protect *you;* we are not royals."

The patience of a warrior is a delicate thing. When respect leaves, the camel quits searching for a way through the eye of the needle. It stomps, until the tip meets the hoof.

Edjer's lieutenants still ate. But Tomias watched helplessly, wishing to engage and stop the banter. He placed his hand on Edjer's shoulder.

"*Stop speaking with him. They want to see the limit to your discipline.*"

Edjer looked over and replied: "*If we don't speak, they think we believe we are better.*"

"Are you planning to kill us with the mute?" asked the Guard.

The lieutenants finished their soup. They did not move; they watched Tomias for a moment before turning to their bread.

"His name is Tomias." Edjer spoke softly, trying his best.

The Guard laughed. He grabbed more ale. Only the men near him enjoyed the banter. The words he spewed were beginning to thread the brinkmanship.

"You, *The Children,* you think you are smarter than us?"

None answered. Tomias moved his bag. He placed it behind him. The Royal Guards could not see him tuck a blade in the lining of his undergarments.

"Our *King*...and the *Concubines*. We see them work in the palace, don't we?"

The men near the Guard stopped laughing.

"What makes the women so sacred, eh?"

Edjer finished his soup and was on to his bread. His lieutenants were watching now. The mood shifted. Khalil and Habiel looked up at Edjer, expecting a response, eyeing their leader.

"I do not know," answered Edjer. His jaws clenched tightly together, muscles protruding.

"*Prince,* it is us soldiers. Our banter, you know, is vulgar."

The Guard's responses were faster, targeted.

"We honor our rules," replied Edjer.

"Great *Prince,* we are men. You are all *brothers* to the King. He does not sneak you in for a little time with the Concubines?"

A blade moved quickly in the air. The men shuddered with fear as it flew. Tomias' hand froze, postured upright. Accuracy required his follow-through to remain steadfast.

Tomias' blade struck the sack of ale the Guard held onto. The soldier had wanted to take a sip after his crude joke, thinking he was close to Edjer's impregnable composure.

The blade was the length of a soldier's forearm, and its width surpassed the burliest of soldiers' arms. The skill needed to hit the sack terrified the camp.

They were all several paces away from one another, seated.

After the realization came, the Guards turned to the brothers. Tomias was ready to fight. Edjer and his lieutenants were relaxed, still eating.

The Guard and a few brave men rose, hands on their unsheathed swords.

Edjer focused on his food. He peeked up at their noisy posturing, prepared: "Come and you will die. Killing you will be an easy task. We will not be reprimanded, nor will your kin care for vengeance. Remember who it is you sit with."

The men behind the Guard hesitated, bringing their steps to an end.

"If the scribe can do as such, what do you expect from my blade, the men I sit beside?"

The Guard took a seat. His fellow soldiers did the same. Tensions rose as Tomias retrieved his knife, but nothing came of it.

The men did not speak to Edjer for the duration of the trip. The feeling of fear for Edjer scarred over into despicable hate the longer they traveled together, as had been normal for all his enemies.

SIX

32 days until the Ceremony.

The hill protected Edjer from the disgruntled Royal Guards. At the apex, an outdoor outpost was decorated in an open field, along a trade route. A stomped path of dead grass led to a table in the emptiness, dressed in white cloth and held down with candles and Tomias' writing materials.

Edjer sat on the same side as Tomias. They were in their respective garments, the white for the Arms of the King, and the black and gold for royals serving Umid. Their arms rested on the wooden table. Flaps of the tablecloth wailed in the mild wind. They felt Khalil and Habiel's eyes from behind.

"Tomias, you must keep check of your emotions. The man today is not one we can play with," uttered Edjer. Tomias nodded in affirmation.

"I apologize for earlier."

"No need."

Their eyes left each other's gaze when a carriage rustled in front of them. Yards away, the carriage was trailed by one hundred men on horses. Like the Royal Guards, the soldiers kept their distance. Pride in the Far East Empire was no different than any other kingdom.

Edjer and Tomias watched the carriage stop steps away from the table. The overseer stomped to let his master know of arrival. The brown carriage was draped in the maroon, red banners of the Far East Empire. A blood-orange Bengal tiger, fiercely growling, was the sigil, a warning to the fierce ways of their soldiers.

A door creaked open as an elegant man appeared.

His face was dignified, confident. The man's golden-brown skin, his tied hair, and well-partitioned attire exemplified royalty in the rough terrain. The driver of the carriage watched as his master walked on the muddied grass towards the white table, retreating once his master took his seat.

"An ugly day, gentlemen."

The man's voice was barely heard as his carriage retreated. Tomias lowered his head to begin writing.

Years passed since Edjer had last seen Prince Debyendu of the Far East. He was the opposite to the eccentric ruler of the Far East Empire.

The king of the Far East Empire was rash in desire. During the Great War, the king had killed the leading nobles of their twelve houses when they threatened to pull out of the war. He had brought the kingdom back decades with his decision.

Debyendu was quite different. He knew himself. He was comfortable in the den of his enemies. Pleasantries shared in his delicate voice masked his masterful negotiation tactics, earning him the name, the Tiger's Paw.

"You have grown, *Prince*."

"You have aged as well," replied Edjer.

"Peace is not what it used to be." Tomias scribbled every word for Umid. The contents of the discussion were desired.

"I wonder of times when it was not a commodity. There would not be use for my men and I if that was the case."

Debyendu chuckled at the deduction. He was relaxed. His eyes darted around in the anomalous silence. He was aware of Edjer's lieutenants, the twenty Royal Guards beneath the hill. The man removed his gloves and brought out documents like Tomias.

"Is this…your brother, from your journey?" asked Debyendu.

"Yes, his name is Tomias, our scribe." Tomias wrote their words and looked up to the Prince across from him. The Tiger's Paw had extended his hand out for a forearm embrace.

"You are as famed a writer in your home as you are in ours. I am Prince Debyendu, prince of the Far East Empire."

"Pleasure to meet you, Prince."

"Pleasure to meet you, Prince," translated Edjer.

"Prince Edjer, you *Children* fascinate me in what you have become. What comes from war is not easily created elsewhere."

Tomias returned to scribbling.

Edjer nodded, his hands now under his chin. He was nervous when others spoke of their history, even with empathy.

"Let's begin, before rain returns."

False modesty was at its end; a discussion was required. The debt was high, not only for the Far East Empire, but for the empires in the known realm.

The Perfugan king before Umid had made a dangerous decision to act as a bank during the Great War. It was thought to be fortuitous. No one could have foreseen the horrific times that would come after the Great War. Perfugan rulers had given the other kingdoms time to pay their debts, but the grace was abused.

Perceiving Perfuga weak, all the kingdoms had refused to pay their debt.

As taxes rose in Perfuga to mediate the unpaid debts, patience became impossible. Continued skirmishes over repayment had emptied Perfugan coffers and antagonized the people.

The Northern Kingdom, the Far East Empire and the Bear Kingdoms had all chosen to attack. Edjer had found himself fighting and suing for a temporary peace each time. But they would renege and attack again. The Northerners had even campaigned for war with the Bear, threatening another Great War.

Succeeding in forming one army, they had fallen to the swords of Umid and Edjer.

With peace on the horizon, the old king of Perfuga had died following grueling negotiations. It was said his heart was weak from the talks. Since Umid's abrupt ascension, kingdoms never stopped eyeing an opportunity to escape from under Perfuga's thumb.

Empires tested Perfuga but all would come to surrender as Edjer began to mount a legacy on the battlefield. He righteously garnered the title of Prince of Death, never losing a battle.

Umid's first years had been a showcase to his people. He had wished to prove his ability. Kingdoms waited for him to spiral, yet he had remained steady. He ruled with a heavy hand, and once crushing the kingdoms in battle numerous times, he had increased their debts and the speed in which he sought repayment.

Policies were enacted, yet Umid had been unable to practically implement and enforce his decrees as time went on. The other kingdoms had utilized the threat of war to avoid paying debts without any accountability.

Umid's own people then turned against him. Once applauding his heavy hand, they began to fear repetitive war in the name of debt. The promise of decreasing ever-growing taxes became impossible, mystical to commoners. Each conflict brought unimaginable loss. Perfugan pride turned a citizenry once full of compassion into one of paranoia. In a state of disarray in the nine years since Umid ascended, the once great Perfuga sat in front of one of their neighbors, the Far East Empire, hoping for a chance at peace through a Ceremony.

"The repayments are the point of my discussion today."

"Does the Far East Empire agree to attend the Ceremony?"

Debyendu went silent in a moment of thought.

"We will attend, like the other kingdoms. We wish to come to a private agreement, however, in case the talks sour."

Edjer looked at Tomias, but his brother did not look back. Both were unsure of the authorization Edjer had: "I can come to a reasonable agreement, but it is King Umid who will agree to terms."

Debyendu lightly chuckled: "We are the same in that our brothers do not see eye to eye with us. However, we differ in that yours shares an undying love for you."

Edjer did not respond. Tomias wrote in calm strokes, thoughtless.

"I warn you not to overstate my position."

"My spies once intercepted a letter, years ago, on one of these roads... I remember sealing it myself before returning it to the rider. For what you have done, secret exile over death means his love is strong for you."

Tomias stopped. He fought every urge to look up at Edjer.

Debyendu smiled: "Perception is our currency in politics, I am sure you are aware. Whatever truth lies in the blank space between perception, it does not matter. Our kings act on this currency, until they veer too far from truth."

"And what happens when truth has distanced from them?" asked Edjer, curious.

Debyendu brought his fists to the cusps of his lips. He blew into his hands, and they expanded like smoke. He laughed, mimicking magic.

Edjer knew Debyendu was right.

Debyendu was a traveler, a listener of the wind, dispatching people to report on its direction, equipped with an arsenal of soldiers to chase it.

"You see, along these beaten paths of grass, all of us marvel at the shared culture, the commodities traded daily. It is a travesty..." interjected Debyendu, waiting for a reaction.

Edjer was brought back: "Why has your brother closed the road?"

"As I said, perception, Prince. The most valuable commodity along these routes are the rumors that opportunists sell. When damaging rumors align with truth, they certainly are... the most valuable commodity."

Debyendu's smile vanished. He stared deep into the fields.

"Cut our debts by half, and we will provide full repayment in reasonable pieces, finished within a change of season?" pleaded Debyendu.

Edjer was puzzled. He feared why Debyendu was surrendering.

"I can plead to King Umid. Half is a steep discount to provide."

"It is the only deal we shall make, or else, I have been instructed to say we will not attend your Ceremony."

"Nevertheless, I believe the people will look at the large price given in a short time and be content." Edjer spoke with confidence.

They both eyed Tomias as he wrote the last words of the trailing conversation.

"Why, may I ask, is your kingdom...retreating?"

Debyendu deeply exhaled as he returned his eyes to Edjer: "Blood has been shed for decades. Our people have yet to mourn their dead fathers and sons. The next time we see one another; I will tell you a story."

Edjer was enticed by the peaceful sentiment. Debyendu's deal was one Umid would be a fool not to agree to. King Umid's initial offer to the kingdoms was to slash their debts by a quarter and provide them with two years to pay. The offer was gracious.

Edjer was unable to shake his curiosity, though.

"Will your brother agree to all we have spoken of?" asked Edjer.

"He will – his supporters search for peace."

"Prince, I ask, what do you fear from the trade routes? Why do you handicap your people?" asked Edjer.

Prince Debyendu took the words as a slight, as if he did not think of the consequences. "It is difficult to ignore information. You have stayed away from politics too long.

"The Ceremony brings you threats, from kingdoms you see, and some you do not. We refuse to be entrapped in another conflict. Your people are angry, your soldiers grow weary of swordplay. The great *Prince of Death* remains a recluse."

"Children's tales," replied Edjer.

"Yet King Umid's guards engage in a game of knives with his kin."

Tomias stopped for a moment, afraid to look up. Edjer held his eyes on Debyendu, fearing the validity of his words.

"Who provides you these rumors?"

"Prince Edjer, it is all a game. The strife Perfuga plagued the kingdoms with during the Great War was shameful. It is now our time to watch what becomes of your kingdom. Be careful with your Ceremony."

Elegantly said, it was not a threat, and the two men knew it. A warning.

"Where does your kingdom lie in this game my brother plays?"

Debyendu, from across the table, placed his hand near Tomias' papers. Tomias looked to Edjer, finding approval. Tomias' pen rested above his papers as he became a ghost.

"Do you trust the scribe?"

"With my life."

"You face a threat you are not prepared for."

"How can I believe you? Was not the Tiger my last enemy on the battlefield?" inquired Edjer.

Debyendu took a moment to ponder, "We have retired from our protest. But must I warn you, the nature of the threat you face now, know I am not aware, nor do I know who approached my brother. However, he personally asked for you today. Were you told?"

Edjer shook his head: "I was not."

"Many rumors show themselves today to be true. I wish for you to understand, Prince Edjer. I concur this is the reason your brother has attached the scribe to our meeting today."

"Did you know?" asked Edjer.

Tomias looked at Edjer: *"I did not... I suspected."*

Edjer did not hide his disappointment.

"Our empire is not a part of any threat; it is vital you understand this. My brother wishes *you* to know, outright and clearly. He will not attend this Ceremony for this reason. I understand he will be the only head royal not a part of a delegation?"

"I was not aware, but from what I hear, he will be the only one missing."

Debyendu sighed as rumors became fact: "Please, Prince Edjer, take that as a warning in itself..." started Debyendu, "Whomever approached him, he has not whispered a word, to even me, but the nature of the threat brings him fear. He pleads his innocence *to you*, personally."

"Why me?"

"Beyond this, I have no words."

Edjer deduced another thought from Debyendu's words that stole his curiosity.

"I do not know of what you wish me to do with this information."

"I presume my brother wishes for your King to cancel the Ceremony."

"He will not do so... Is there any way to learn who approached your brother?"

They remained at an impasse. The wind blew the tablecloth's flaps wildly in their silence. Allegiances withheld their wish to speak freely.

"Would you leave your kingdom, if pushed to, Prince Edjer? My brother asks this of you."

Edjer did not move.

"Any kingdom would welcome you. As a citizen, without the requirement of wielding a sword. If you are not content, we would welcome you."

Tomias and Edjer were struck by the offer. The vague attempt alluded to Edjer that Debyendu held back details.

"No."

Both Tomias and Debyendu knew he had lied.

"Tell King Umid, if he agrees to the tax deal, I will be in attendance. I will do my best to relay any information I find. Will you be at the Ceremony?"

Edjer watched Tomias jot down what was spoken in detail.

"I will…need to."

SEVEN

200 days until the Ceremony.

The story is known. It is not that it is forgotten but ignored. Here, ignorance becomes death, and I have seen death. It is shapeless, not black, but a void. The careless nature of its movement is confidence, knowing it shall triumph.

To not acknowledge *The Children*, our journey, is to know the ugliness of war and death.

I ask that you remember, I am one of them. The story, whether for those too young to know, or for those who have forgotten, is one demanding accuracy.

Believe these words, for my journey here, like those I came with, was not an easy one.

The Great War began as the great kingdoms beside Perfuga, both left and right, above, and below, engaged in battle. For what reason, we debate.

Rumors within the Far East Empire were quiet. Amala, sister of the Far East king, had united empires in marriage, gifting her to the Bear.

Her marriage to Azazel of the Bear Kingdom was to bring everlasting peace. The marriage was not only to bring prosperity in the known world, but to her own home as well.

She was to be a beloved queen. The future envisioned for her immediately went awry.

Ruinous events transpired, of which, few know. Most believe the Bear Kingdom is to blame for having jailed Amala in secret. The reason still eludes us.

Soon, the word spread. The Far East Empire was shocked. Sudden news of her imprisonment triggered reactionary rulers. Distrust festered as details of her captivity remained hidden. No spy could penetrate the Bear.

And then, she was executed.

Balance was required.

Armies mustered and banners were called. The Great War was nothing to be forgotten. The Bear Kingdom, with its hold over agriculture, called upon the Northern Kingdom, its trading partner. The Nation-States were forced into a pact with The Far East following the Bear's encroachment.

Before her marriage, the Far East rulers had toured around the known world with the Princess in the name of peace. Amala was dearly adored, and the news of her death brought honorable men to the battlefield in the search of noble retribution.

Warriors desecrated her memory in the name of war. Legions of men fell at the tip of a sword. Generations of orphans grew with memories of villages raided, mothers and sisters raped, and fathers with no allegiance murdered. Great warriors never returned, buried in empty fields, or trampled into the dirt by horses. Those times do not deserve more words than necessary.

What requires a moment, however, are the deeds of Perfuga. Like others, the kingdom grieved Amala's death. Yet, Perfuga sheathed its sword, and demanded its armies do nothing. The Perfugan people benefitted from this moment of wisdom.

Closing its borders, and with its famed mining deposits and stored provisions, Perfuga was able to maneuver through threats of war. Allies and foes attempted to pressure Perfuga into choosing a side due to its geography as it lies between The Bear and The Tiger. The closed borders forced the fighting further south.

However, it became a bloodbath for the Nation-States. For seven years, raiding and raping, the kingdoms fought in the name of Amala.

Victims of the war came to despise her in the end.

To us in the south, as war ensued, there was whisper of a kingdom that held peace together, respected by the warring nations. The promise of heaven's existence seemed impossible for most, for many died seeking peace. But there was a group that searched for its gates.

Children, then, with a few older than myself at the age of nine, were in one of the southern Nation-States, near the Red Sea. We were doomed, trapped by the Great War. As the armies fought towards the South, any who chose peace were objects to be conquered.

Refusal was death.

My father was once a noble of a Nation-State, Ambassa. He had declared his land to be a harbor for fleeing refugees. Even as innocents flooded in, we chose ignorance, believing the fighting could not venture to the southernmost Nation-State. War had to have limits.

When the Bear Kingdom came, there was no option. My father, with my older brother and mother in the room, warned us. If we had survived, he ordered us to find 'Perfuga, The Kingdom of Hope.' He must have known what was to come.

When soldiers demanded the location of our refugees, none of us spoke. Yet, refusal was death. They executed my father with one swift slash across his neck. As I screamed, they did the same to my mother after asking her again.

I continued to scream.

The soldiers did not stop. They put my brother to the sword and begged me to end my shouting. I could not, I was terrified. For that, I lost my tongue. They cut it out with impudence. They demanded, if I wanted to live, to bring them to the refugees. As I walked out, I saw my nation on fire. I witnessed the deflowering of my village, cut down by men scarred by fear and war. They threw children who disobeyed on spikes, and others into bowls of tar. Soldiers were content with this foul display of humanity for they knew it would be a decisive victory; one they needed for morale. I watched them take our young men as slaves and demand they kill their own mothers and fathers, brothers and sisters, if they were to survive. It was treachery.

In my greatest moment of shame and fear, my mouth gushing blood, I brought them to the doors of the sanctuary that housed hundreds of refugees. The soldiers did not wish to enter but instead covered the compound with tar. The smell of burning flesh, I am ashamed to say, was no different than the meat cooked in our kitchens.

I ceased crying. The pain in my mouth, the blood, it all had stopped.

I have spent days on end pondering my father's choices, the decision to separate the children of the refugees before the Bear soldiers entered. I do not know if he expected me to live, but I lose hours in the night thinking. He must have known what was coming.

My nightmares ask the question: why did he not run?

The great fire burning the refugees brought the soldiers together. The blazing spectacle signaled victory. The soldiers had thought of throwing me into the fire. I saw it in the reflection of the flames in their flaring eyes. They must have expected me to pass on as my cut worsened, so I simply walked away, and was forgotten.

They did not care to look at me.

Once the soldiers were behind me, I walked into a house and grabbed the first knife I found. I have never been known for more than my ability as a scribe. The word bravery has never been used to describe a man as I.

Now armed, I left. I knew I had not had long to live. I dipped my instrument of death in a pool of fire, where compatriots of mine lay dead. I warmed the blade and cauterized the wound. No more has to be said of it.

I left my home a bloodied citizen marked by war. I walked to a farm south of my state, where children of refugees hid from the screams of my home. I opened the door, and immediately, ones I would call brother, sister, they understood my tribulations. They had seen the face of distraught before. All shared similar scars and wounds.

In their eyes, I could see it. They knew.

They were devastated for me. The unbothered son of a noble had become one of them. Innocence had been taken.

Seventy-six children were in the barn.

There was nothing to do but die. We did know what lingered south of us. We did not want to follow the fight. But in the Deep North, my father had told me, there was a place to hope for. Perfuga.

If survival was to be had, this was the answer.

Seventy-seven of us now, the youngest being five, the oldest eleven, journeyed through deserts, jungles, and wastelands. We stepped over ocean waters, seas of blood, and ventured through deserts of emptiness.

Some days it was the heat. Others, hunger. Our numbers began to wither and with that, hope diminished. Refusal was death, as was submission. We evaded soldiers, hunters, animals, and at a point, the distinctions were needless.

Nature is its own beast. Seventy-seven withered to forty-one.

When we reached the borders, we stayed on the outskirts for days as Perfuga pondered our fate. Fervent arguments were said to have been had. Many demanded Perfuga remain closed. For they feared what would come if the borders opened.

We waited and waited. Benevolent provisions were offered.

Suddenly, the royals began to take notice of our leaders, specifically the two eldest boys. The royals admired them, as all did. They were fierce, with extraordinary compassion. The darkness of our journey need not be discussed. We do not speak easily of the days, but they recounted the story to the Royals. Empathetic, the Royals had crumbled in dread.

Within days, Perfuga made the decision.

When we entered, the elders carried the wounded in. The marketplace was closed, yet the people were out of their homes. They had watched in horrific fashion. What weakened my legs were their hands, they were so clean. The Royals demanded the kingdom, its citizens in the Capital, see the brutality of the outside world. We marched through the city, watching tears fall for our sick and maimed, for our dirtied faces. I remembered as we made it to the palace.

Days later, our two leaders, Umid and Edjer made a plea to the Inner Council. They pleaded for asylum for not only us, but for their dead fathers and mothers, their dead kin. The two demanded the borders be opened for all fleeing war. The council was impressed, but none more than Prince Jabez. The rest of the story is known with Jabez ardently arguing for the borders to open and a school for us, the first refugees, to be created inside the palace.

As I said, the story is known. The adoption of my brothers made them beloved by all. Many in Perfuga declared them the Two-Headed Beast, a creature of two minds, yet one in wit.

The Great War, our pilgrimage, they are great stories of the past. They are, however, not simply stories, but truth. As another deadly Great War looms, it is important to understand our history, and how my brothers and sisters suffered.

The air speaks of similar days to come, and it is time to recall the implications of past mistakes. The Ceremony is the beginning of a better future.

Tomias, *The Royal Scribe*

To Perfugan Royals, The Journey taken by The Children

EIGHT

30 days until the Ceremony.

His plans and schemes wished to restore the kingdom to the mythical glory of the past. He did not wear the royal white robes, held together by an engraved Bear pin, without reason.

Semjaza pondered how the task could be done when the people's morale was horrifically low. In his lifetime, The Bear Kingdom had suffered. Deception clouded their past actions, and with a loss in the Great War, their bear emblem and hunter green banners triggered people's ridicule. Following their defeat to the Far East Empire, then multiple losses to Perfuga, he had one more opportunity to restore the Bear Kingdom.

The queen eating her royal dinner in front of him was an opportunist. She was a representation of the citizenry he hoped to cleanse. She was once a keeper of a brothel, whose station had enabled her to extract information from royals for coin.

She rose in stature as the information grew in value. Her network of brothels and willingness to listen allowed her to trade for status. Her reports lead to the assassinations and imprisonment of two hundred officials and spies. Queen Liliah had cemented her legacy by best conning a grief-stricken king.

Semjaza respected the network Liliah had built. Her spies, the information she uncovered from trade routes, kingdoms, brothels; she seemed indispensable. His plan was built on her reports. For the moment, she was protected. When the time would come for the Bear to rise once again, he wished for another to take her place. Semjaza's plans required only patience.

Everything came down to patience.

It was midday. Semjaza finished his green soup and poured himself tea. He and the queen were not the only inhabitants of the room.

The woman who once hung, she had been lowered. The *Desert Woman* was chained and covered in a white sheet. The information they sought had been confirmed, and as such, cruelty was no longer demanded. Her wrists were scarred. The burns on her feet were slowly healing, however, they were puffed and white, full of pus. The white, silk dress and blanket she wore to cover her body were stained black with her blood. It took time to overcome the chill of the hard, cemented floors but fear of the coming days kept her alive.

Only her head was visible. Her chained arms and legs were covered, connected to an unlit, steel fire pit. A sliver of yellow-orange light scarred her eyes each time she attempted to look up at the windows.

"What do you stare at, witch?" asked the queen.

The *Desert Woman* hissed at the queen.

Her hiss turned Queen Liliah's face sour. Liliah quickly grabbed her knife to take her payment for the insult. Semjaza watched intently at the rage.

"Do not touch her, Liliah."

The sound of the order froze Liliah, steps away from the golden sofas in the middle of the room. She turned to her brother by law.

"Your words sound too much like instruction."

"You have grown ungrateful to the crown placed on your head."

"Semjaza, you forget who shares your brother's bed?"

"From what I hear in the palace, your talents are not what they used to be."

She walked back to the sofas: "Those garments will not protect you. Do not overestimate your place here, nor outside of it."

The threat brought a distaste to his mouth. The swift stroke of his daggers could take the queen's life away. The knives were attached to holsters tied around his quadriceps and hamstrings, hidden by the garments hanging near his knees.

He instead grabbed a piece of bread next to his plate.

Semjaza was a lengthy man. He was older, the same generation of statesman like Jabez and Debyendu. His pale, clean face and the symmetricity of his tendons and muscles hid the skill of a rabid warrior well. The dust of his brown sandals skidded across the hard floors as he strode to the fireless pit with bread and water.

He grabbed the bottom of his sleeveless garbs, kneeling beside the chained *Desert Woman*. He broke a piece of the bread, the fresh fluff of flour opening up. His attempt to hand her the piece failed. She was too weak to reach from below the blanket.

The woman had refused food for days in protest. He needed her for one more task. He required her well-being, enough to stand. Mercy was given with a hand of respect, and another hand of necessity. He fed her himself.

"Your principles baffle me."

"This woman knows more of principle than you can ever wish to obtain."

Semjaza and Liliah watched as the flavor heightened the chained woman's senses. The bread brought spontaneous tears to her eyes. The water fell silently at the realization of her predicament, the sweet bread meeting the roofs of her mouth.

He whisked her tears away with the stroke of his thumb: "We make mistakes in this world. Yours brought you to me, mine to you. We share the fate of those who acted on impulse."

Semjaza lit the pit behind her. His thumb could not wipe all her tears away, as he eyed a few fall to the cold floors. He watched a moment longer. "Be strong, flowers of your like do not wither in the face of brutality. What remains will no longer be of the physical. You will need to be strong." Semjaza gave her water and returned. The doors opened moments after he sat down.

Lomotos arrived with Azazel, a smile plastered on his face. He could not contain his excitement: "The Ceremony is set. King Umid's representatives have sent word."

Azazel sat next to Liliah, eyeing the chained woman's tears. He watched them fall as Semjaza did.

"Semjaza, the representatives explained they would forgive up to a quarter of our debt." Azazel spoke calmly, in a faint voice.

"That is all they offered?"

Lomotos was dismayed by the direction: "Why discuss this?"

"They are open to a timeline of payment. If another kingdom finds a better deal, they will grant us a similar offer," said King Azazel. He spoke timidly, with fear.

Semjaza recognized his brother Azazel did not desire another large conflict. Their treachery could repeat the bloodshed of the Great War.

"Azazel, you are the king, and as such, you must know we have an opportunity to end our debt, and the debts of our allies."

King Azazel rose from the couch, nearing the chained woman. He looked at her, into her bloodshot eyes. He did not wish for his people to feel her torment. Their plots were daring.

"If the Far East reveals to King Umid—"

"Azazel, they will not. After they refused us, I sent a letter. I promised what only we can give them," interjected Semjaza.

Lomotos smiled at his conniving brother.

"Azazel, in the end, we will rise. We will be out of this horrid debt. We will fracture our true enemies!" Semjaza spoke with passion. With vision.

"Semjaza, our spies in Perfuga tell us Prince Edjer travels with news from a meeting with the Tiger. They have agreed to the Ceremony." Lomotos was eager himself.

"Good. It is time to decide Azazel?" replied Semjaza.

Azazel moved to the chained woman. He again looked deep into her eyes. He was regretful for the pain he caused.

"My dear, a king's burden is never easy," whispered Azazel.

"Azazel?" asked Lomotos.

"I want her clean and dressed. Our healers must tend to her wounds... prepare our delegation." Azazel's decision was final.

NINE

28 days until the Ceremony.

Edjer and Tomias rode in the middle of their dispatched Guards. Habiel and Khalil covered their flanks. The East Road spanned through the known empires in every direction, the focal point being Perfuga itself. Orders from the empires to stall traffic of trade routes for the Ceremony limited their interactions on the road.

Prince Edjer hated nature's silence. The bliss from whistling trees was an illusion. Edjer despised the wetlands, the jungles he crossed, the empty deserts on the path home. His black horse was as on edge as he was, aware of the eyes watching them. Surely spies and emissaries eyed his return home.

Edjer wondered during the whole trip whether Umid was aware of the risk presented by this Ceremony of peace. He could not stop thinking about his brother's dilemma.

Umid's people grew in number since his reign began. The sins of the father became a penance needing payment from his sons. Old opportunistic decisions were shortsighted. Debts, sovereignty, and annexation were thought to be beneficial. The problem fell to Umid and Edjer.

The demands of the kingdom, wondered Prince Edjer. The demands. He had sworn to protect Perfuga, his oath was his bond. But the demands of the crown had been the reason for separation between Umid and Edjer. They had created distance between themselves and the tenets they had adopted to survive. The need to separate their internal feud, with news of propagating danger, was all a puzzle for Edjer to solve.

Embedding Tomias in talks with Edjer was purposeful, for Edjer was loyal to the kingdom, always the kingdom. But rulers could become obstacles to their own lands.

Umid had always wanted Edjer's loyalty to be solely to him.

But Edjer never could give it.

The traveling party encroached on marketplaces along the trade routes. Heads veered to watch the feared Prince of Death pass on his horse.

The growing number of traders alerted Edjer that they neared their borders. They would rest on the Eastern Road, near the mining cities before they left for the palace.

Edjer caught sight of a long river, a tributary that bled out to the sea at the border of Perfuga. They moved toward the famed mining city on their Eastern borders, finding small detachments of people hard at work. They needed to travel for the rest of the day before arriving inside the city, their designated lodging for the night.

The Eastern border itself had no walls. The river was the only security, providing a natural barrier for the citizenry in the insulated mines. Towers watched the border, where warnings could echo to the people in the walled city nearby.

The Cities of Mammon were the prizes of Perfuga. They were established as mining cities that maintained the financial backbone of the kingdom. Wealth from the rich earth bed of the cities guaranteed stability, awarding Umid and his predecessors the ability to fund most campaigns under the guise of carte blanche.

Long before Umid, when the stored wealth in the mining cities had been realized, brick and mortar had been used to erect physical barriers on the outskirts of each of the cities of Mammon. *Mammon,* the ancient word, was easily translated to what the kingdom was given from the earth, wealth.

King Umid, dealing with an astounding number of refugees during his ascension as king, wisely put men, women, and children to work in these cities. Along with overseers, caretakers, and brothel keepers, each mining city was manned and worked by over 100,000 people. The cities bustled, wealth was stored, shipments were exported, and royals funneled the wealth into markets and royal banks.

The luxury enabled royals to act with freedom, so in return, they allowed the cities freedom in their actions. Crime was still outlawed, but the walled Cities of Mammon, over time, shifted into cities of vice.

Edjer and his men entered the easternmost city of Mammon, Libonia, before nightfall. Just outside, farmers were entrenched in the fields. Thousands upon thousands, dispatched with soldiers, worked in the wet Spring weather. No matter the conditions, they worked. The refugees learned to invest in their own livelihood. What could be imagined, could be bought in Mammon. The people of these cities took pride in the work of their hands. Splendid nights in the artful hands of delicate prostitutes matched with unyielding pride were powerful in motivating the citizens to rise and ride out with soldiers to the fields.

Each city in Mammon's grasp held pride in the element harvested or mined. Agriculture, to gold, silver, rice, salt, oil. Work was available.

The Cities of Mammon were the only cities with no senators, no representation. They did not require representation. Demands of the city required an ear to be heard.

Time had passed since Edjer had last stopped in one of the cities. He looked at the workers, watching him. Men, women, children as young as six worked the field. Their loose, cotton garments, stained with the smell of ale and tea, separated the earth from their souls. From Edjer's view, it was difficult to tell if they were part of the soil or not.

Muddied faces looked up at him, with bright white eyeballs widening at sight of the rare man.

Shame. Shame befell him.

Reprimanding the workers felt incorrect. Moments like this would be ingrained in their minds for posterity. Soldiers and field hands alike, in hundreds of rows, watched Edjer as he went deeper into Libonia.

Edjer eyed them, embarrassed. His black horse, the uniform, the dignification brought about a feeling of catharsis. Luxury was not of his lineage; he was gifted the opportunity.

Blood was blood, flesh was flesh. The tragedy of his life had shuddered him from the people. He had always fought with the memory of those lost in the deserts he crossed, with the ferocity the journey he took as a child required.

His head lowered as the people looked upon him. Years in power surrounded him with royals who enjoyed their positions without the appreciation required. The clash within him, as he eyed the field hands and soldiers overseeing the mines, stemmed from the belief he should be there with the workers.

His eyes widened as the thoughts fermented. The prince's dilemma, the battle between humility and the requirement to serve was always visible to the people. This was the source of their love for their prince, the first refugee.

They knew his plight.

Rows of uncountable fieldhands, manning the gardens, bowed to the presence of their Protector. The silent air carried the whispers of their knees meeting the wet marshlands. They rose as he went out of sight, rising full of pride for their champion.

Edjer had hoped the tavern would separate them from the noise of the workers meeting the town's amusements. Umid's Royal Guards had long left them to join the commoners in pursuing the city.

The tavern was at the end of the street, with two candle lights above the door, where the brothers knew peace could be found.

"Mammon, Umid truly despises us," said Habiel.

The antithesis to the roaring city, the tavern lounge was quiet. The four men sat in the back. Their white garments stuck to the ale-stained table. They sat together. A few patrons were scattered around them. A bar hand served drinks to two men seated by a window before he caught wind of the esteemed warriors.

Behind the bar, a woman cleaned four mugs she was to serve to the men.

The place had two floors. The upstairs had rooms for merchants desiring privacy. Candles were connected to each corner of the room, with another two above the door. The candles were fresh, and the aroma was that of honey, sticking to the wooden walls. Near the bar, frankincense burned, Persian in nature. Rare in the Cities of Mammon, these places were for those who did not wish to partake in the festivities, but to discuss business.

The woman was not courteous in her placement of the four mugs, annoyed by the presence of Edjer and his men. She poured them rum, leaving the bottle. She was like them in age, dirtied from the work, yet elegant to the eye. The tawny skin, her mahogany brown hair, she was remarkable. She needlessly returned to the bar.

"She did not speak to us," announced Habiel.

Edjer's eyes were glued on her. When she left, he watched his drink carefully.

"Leave her be," said Edjer.

Edjer modestly poured himself and his men a second drink. Umid had sent word with a rider for his Guards to stop in Mammon for an errand. Edjer was not privy to his reasoning, nor did he care. They all needed a drink, and rest.

"Edjer, will you tell Umid what was discussed?" asked Habiel.

"Tomias will tell him everything that was said... everything, Tomias."

Edjer looked over to his right. Tomias exhaled, a burden awaiting him.

"Umid is showing his arrogance if he does not think each kingdom wants flesh. He cannot think they have forgotten how many we have killed," added Khalil.

"Tomias should warn Umid of this as well," said Edjer.

Puzzled eyes gazed upon Edjer for clarification: "If Tomias was sent to spy on us, let him report *all* of what was said. Include our own conversations."

They all nodded before entering a shared silence. The men considered each other siblings, as all forty-one of *The Children* did. They knew they were not of blood, but the term was easiest for them to use to describe their shared tribulation. They each drank, for a release, not numbness. Dreams and nightmares would regardless appear in the night.

Habiel broke the silence in hope of being the voice of reason: "Umid would sacrifice the kingdom to be in your good graces again. If you position yourself against him, Edjer, he will listen to those who wish to discard you."

Edjer hesitated. "I...I do not wish to go against him."

They believed Edjer. The discord between Umid and Edjer had created division. *The Children* were undoubtedly for Edjer, however, some wished to distance themselves from the conflict. One had even chosen to leave.

"Habiel, when we arrive, we will surround the Capital with men who will watch the city."

Habiel nodded to his leader.

"Khalil, I will ask for our men to be placed in the palace. Umid and Niobe will need protection."

"I can, but our *sisters* will need to be told as well, Edjer."

Edjer did not want to bring them into this. The Royal Concubines loved Edjer and would die for him. However, he wished to protect them from this. The times forced his hand.

"I will ask."

The pilgrimage for power was both unquenchable and cyclical. The Bear Kingdom had become too quiet after ceding lands following their last loss to Edjer. The Northern Kingdom could do no damage alone, and the Far East Empire had momentarily chosen peace.

Nation-States, would they? Many aligned with Perfuga or the Far East Empire. A few remained free, but they were no threat alone. Their tiny delegation for the Ceremony was in name alone. They had minimal debts Umid would forgive if the people were not overly proud.

Edjer came to the conclusion more than one conspired in their demise. Each kingdom had attempted in the past to undermine Perfuga, but each had failed alone.

As they poured another drink, the last of the patrons walked out. They were alone, the boisterous city's roar funneling through the open door for a moment, becoming a continuing void once it closed. They were alone with the woman running the keep.

The brothers watched her. Before cracking the door open, she licked her fingers. Shuffling voices entered again as she robbed the candlelight outside her door of the fire.

The long sleeves of her garments were loose from the day's work of cleaning her inn. She was nearing the end of the day, an eventful one at that.

Returning inside, her hands reached to the top of the door, locking it. On her toes, the extension of her arms revealed a purple flower, marked on her right wrist. She shared the markings with only a few, the same on the arms of Niobe. Grabbing a bottle of wine from the bar, she walked over to the men.

She grabbed a stump from a neighboring table, dragging the bottom along the uneven, cracked floors. She looked at each of them. A sadness protruded from her eyes.

"Why did you come here?" asked the woman.

"You did not speak to us," replied Habiel.

She gave her brother a piercing look. She scowled at his childish comments.

The Children were everywhere.

"Why did you come here?" said the woman to Tomias, moving her arms.

Edjer smiled at how angry she could become. She was the surviving twin of the girl who had fallen from Edjer's grasp years ago.

Kiliea was one of the forty-one who had lived through their journey. She was the only one to ever leave the palace on her own will, leaving the Capital when given the choice. One could not wishfully leave without the King's approval. Umid would not hesitate to free any of his brothers and sisters, nor did he allow them to return if they left.

"Umid wished for us to stop here after an assignment," shared Tomias.

Kiliea held onto her anger in her reply, *"For what?"*

"He said his Guards had a task to complete," calmly answered Edjer.

She exhaled. They reminded her of the life she wished to forget.

"You came here because he wants you here. Punishment for both of us. He still uses me as a conduit for his spies on the road."

Kiliea was younger than most of *The Children*. Her twin sister's death had brought her closer to Edjer. But the feud between Edjer and Umid after all the loss they had endured made her blood boil. She wished to be free of them, the politics, and yet, she could never force herself to leave the kingdom outright.

Her small tavern, in the corner of her new home, was her prison.

"We can leave?" interjected Khalil.

"What would that say of me? You would report back the instability of the sister that left, wouldn't you Khalil? Drink, pay me, then leave."

"You believe us capable of reporting that?" replied Edjer.

She rose slowly, then returned the stump. She snatched the fire from the rest of the candle lights, leaving only the candles at the bar lit.

"I will lock up on your departure."

Edjer was the only one to ask: "You do not wish to drink with us?"

After rising a few steps atop the staircase, her head lowered in fear of turning away family.

"It is rumored the Prince of Death's exile is at an end?"

There was a slight pause in response. The men looked to Edjer. He replied, "Umid needs me, then I am sure he will require my departure."

She sighed, hiding a chuckle. She turned her head, the purple flower on her hand fully visible as she pointed at him.

"*She* would be ashamed of you, now." They watched each other in cold silence. "There will be no embrace for you here."

Kiliea ascended to the top. Moments later, they paid their fee, leaving the bottle at the table, the four mugs with it. Reaching their inn, they awaited their nightmares.

TEN

27 days until the Ceremony.

Prince Debyendu wished to clear his mind but like his steps, his mind circled. Sweat dripped from his forehead as the spiraling steps took their toll. He prepared to see his brother.

Winds whistled, sneering past his frosted ears.

Debyendu, blowing warm air into his hands, was draped in his royal robes and furred overgarments. The insignia of the Bengal Tiger on his metal clip held his coat up.

King Akshat of the Far East Empire was a man known for insecurity and was as paranoid in ruling as he was a strategist. He had devastated the future of his kingdom. Akshat could not share with his people the mistakes, the whispers, or the truths of the adventitious events that had led to the Great War twenty-five years ago.

Like all others, he wished to avoid another.

Debyendu remained the glue to the wavering confidence of the Far East peoples. He walked down the dark hallway, on the blood red carpet leading to King Akshat's black throne.

Prince Debyendu looked outside the open windows; wooden covers were fastened to the brick walls. Three torches on each side guided visitors through the long hall.

Were the people visible, thought Debyendu, from the open crevices up in the tower? Rarely did he come to his brother here, but political matters had soured, and he had questions.

Akshat and Debyendu were the last of their bloodline. Debyendu's wife had passed away from the plague, and his sons had died fighting his brother's wars. Akshat never married; no queen existed he could trust.

Their flag, the ravenous Bengal Tiger, on a blood red banner, hung behind the throne. A room of soullessness, a sunken void of sadness stunk the air.

"What news?" murmured Akshat, from his black throne.

The chilled seat was shrouded in his kingdom's sigil on the back rest. The Bengal Tiger insignia had faded long since he took the mantle.

Debyendu approached the throne. He found Akshat's eyes wandering.

Why does he dress like this in front of me, considered Debyendu.

The king's once golden face lost its vibrance. His features sluggishly sagged. His cedar skin was without expression, without energy. Akshat's mouth moved in repulsion to his stagnant body.

"I have told the Prince what I have been instructed to," replied Debyendu.

"What does he suspect?"

"He knows nothing, for now…"

"What of the deal?" asked King Akshat. He rose, his cloth hiding his frail body. He looked to float slowly down his steps, walking over to the blazing torches near the windows.

"A fair transaction, according to Prince Edjer. He accepted."

Debyendu's eyes temporarily focused on the backrest of the throne. He could not move from the hold of the faded tiger, its significance. His eyes steadily shifted to his brother, watching him near the warming fire.

In the flames, Akshat felt peace.

"We may yet be freed of all debt...Does he question my reason for avoiding the talks?"

Debyendu closed in on his brother's torch, eyeing the same inferno. He cleared his throat to speak: "He properly fears your reason for doing so, as I do..."

King Akshat sighed, weighing a decision. His hands did not plot; they did not connive in the name of power. What Akshat knew; he would never utter. The victor could be either side, but the plot itself was daring. He would benefit if he warned one but become a mortal enemy to the other.

"A commoner's morals, Debyendu, you must forsake these."

"What do you speak of?"

"We cannot act on honor, nor do we become rulers based on a commoner's beliefs. You do well to remember."

Debyendu let himself ease into a tiny chuckle. He ended, abruptly: "Who do we serve then?"

Akshat did not wish to answer, losing himself in the blaze. He whisked himself away from the flames momentarily. He headed towards a window.

"We have tried to plague Perfuga's people. We gave refugees coin, ideas to disseminate, yet they have succumbed to the opportunity Umid offers. His walled cities keep them occupied."

Akshat balled his fists.

"What do you fear?"

"What I cannot stop," replied Akshat quickly. Smoke near the torches escaped to the windows. He continued: "Umid's own people despise the refugees. He has done well to position them away from his citizens."

"He is well in tune with the people."

Akshat laughed.

"They play with people, like all rulers do. We are not blessed with walled cities of gold, brother...We have made mistakes."

"What mistakes?" asked Debyendu.

"My mistake, brother. They have been my mistakes." Akshat let the sentiments sink in. "We wished to plague the minds of the people, we—I, know better. To weaken a kingdom, our enemies knew. The parasite must grow within the mind of their royals, their *King.*"

Stupid metaphors. Debyendu despised the aristocratic dance. Akshat spoke of decades prior, reincarnating the times in the present. Debyendu sought the correlation.

"Do you speak of Umid, or yourself?"

Facing each other, both leaning on the flaps of the window doors, they locked eyes. Akshat appreciated his brother's boldness: "Once a king's mind falters, he acts on the fear of each previous decision."

"You acted on instinct."

"I acted in rage. I should have killed *everyone*, everyone Debyendu, those that opposed me. A few plotted, but I should have killed them *all*. Umid will need to make his choice now."

Akshat continued, "If Umid wavers, the kingdom will fall. If he remains upright, his people will splinter. Debyendu, this is not a game."

Debyendu flinched at the misdirected accusation: "Each lives by principles," said Debyendu, mounting a soft defense of his own.

Akshat, stepping forward, stood in front of his brother. He grabbed Debyendu's coat.

"You admire Edjer, but what can make a king buckle, Debyendu? What can make a ruler shake, with hundreds, hundreds and thousands willing to fight for me?!"

The answer was one Debyendu deeply required.

"I heed the words," said Debyendu, wishing to be free of the hold.

"Debyendu, look into my eyes!" Debyendu could only nod.

"Look at me!" Akshat demanded attention. He waited for Debyendu's breathing to find a calm cadence.

"I will have you executed if you interfere in these accords. Understand this warning."

Debyendu fell victim to the terror ravaging his brother. To threaten him, Debyendu wondered if Akshat was finally lost. But this felt different, Akshat was afraid. He trusted this fear as he left the tower.

Debyendu's dealings, long ago, had steadied the hand of unruly rulers. But he pondered, what was a man without principle?

ELEVEN

27 days until the Ceremony.

The clouds in the sky were dark with occasional clear, white distortions. Prince Edjer, seated next to Tomias, watched them float, awaiting permission to enter the halls. The two men sat in the royal gardens, surrounded by beautiful flowers in the wild habitat.

Before the arrival of *The Children,* years were spent by palace overseers accumulating the most elegant, wild seeds to decorate a once empty courtyard. Serving as a popular sight for visiting delegations and royals, the garden smelled of free lands. Edjer knew, however, that whatever beauty stole the eye, something else lay in the garden.

Rows and rows of plants, their placement was economic. There was no roof to the castle courtyard, allowing for rain and shine to enter indiscriminately. Two dozen overseers cared for the garden, under strict orders to not let one plant waste away. *The Children* were once the only threats to its homeostasis.

In the breaktimes afforded between classes, they would step into the courtyard and walk the grounds. Their horseplay had always damaged something. Classes for the orphans had always been conducted in the open hallways around the yard, stemming from Edjer and the others' fear of enclosed quarters.

The rows of plants in the elegant garden led to a tree in the middle, sitting opposite the Headmistress's class. When *The Children* arrived, the ash tree had been the only plant near its full growth.

Years passed since Edjer had forfeited his familiarity with the castle. He had accepted his exile, needing a moment away from his anger. Yet, in recent days, he found himself at the behest of his brother, knowing memories would flood in at the requirement of his presence. He sat like his overseers once did, contemplating.

Edjer watched the palace children in their lessons. He felt their desire to escape. His eyes slowly veered away from them.

The Prince of Death became a slave to the flowers, swaying peacefully in their sights.

Edjer wallowed deeper in sinking thought. *What would the desert locust be if introduced into the garden?*

The locust immediately would believe in its own ability, for its way of life had been innate from inception. Whether in a swarm or alone, the predator would believe itself a destroyer of worlds. *Foolish,* Edjer thought. The locust, introduced into an environment it did not know, would become the prey. Could the destroyer learn to be otherwise; Edjer hoped it possible.

The Children had been awarded roles in every sector of the kingdom. The boys became the inductees of the famed Arms of the King. The women, however, served the palace. They were marked and deemed Royal Concubines with a tattoo of a flower given to the fierce, refugee women. No woman would be given the role after, nor did any deserve the title. These women were like no other.

An intelligible and brave group of forty-one, *The Children,* became a force, with no loyalty but to the kingdom which saved them. They had grown since their arrival. They were disciplined in servitude. No term existed capable of defining the love *The*

Children had for one another. But, when Kiliea had chosen to leave, their unity had chipped.

Edjer, as well as the two youngest who had arrived in Perfuga, Khalil and Kiliea, had been the most favored. These three had been elegant, dignified, matched with ruthlessness.

"What troubles you, Edjer?" signed Tomias.

Edjer's eyes lowered from the branches of the tree above him. They were surrounded by fallen leaves. He sighed, "Am I a fool, brother?"

Tomias tracked Edjer's eyes. He froze, finding the flower Edjer watched.

Strobilanthes Dyeriana.

The Royal Concubines had been marked with the fierceness they embodied. Smooth green leaves shared a stem with the dominating purple flower, known as Strobilanthes Dyeriana in the old language. Grown in warmer climates, the main stem was strong, durable, and represented defense. It was once a gift from the Far East Empire, years before the Great War, and grew in the royal garden with the first tree. The stem was marked upon the forearm of the women in detail, with the purple flower etched into the outer palm of the untouchable concubines. They were trained for far more than lust. It was forbidden to defile the women.

"A fool you are not."

They began to hear the children from the inner halls.

"I will bring another into the fold, the first in years. Do I falter?"

Tomias' face twitched at the question.

The momentum of The Arms of the King withered. Of the original seventeen men, all still lived, but castle duties stole Tomias, Demetrius, and Umid. What could Edjer do with fourteen war-fatigued men?

"You need men. You win the king's wars?" The statement was true. *"Is the boy correct? Does he know what he is to be given?"*

"The boy learns fast. He ingests every lesson, every piece of information. He is no different than any of us."

Silence. The boy would be the first to join the group since its inception.

"A ruler must do what they must, to whatever rule they subscribe to. If it be cruelty, may it be wealth, or power, a ruler must remain loyal to the virtue they serve." Tomias fully committed his body to facing Edjer. *"What do you seek, Edjer, truly?"*

"I hope the principle of loyalty will outlast the crimes committed against us."

The bold statement struck Tomias to the core. *Crimes.* The word was justified. Nonetheless, it brought Tomias worry.

"Tomias, speak truthfully," commanded Edjer, his voice pleasant. He focused on the cluster of flowers as he spoke. *Strobilanthes Dyeriana.*

"Are my days numbered?" asked Edjer.

"Those who have the King's—"

The Prince's battle-ridden hands reached out. His hand steadily clamped Tomias'. He looked his brother in the eyes. He felt the coming burden of the times.

"I do not wish to know who instructs or advises the King. I wish to know if my days have been numbered?"

"You answer his every command; you win every campaign he sends you to. Your motivations are unknown, yet you serve diligently. You inspire love in the people, and fear in your King and his advisors."

"You dance like your friends, Tomias. I simply ask for an honest answer?"

The leaves shifted, caused by the entrance of a strong wind. *"You hold the King prisoner, Edjer, in this distance you create with him. His advisors and senators see you as his weakness. They wish the King to admit this, but he will not. I do not suspect you will see the new year."*

Edjer's exile had slowed the continuity of the kingdom. Only *The Children* knew of his exile. To others, Edjer fought and led his brother's campaigns. If commoners or refugees knew, they would revolt.

"This conversation is another one I wish for you to share with the King. If I am to be executed, when the time comes, take me home."

Home. The small nation-state swallowed by politics, Edjer desired a return to his homeland before he found death. He was blessed to be one of *The Children* who could remember a different life before Perfuga.

Tomias became fearful of what he triggered from his confession to Edjer.

"They will not bend to him, Tomias, they must be all allowed to leave."

"He is aware of what the cost would be."

The conversation came to an end. Edjer did not wish to divulge his confessions, his desire to disband the Arms of the King, to become a lost traveler. *How did Debyendu know?*

Second sons knew of love's hold. Edjer knew he had become unrecognizable. His own sisters had long since seen his face.

Edjer awaited whoever was to come fetch him for Umid. The clouds began to separate, becoming anomalous in the blue sky. The children's yells neared the door to the courtyard, across the bushy garden.

Brief, but nonetheless desired, the sun was able to escape. The students had found the freedom of the garden.

Many of them began their break time running around. Deviants pestered the Royal Guards, hoping to force one to unsheathe their sword. The Headmistress Manissa attempted to wrangle a few of them.

While many of the children ran back to the hallway, and others continued to toggle with the guards, outliers put their focus elsewhere.

These children encroached into the garden.

They were few, four in number, walking through the terrain. They snuck in between the rows, where the plethora of leaves, and tall bushes hid them from their Headmistress. It was difficult to see across the middle of the four hallways due to the plants and trees growing to their full potential. A jungle existed amidst the castle. But no one could hide from Edjer as they searched for a muse to their curiosity.

"Tiptoeing in the wild, you will find yourself being offered to a predator by nature itself."

His words found the ears of fearless students.

Four children walked deeper into the plants, careful not to brush into unknown flowers. They did not recognize the voice. Leading the pack was the boy who had spotted Edjer first, days prior. His boldness, he was a prospect to many in the castle. He walked forward, leading three behind him, two boys and a girl.

"Isaias do not venture far," yelled Manissa blindly.

"Yes, Headmistress!" answered the boy.

The curiosity of the sheltered children rose sharply. They found a man many could only imagine meeting. They slowly realized the actuality of Prince Edjer, and bowed.

"Do not bow. Children must never bow to me," uttered Edjer. He let the kids smoothen his gleaming mood. "Danger lies in the poisons of the garden."

Isaias paced forward, finding the tree's shade. He was African, a child of dead refugees. Behind Isaias, two Persian boys, twins, followed. The last of them, a girl, was African as well. A roughness existed in their faces: sharp features, ungroomed hairs. Some children were born within, with others found and brought by emigrating travelers.

Under the great tree of the past, congregated outliers of a kingdom.

"The poisons of the garden can be avoided," replied Isaias.

"Perils can never be avoided, boy."

The African girl, she signed in the hand language, "*Attempting to avoid peril is the road to a dishonorable death.*"

Edjer turned his head to Tomias: "We teach our language to the students?"

"*I taught her. She is mute.*"

Edjer nodded: "Honor is an achievement bestowed upon warriors, by cowardice men."

They looked upon Edjer with surrendering eyes, entrapped by his presence.

They were interrupted by their worrying caretaker. Headmistress Manissa ran through the dirt part of the garden after they did not answer her calls. Behind her, an attendant.

"Edjer, Tomias, I apologize for the kids' intrusion."

Edjer smirked at the children. They calmed him. Tomias saw firsthand Edjer's power over people, both commoners and children. The Prince of Death was truly a man to fear.

"It is all right Manissa, they are like us. We did not listen, either."

Tomias and Edjer embraced their sister with a hug. Manissa was shrouded in a black dress, down to her ankles, covering her arms. She, like the rest of the Concubines, was marked in the hand.

—

Edjer stood in the Inner Council room, awaiting Umid outside his chamber door, the attendant and Tomias with him. Behind the chamber door, yelling.

"Niobe—"

The conversation intensified. Voices carried into the quiet Inner Council room. None could avoid overhearing the argument.

"It is my responsibility!"

The doors opened violently to Niobe fuming out of Umid's chambers.

"Leave us with Edjer. It will just be the Prince today."

Tomias walked out of the council room with the attendant, satisfied, without a goodbye.

Edjer met Niobe at the chamber door. She was slow to open a path for him. He walked in to find incense burning by the fireplace. The King's desk remained packed with papers. Candles were lit on the desk while a calm fire brewed. The midday light gave ample vision to the inconceivable stress overtaking Umid's composure.

King Umid leaned against the mantle of his fireplace. His sweat reeked through the loose garments he wore.

Niobe closed the door behind her. Edjer took a seat. Umid's eyes remained on the fire while Niobe waited by the door. The air was off, a complication of some sort.

The King spoke sternly: "Did you see Kiliea on the road?"

The brothers could not see Niobe's eyes widen. She betrayed her own composure, attempting to straighten before the men saw her. She awaited Edjer with remorse.

"I did."

"What news?"

"No news. She remains alone."

How is she? Niobe wished to ask the question.

Umid left the warm fireplace to face his brother. He took his seat.

"Do you hear our arguments?" asked Umid.

"Umid, do not," uttered Niobe. Her voice was vulnerable, a command turning into a plea.

Umid scoffed. The patience he had for Edjer, Niobe, and the rest of *The Children,* wore thin.

"It seems Niobe and I are unable to produce a child."

"Umid!" shouted Niobe.

He took a deep breath. "Niobe does not wish for you to be consulted. She fears… your allegiances." His comical tone danced around the severity of the news.

"I am but an exiled Prince," answered Edjer. He was upright, rigid.

Silence took the hall. Umid took a moment to just stare at his brother.

Edjer knew Umid was unarmed. But Niobe held *the blade*; the knife never left her thigh. His own was in the rear of his waistline, but to engage Niobe from behind, she was one of the deadliest of *The Children*.

Neither left unscathed the last they had crossed swords.

"I confess, I have sought other means for a child. The game of odds proves it is I who is the problem."

"He wishes to take a child from the palace," interrupted Niobe.

"I wish to take a boy and a girl, as children. I will take an Arabian, and a fairer boy, similar in look to myself."

The boy must resemble Umid. Psychology, perception, the semblance of visual continuity was demanded for a smooth transition.

"It is of no consequence to me."

Umid turned away. He tightened his hand.

"What news do you report?" asked Umid, visibly frustrated.

Edjer waited till the tension momentarily subsided. "I ask that you speak truthfully to me now. What news do you hear of the Ceremony?"

Niobe motioned towards Umid.

"Threats circulate, Edjer. There are those who do not want to see peace. Most is brothel talk, but others speak of true danger."

"From whom do you hear this, Umid?"

Umid was speechless. He did not know.

Edjer found confirmation in Umid's fearful look. Even from his talk with Debyendu, he had believed the threat came from the Bear Kingdom. Patience lay in their audacious royals. The loss in the Great War, and the concession of lands in recent skirmishes became costly. Misguided portrayals of honor motivated their desire to plot, Edjer knew it to be so.

"Why these questions?" solicited Niobe.

"You were right to fear a plot. A play will be made to weaken Perfuga."

Niobe and Umid did not know if they could believe him.

"What of the Tiger's Paw?" asked Umid.

"They have closed their routes; all trading has ceased. They fear repercussions. A delegation without the king will be sent."

"Repercussions in what manner?"

"War, Umid. Which heads of the kingdoms have agreed to travel?"

"The Bear and the Northerners have agreed to send their kings. The Nation-States will send the ruler of the biggest state to settle their debts."

Edjer looked into their faces: "From what I gather myself, the Far East royals were approached with an offer, I do not know of what kind. Akshat does not speak of its nature to Debyendu, nor does he plan to. He will not leave his castle."

Edjer gave Umid and Niobe a moment to think this over. "Can the Ceremony be stopped now?"

"Edjer, the talks could provide us with lasting peace."

Edjer looked across the table: "Listen to me then. Any kingdom's delegation with a king or queen is not to be trusted. Akshat is no friend of the Bear. If the Bear sought after the Tiger, others were given an opportunity to plot. I fear we will be surrounded by enemies.

"This is no small matter, Umid. For Akshat to shelve himself in his tower, this goes beyond an entente of kingdoms. If not soon, then during the Ceremony, they will all attack," continued Edjer.

Umid sank his head in shame. He stammered to speak: "Edjer, I allowed King Azazel's party to travel with nearly six hundred soldiers. They will march to the last trading post."

"Revoke the approval!" declared Edjer.

"I cannot! The approval was given before you arrived. Azazel and Lomotos were met on the road, with terms discussed and signed."

"You allow an enemy army to march towards you unopposed?!" shouted Edjer.

"I do not prepare for fucking war, Edjer! I bring peace!"

"Only after my sword plunged into the bellies of their sons!"

Niobe motioned forward from the table; her hand pressed against her robe. "Careful, Edjer."

The warning forced another silence.

Edjer himself had not noticed his hands lowering to his sword. He calmly retreated.

King Umid looked at Edjer's hands as Niobe approached closer to Umid.

Edjer calmly stated: "Tomias will share with you the terms of their arrival."

"How can we trust Debyendu?" asked Niobe.

Edjer found her eyes: "We cannot, he is either central to their plot or his fears for war are as real as ours should be."

Niobe and Umid began to truly worry. Edjer stopped before he walked past the door.

"Khalil will now protect you in the castle. I do not trust your Guards. He shall ask your permission to alert the... Concubines," concluded Edjer.

Niobe and Umid shared a look. The formality in Edjer's voice terrified them.

"It will be granted."

Before Edjer could reach for the door, Niobe uttered: "Where does the prince lie his head in the Capital?"

Edjer sighed, beginning to lose his composure. "I shall retire where I belong."

"Umid, he must stay. People are aware of his presence now. They will assume disunity."

Edjer fumed. "Do your nightmares differ from those of our brothers and sisters? Do you not fear to ask me this? Recall the dark times before we are surrounded by enemies!"

The royals did not move from their position, suspended. They cowered in shame from the thoughts he harbored of them as he left.

And like others, their feelings scarred into anger towards him.

TWELVE

27 days until the Ceremony.

"They will kill me, Uncle!"

Jabez looked at his nephew, Edjer. Bags of darkness under his pupils hid the fear he had for his nephew.

"Paranoid men have your ear," shared Jabez.

They sat deep within the compound of the Arms of the King. Night befell the land, and with the Ceremony approaching, curfew orders kept streets silent.

Near the fireplace, Prince Edjer and Prince Jabez sat in a library. The space was vast. Grand in stature, the hall held thousands of pieces of literature: scrolls, journals, and books, on all topics. Unfinished canvases and paintings stood on easels near the bookcases. Bookshelves, the height of two men, were pressed against the outer walls surrounding the Arms of the King in more than just knowledge. But hope.

The library doors were open.

At the edge of the hall, near the doors, a row of bookcases was lined together. Seven wooden tables, enough to hold fifteen men on each, were in front of the cases. The compound housed the Arms of the King, their armory, an outdoor and indoor training yard, and a bathing room. This was a warrior's palace, where secrets and traditions were kept, by men who served Edjer.

Jabez was the first to formulate the idea for separate quarters. The identities and traditions of the Arms of the King were hidden from imitators. They remained in a sector designated for refugees, whose differences from Perfugans demanded separate living.

The Native Quarter was built on the trust and reliance of each citizen. In the quarter, the Arms of the King served as healers, protectors, and guardians.

And for that, the people safeguarded their privacy.

The two men eyed one another. The time for a coronation neared. Another man sat with the princes at the edge of the table, a former member of the Arms of the King, Demetrius. He watched his master Jabez reiterate the same statement.

"Serve, until you can no longer serve."

"I serve my King, Uncle."

"*I serve my king...* The time of kings, many believe, is coming to its end."

Jabez's was under the influence of ale. Their cups were full of hot tea, yet Jabez looked to have a drink of strength in the cup.

"What do you believe, Uncle?"

"Three seasons have passed, and garden attendants tell me one must wake before most if they are to catch the shine. The sun wishes to elude us men now."

"You believe the kingdom cursed?" asked Edjer.

"I believe all men cursed. We are warriors, you, I…Demetrius. Not many will understand."

Demetrius did not like the morbid tone Jabez held onto. At this point in Jabez's grief, even Demetrius could not hide his debauchery.

"Your eyes have not known sleep."

Jabez snickered: "We recognize ourselves in others."

Demetrius watched them try to anticipate the other.

Edjer waited for a comforting silence. He did not know if he could trust his Uncle's loyalties.

"What do you report?"

"Demetrius, what were the orders?" asked Jabez, disgusted with his own inability to remember.

"Sire, the Native Quarter."

Jabez left his seat, pacing towards the fire. "Your brother wishes for your aid in reaching the senators in the Quarter."

"To what end?"

"He wishes you to accompany Myawi. With the Ceremony at our feet, they decline an invitation for all the Senators to speak prior to the Ceremony."

Edjer watched the candlelight in front of him. "I do not meddle with politics."

"Their constituents adore you. You will accompany him and need not speak. Myawi will set terms. Your presence guarantees their attendance."

Edjer knew this to be true. "Where?"

"There is a hall, I believe, you set up for the Natives years ago. The Hall of Healers?"

Demetrius mirrored Edjer, tightening. Years before, at a different time, he had created a clinic in the Native Quarter. But it slowly had become a place of pain for him.

"Do you and Umid wish to antagonize me, Uncle?"

"Grief is not a monopoly, dear nephew. Like mine, yours has yet to pass. I long to hear my son's voice, do you wish to hear the dead, Edjer?"

"Sire…" whispered Demetrius.

"I do not care to take part in potions… Tell Umid I will serve the King."

Jabez returned to his seat. "*I serve the King, I serve the King, I serve the King.* A time will exist when kings will watch their children's heads on spikes, before theirs follows!"

"Sire!" shouted Demetrius.

Edjer hoped the words to be afterthoughts of a man poisoned by ale and potions. Ale always masked sentiments Jabez wished to plainly say.

"Come, Demetrius. I hear the footsteps of a wild one. Let us prepare," ordered Jabez.

Their hollow footsteps motioned towards a seemingly empty hallway. They crossed paths with an Arabian boy, nineteen, on the way out. The boy bowed as they passed, but he was ignored.

Ignorant to the traditions prepared in his name, the boy frantically bowed seeing the Prince of Death by the fire.

"My Prince," said the boy.

"Children do not bow to me," declared Edjer.

"I am a child no more, Prince."

The boy had been training for two years. He started slender, with a clear face and youthful eyes. The boy kept the eyes, but blackness bordered the circular spectacles. His face had roughened; hair contagiously grew around his face. The boy wore a short-sleeved garment, tight around his neck. His pants were plagued with holes, his attire the result of his regulated regiment. For two years, he had slept in stables with the horses of the Arms of the King. The animals had kept him comfortable at night. Combat had been his occupation when light reigned, and cleaning the expansive compound had been his responsibility once the sun had begun its descent. Long days, endless orders, these were the conditions he had chosen to endure.

From the first lessons, the boy had learned the reason for the unit's rumored divinity. The fast-paced training had left him whittling away, but wisdom had never been lost on him. He had learned and steadily adapted. He found that he had been left alone most in the library, given the opportunity to read, write, paint, and simply move about the way he had chosen. This had not been a mercy. In the training grounds, he had learned to fight as they all had once did, but they also had taught him to humanize. He had quickly recognized the skills differentiating their discipline.

The boy was at his last test.

He had not been given food for three days, nor water in the last two. His officers had withheld library privileges over the last few months, robbing him of sanity. Training had not changed since Myawi and Jabez taught all *The Children*.

Brief stoppages occurred during the physical training. Each member had interrogated the boy. He had been given three tenets to subscribe to: he could not lose his composure, he could not deviate from an order, and he was bound by secrecy. The boy had complied, losing his composure only when alone in the deep nights. The farm animals could not warn the boy of the soldiers' presence as they had watched him at his loneliest moments. He had endured training purposely created to exceed his limitations.

The boy had never met Edjer due to his exile. Edjer had handpicked the boy years prior and had kept note of him for years. Khalil routinely had sent messages of the boy's progress.

If he did not pass his last test, Edjer held poison in his hand to end his life.

"Sit with me, Tafari."

The boy slowly went towards the fire, eyeing the man he least expected to see. He took Jabez's seat. Shuffling began within the compound. The main doors opened outside, as murmurs of a growing group amassed.

"Yes, Prince."

"No titles are used here."

The boy wished to apologize. He opened his mouth to speak but Edjer raised his heavy hand. "You are near the end, you sense it."

"I do, *Prince*. Oh, my apologies*"*

"Edjer, Tafari, beginning today you may call me and your masters by our names."

He nodded, looking up, amazed. Tafari did not know when the day would come.

"I ask that you listen to the words patiently, Tafari. I will share this with you, then, you may ask your questions."

"Yes...Edjer."

The Children had adopted another tenet in the bowels of this training: death would be the only unconquerable impediment from finishing.

"Who do we serve, Tafari?"

"The people."

"What are your orders if you can no longer serve? Recite it."

"The vessels, where the rivers of red meet the broken hands of a soldier, they are to be sliced clean, the stroke of the knife against the wind."

Edjer pulled the boy's hands. They looked upon his wrists together.

Tafari was well received by all. What no one knew, however, was Edjer was grooming him to take his place.

"Tafari, there is no religion that is incorruptible, no virtue absolute, no love unbreakable. Any belief in an absolute, in men's hands, dares not exist as truth. You understand?"

"I do not," said Tafari. His eyes grew wide.

Edjer desperately desired fairer times for the boy, but the conditions of the kingdom were becoming dire. He dared to wonder if Tafari could face the burden of the role.

Edjer sighed. "The heart's desire will outweigh the trained mind in your clouded moments. We observe a man at his weakest to learn of his character.

"You were watched; the moment you were given the purple flower. We wish you to submit to one rule, loyalty. The heart's demands are quite powerful. When the time comes to pursue yours, fight them. If you cannot separate indulgence from duty, you have failed."

"I will not fail you." Tafari spoke firmly.

Edjer placed a blade on the table. It is the famed blade given to all *The Children;* the same Tomias used to defend his sisters' honor.

"Is the brotherhood one you wish to enter?" asked Edjer. Tafari quickly nodded again.

Edjer left his seat, reaching towards the mantle above the fire. Blackened firewood held the flames strong, blowing dark smoke through the chimney.

An inscription, painted in black, decorated the walls above the fireplace. Below the one-word inscription, two chamber pots pressed against the bronze walls.

Edjer fiddled with the contents inside one of them, a poison, a *clearing metal of sorts.*

"Do you wish for a drink, Tafari?" asked Edjer.

"Yes, please."

Edjer threw the poison into the fire. The fire, as it met the metals, brightened like a star. It shined into a deep blinding white. The smoke softened from darkness into a powder like vapor. Edjer placed a transparent, thin barrier in front of the fire to shield from the light.

Edjer discarded more strands before returning with the second pot.

"You know we draw close to an end, and you are within the grasp of what you seek. Ask your own questions."

Tafari placed his drink down. He tightened. "Why me, Prince?"

"You were well regarded by Myawi… as well as the previous Headmistress."

Tafari smiled. He remembered his old Headmistress when he was an orphan in the palace. Tafari knew she had looked upon him with care. She honored him with the time she had invested in his teachings.

"I…" Tafari cleared his throat. "I took part in the Second Exodus when the plague hit. I was carried into the Capital by my sick mother. The Headmistress could not save her, but she took me in to be a palace child."

"When you outgrew the Headmistress's instruction, you returned to her? Why?"

Tafari reminisced: "She was what nature left me as a mother. After the students were given to royal attendants, I returned to help her teach those like me. She was my mother in more than name."

"Most believed you could have been a politician if you pleased. They speak highly of you."

"I was aware of the world we choose to be blind to, Prince. The role did not suit me."

Edjer hid how impressed he was from Tafari. Something changed. He began to fear him. His intellect.

"Before you left the Capital, you graced the classes often if I am not mistaken?" asked Tafari.

Edjer did not expect the question: "I helped the castle in its objectives."

"What objectives lied in telling stories to children?" continued Tafari.

Edjer stammered.

"I helped the Royal Concubines, the Headmistress, with their responsibilities."

"I apologize if I offend you, Prince. They are not concubines. I ask you to avoid this term. My Headmistress Lady Asiya, she was no concubine, Prince."

Edjer froze. He despised the return of memories before his exile. Those were turbulent times. He rose out of his seat to the fireplace, injecting metals into the fire.

Tafari eyed the Prince the whole time, wondering if he had overstepped. He exhaled watching Edjer return to his seat.

"You trained with our linguists, Tafari. You see the word painted above the mantle?"

"Yes, *Pignus*. It is of the old language."

Edjer demanded more from him. "It's translation, Tafari?"

"Pawns."

"A welder produces, farmers produce, blacksmiths produce. Workers of this kingdom work blindly; we do not. We are the King's warriors, but we are autonomous. Understand the privilege set upon us. We do not suffer the burden of blind servitude."

"That is what these books are for. Are they not?" asked Tafari. His deduction reassured Edjer. Tafari passed the final test.

Edjer took a moment to sip his black tea. "Perfugan royals trained us when we all became of a suitable age. When we completed the training, we formed the Arms of the King." He took a moment to remember the day they were placed in their roles. "The women, like your old Headmistress, trained with us, and were marked and given the title, Royal Concubines.

"We act as pawns, but for the people. We are trusted for expanding our skills beyond the sword and dagger. Within the Concubines and the Arms of the King, there are artisans, artists, poets, and authors, those who provide more to the world than the blood of enemies. We earn the loyalty of the commoner by how we act in our autonomy."

"To what end?" interrupted Tafari. Tafari contemplated the philosophy. He subscribed to Edjer's wisdom.

"I feared you would turn into a man seeking blood. We taught you of life, avoiding the path of an animal. An animal can be trapped, it can be distracted. A warrior taught to understand can expand and conjoin into a unit more than oneself. Do these words find a home, Tafari?"

Tafari heard the words. "Prince, are the Arms of the King allowed to leave your service?"

"Do you wish to leave?"

"No. I ask, for I assume my purpose is to further your unit. You... you want me to bring others."

"They speak properly of your intelligence. My years away have been disguised as my leading Umid's campaigns, but I have been exiled and return only for this Ceremony. It will be you who shall take my place in years to come before I am – killed."

Tafari's concerns grew: "Why expand?"

Edjer recognized a growing mind.

"I know not of the kingdom's direction. Like you honor your Headmistress, I honor mine, the place that saved me. I will not leave Perfuga to rot. It means nothing to me if others do not keep their word. I will keep mine."

The shuffling in the hallway increased in volume. Eyes became white glares in the dark walkways. They peered in, awaiting the coronation. The signal had been given, and many awaited the hue of the fire to truly complete its turn.

Edjer returned again to the flames, depositing the clearing metal. He watched the shift in real time.

"You have become mute. Do you succumb to fear?" laughingly asked Edjer.

"You burden me with information I did not expect."

Edjer spoke calmly: "You will have time before you are burdened."

"The robes, they differ from the robes of the King's men. Why?"

"The black on the robes of royals and attendants represent duty, servitude. We choose white, however, for stealth, for purity of action."

"May I ask questions of personal matters?" inquired Tafari. He waited for Edjer to sit. Edjer granted his request with a still nod.

"Do you believe these positions given to you, and your sisters, honorable?"

Edjer eyed the chamber pot next to his cup. He poured more tea before speaking. "I do not know, Tafari, truly. At that moment, Umid was given a crown, and all the others, our roles. We were young."

Edjer sipped his drink. The eyes of his men spying behind the door grew in number. They shared his opinions on the matter.

"Balance and honor are important to understand. Religion teaches us there is a balance in the world. We misconstrue the belief and wish it to be a singularity." Edjer held his blade up. "If I am to strike you with this blade, the idea of balance to all men is that your family will strike me down. That is balance, done in the name of honor. The balance of nature, gods, whomever, it is not singular. A wrongful death can be remedied kingdoms away with a stay of execution on an innocent man, and nature would rest. Insanity brews in those who cannot comprehend this, and it remains a fact you must understand to do this."

"Why do you not leave? Have you never wished for another life?" inquired Tafari.

"I swore by my name, only death frees me," lied Edjer.

Tafari was not a novice to the topic. His mother was once broken down as she held a dying boy in her hands. She had hitched rides with soldiers and merchants, providing payment to Royal Guards to take her and her son to Perfuga with her body. He understood at a youthful age the balance existing in the world. Excitement died down, and realism set in. This was no fantasy joining the Arms of the King. Tafari was entranced by Edjer, however.

The mystique of the Prince compounded on a single conversation, for already, Tafari loved him.

Habiel and Khalil brushed past the intrigued warriors. They walked through the bookshelves with candles. They stopped at the end of the shelves, near the long tables.

"The smoke is ready, Edjer," warned Habiel.

White smoke emptied through the chimney. The palace, the people of the Native Quarter, would know another joined the ranks in the Arms of the King, the first in years.

THIRTEEN

27 days until the Ceremony.

Seated next to her door, Niobe stared at her bare body reflected through the glass. In front of her, a soulless reflection stared back. The candles by her mirror could not radiate her dulled emotions.

She turned to find Umid for comfort, but she could not locate him. Behind the fireplace, Umid sat in silence, washing in private.

Niobe rose. She eyed her glowing skin, the bulging breasts she feared would never feed a babe. She held her position, naked in the mirror. No one watched her. It was a moment of safety, guiltless from her decisions.

Niobe was never the same when Kiliea had marched out of the Capital, demanding Niobe end the infighting between Umid and Edjer. Niobe's refusal, her staunch loyalty to Umid against *The Children,* secured the crown she adored.

In *The Children's* past journey, Niobe had represented strength. Edjer and Umid were leaders, but Niobe was the unbreakable backbone. She had never withered along the path.

Yet, all of Niobe's troubles led to Edjer. She never could trust him once he had let the young Sevina slip from his grips and meet her death. She had, and still did, love each of her brothers and sisters dearly.

Every single one.

But Niobe's nightmares did differ from her kin. Hers were self-inflicted, darker, bathed in regret and disdain. She was taken hostage in the bowels of castle walls by immortal guilt. Moments of solitude forced her to think of her betrayals, her actions of self-preservation.

King Umid opened the door to find Niobe looking out the chamber window. He was like her, bare. Their bodies, both, were scarred all over. Hunting wounds from the wild animals encountered on the journey stained their backs. Remnants of broken bones and dislocated joints were evident in the radiant skin of Perfuga's King and Queen.

She held far more scars than he, from a battle unspoken by decree. This battle had led to a man's exile. The Prince of Death's anger had shown itself brutal on that day.

Umid grabbed a robe from behind his desk. His hair was wet, slicked back.

"Why, Umid?"

He knew of what she spoke. "We need their loyalty if we are to survive what is to come."

Niobe continued to look out the window, a slave to the cloudy sky.

"They despise us. They will always despise us."

"I am their King."

"They would kill you at a moment's notice if he gave the order."

Umid smiled, hiding from her slight. He looked down at the papers on his desk. The duties of a King were innumerable.

"Indeed…"

The night was to return the past to her. "You boys were trained to restrain yourselves by cleaning brothels, and still, our peace and quarrel are held together by women."

Umid disliked her feelings towards his weakness. He replied in kind: "They distrust me, but they would murder you first, far before they take me."

"Your allies wither...King."

Niobe was keen to find a place in his heart, between the love he also shared for his brother, Edjer.

"The white smoke arises..."

He closed his eyes. King Umid was tactical in his ploys, but tonight, he had none. He called for his attendant.

Umid spoke as she came in: "The white robes, we will need them tonight."

FOURTEEN

27 days until the Ceremony.

Warriors turned to children, peering into the library, curious. They watched Edjer, alone now, continue to cure the fire of its red hue. All were worried for him. Edjer's men remembered him at the beginning of his exile. They did not wish to see him lost again. The trail back to the living required too much of him before.

"Enter!" shouted Edjer, without looking.

The Arms of the King emerged from the outdoor hallway. The men walked in and held in their hands, an unlit candle in a metal holder. They emerged in an orderly fashion and pushed outwards to the walls.

Behind the men, came the women. The Royal Concubines wore white gowns like the soldiers in the room. Their garments were gold on the neckline, with the rest, clear white. Against the cusp of their breasts, the kingdom's sigil, a golden sword upright in the sand. They held their candles up and enclosed the circle made by the men. Nearly all of the forty-one were together again, under the guise of one joining their ranks.

The faces of the women were shrouded in golden, bridal rhinestones over their braided hair. Transparent white cloth hid their faces. They were not to be removed until the candles were lit.

Royal Concubines were told to be covered and always preserved outside the castle.

Edjer pushed the screen away from the fire. Anyone gazing into the light would be blinded. The flames were a silky white against the blackened bricks at the root of the chimney. Crisp firewood beneath the white smoke highlighted the spectacle.

Edjer placed a torch in the pit before he began. Within seconds, it burned with a white flame.

Edjer met each of them with a spark. He said their names, slowly, before lighting their candles, waiting for the wax to drip before moving to the next. He basked in the momentary happiness. As the flame of a candle sparked, the faces of his men lit up. Edjer did not see their adult faces immediately. Rather, he saw their youthful gazes, muddied cheeks and bodies frail from fear and hunger; they were children he had survived with. Their familial bonds were stronger than blood.

Edjer did not hide his smile as the women lifted their veil to his flame. They did not either. He became a child again, a teasing smile taking hold of his face. These were kids he once hunted for, a family he had inherited. They were the people who held him up when Sevina had slipped from his fingertips, when bloodlust nearly overtook him in his exile. Pain was unforgettable, as was the continued support. A sense of shyness emerged in each of their gazes upon one another. The boys had not seen the girls in some years and did not expect their beauty to be what it was. Clear smiles, smoothest of skin, eyes of a glimmering gold, the flame could not better highlight their enchanting charm. The golden Arabian skin of some, with the vibrant Black hue of others, the women were known to be the most distinguished in the known world. And still, they were shy, modest in the eyes of family. As each veil rose, the initial cheeky smile closed, and eyes darted to the faces of lost brothers and sisters. Edjer neared the end, and still, the face of each brought a renewed joy.

Titles were not important to *The Children*. Edjer and his kin were children no more.

As Edjer passed the last of the concubines, smiles ceased.

King Umid and Queen Niobe stood at the entrance.

Darkness hid the royals, but the eyes of *The Children* had long evolved from human eyes. Nature taught them the instincts of a predator. They saw who lingered behind the bookcases. Faces turned stale at their entrance. Umid and Niobe were dressed in the proper garments, but the ambience shifted, like a foreign element obstructed a rare purity.

Umid strutted with confidence, whilst Niobe did not cover her face.

Edjer hid his shock well. The Prince of Death knew Umid needed favor with the warriors and intellectuals in the room. He finished lighting the flames before shifting towards the royals. They waited behind the encircled concubines.

A path opened on Edjer's order.

Umid walked through to follow Edjer. Niobe stopped to fill the open gap in the circle. She held a candle and waited. Edjer lit the candle and said her name. *Niobe.* Neither hid the distaste of her recognition. They became stone. She became uneasy as she watched Umid and Edjer walk side by side, the famed Two-Headed Beast. Every set of eyes was placed on the joint walk. The room intensified.

The brothers stopped in front of the fire.

The Children were split in ideology. Killers were prostrated within arms distance of one another. Many wished to kill Umid, while others, still holding disdain for Umid and Niobe, did not wish to cross that line. The women, however, were together in their hatred for Niobe. Her betrayal was to the highest degree, an unforgivable deed.

If Umid ever chose to disown Niobe, she would not survive the night.

Umid's own survival was dependent on a number of stipulations. In the end, orders were given by a king, and he too, was a culprit.

Niobe felt their hatred immediately. Once Umid left her side, her own fears were realized. Tradition demanded separation. She had believed herself prepared, but she was not.

Would they forgive me if they knew, she wondered.

The flames danced behind Umid and Edjer. The brothers waited for the new member to enter with Khalil and Habiel.

Shadows from the light showed them to be a conjoined beast.

Jabez and Demetrius were the first to emerge through the doors. A path opened. Jabez nearly stumbled at the sight of Umid. Demetrius guided him to the end of the tables in front of the burning fire.

In Demetrius' hands were two pots. He held them by the handles and gave one to Umid and the other to Edjer. Demetrius then grabbed a candle and waited for Edjer to light it.

The coronation was nearly ready. Jabez held a golden thurible in his hands. He brought it into the flame to light the frankincense inside. Jabez powerfully shook the thurible four times to mark the beginning.

They all looked to the dark hallway for who was to enter.

Tafari was blindfolded. He was led in each arm by Habiel and Khalil. Jabez began shaking the thurible. Smoke quickly escaped and clouded the room lit by white flames.

Khalil and Habiel had clothing over their shoulders as they walked. Slowly, careful to attend to the boy, they placed Tafari in front of Jabez. Jabez kept ringing the thurible till the boy came to a full stop. Khalil and Habiel stayed behind Tafari while he faced Jabez, blind.

Behind the unstable Jabez, Edjer and Umid stood upright with a pot in their hands. Tafari's full stop triggered Jabez to ring the thurible, again, four more times.

The ringing ceased. "How many wish to be crowned to the Arms of the King?!" shouted Jabez.

"One, one awaits the burden," yelled the room.

Jabez rang the thurible four more times. Smoke filled the empty spaces of the room. It was meant to have no scent, but instead, heighten the senses of its inhabitants.

"Who is the one who wishes a profession of limitless duties?!"

"Tafari, a motherless boy, a fatherless pupil, as his brothers and sisters before him." This time only Habiel and Khalil spoke.

The words hurt Tafari. He remembered his mother; he thought of her sacrifices years ago. His apprehension was no different from the others in the past.

"Who can speak to his training?!"

"His brothers!" declared all the Arms of the King. Unison.

Four rings followed.

"What says his protectors?!" asked Jabez.

"Let him pass!" declared Habiel and Khalil, together.

Four rings. "Boy, do you wish to continue?!" asked Jabez.

"The boy is no longer Boy! He returns to his title, Tafari!" replied Habiel and Khalil.

Edjer watched the proceedings in agony. A boy lost his innocence.

"Tafari, do you wish to continue?!"

Tafari was much in awe to even answer. He nodded his head and was acknowledged with four more rings.

"Remove his blindfold!" ordered Jabez. His voice rose. As it thundered, Jabez endlessly rang the thurible. Tafari's sight was cluttered with smoke and white flames he had yet to see, a new beginning. The rings stopped after Tafari refocused his eyes. He was shocked to find his King. Tafari brought his head low in fear.

"Young Tafari, understand this duty is more than man can comprehend. You will be asked to kill; you will be asked to commit acts commoners would be punished for by death. You must remain loyal, desirable in the eyes of your King and Queen.

There is no act beyond the act of loyalty that is everlasting. What say you?"

Tafari hesitated in his words. He was still on his knees. "I am."

"Strip the boy!"

"Do not move Tafari," whispered Habiel. He and Khalil ripped Tafari's clothes with the knife they were given as children. The two were slow removing his garments, taking great care of the brother they were introducing to the order.

As they removed his clothes, Prince Jabez hailed the great sermon whilst ringing the thurible: "Young Tafari, heed these words for they are testaments to oaths taken in every kingdom. Understand, a demand of this magnitude is upon the honor of the individual. You have been vetted in a process punishable by death. You are trusted. But know, you are now protected."

Tafari's clothes were removed, and he was brought to his knees, bare.

"Tafari, Tafari, we weep, for this honor is matched with a burden! You are now a loyal man and a loyal man's nature is preparedness to die!" The thurible continued ringing with the booming voice of the grief-stricken Jabez.

"Submission requires one to become a slave, servant, and soldier!"

This much, each slave in the room agreed to.

"My son, my *son...*" stumbled Jabez.

The room went silent at the mistake, awaiting correction. Demetrius nearly left his post to go to Jabez.

"...my son, know as a loyal servant, you cannot betray another. If you were loyal to any before this, the oath dies. Betrayal is no longer your nature. How can you take a woman for betrothal, bend your knees to gods, pledge your sword to another man, for you would betray them all to fulfill this promise of yours today? No man or woman in this room will betray these oaths for they are punishable by the sword you are given."

The room waited for the finishing piece.

"Do you understand the meaning of oath, of endless loyalty?"

"I do."

Jabez whipped the thurible to signal the cleaning.

"The power of the ruler and the warrior will be bestowed upon you to provide the courage to answer the calls." The brothers behind Jabez whipped their pots around to mix the liquids inside.

"Close your eyes," said Edjer softly. He poured his pot slowly over Tafari's head.

"You will be purified through oils, from the seed of jojoba. It will cleanse you, an anointing oil for the warrior to rise!" Jabez ended his words with four rings.

After Edjer finished, Umid stepped closer to whisper: "Wash yourself as I pour."

"You will wash from the waters of the Jordan where rulers and prophets arise to be the wielder of this kingdom's sword." Four rings followed. Tafari washed himself of the silky oil. His hands were thorough in cleansing his body. The soldiers and concubines watched, even Myawi, hidden in the darkness of the hallways.

"Young Tafari. Arise! Arise! Arise! Arise no longer an orphaned boy. You arise now a soldier! Arise, taken in by brothers and sisters of a cloth prepared to be the first and last shield to Perfuga! Arise! Arise! Arise!"

As Tafari rose, the thurible made boisterous sounds. All spoke the same words as Tafari found his footing: "Arise! Arise! Arise!"

Jabez allowed the thurible to become its own organism. He spoke as loud as the sound it made: "Clothe the boy!" Khalil and Habiel began with a long robe covering his skin, his arms, falling to his ankles. "You become a symbol to others of the oaths you take. You are a slave to the demands." Khalil was the one to place the overgarments on Tafari. It lined over his shoulders and chest and was tied around his waist by Habiel.

He became an arm to his King Umid.

"He was nothing. But he has joined us to be One. Brother Tafari."

The thurible rang four times: one ring for the bondage of a slave, one ring to acknowledge his servitude, one for the soldier he had become, the last, for the realization of full submission. He had become Brother Tafari.

—

Celebration was due for the new member of the Arms of the King. The candles were dumped into water and a prepared feast was brought in. Honey wine had been fermented for the celebration, paired with slaughtered lamb and tender beef. Edjer had chosen the tastiest of spreads for his family. He expected Tafari's celebration to be the last opportunity to consolidate the group.

The library was relit with different candles to dispel the darkness of the coronation. No white flames were present. Firewood was reintroduced into the brick pit for a proper fire.

Voices rose once all were seated and began to eat.

Formality was absent in the voices of dignified citizens. The games and jokes were informal. In a moment of peace, guards were lowered. Days of old returned.

To the far left, reality existed in fantasy. Taking half the table, leaders sat quietly across from one another. The family took part in a meal amid impending terror from the Bear Kingdom. Edjer sat next to Khalil and Habiel, representing the Arms of the King. On the opposite side, King Umid and Niobe were at the edge, Jabez and Demetrius next to them. Alongside Demetrius, Manissa, the current Headmistress.

King Umid followed the ruckus himself, envying the happiness of the others. Niobe tried to hide her peering curiosity as well.

"Umid?" Edjer spoke up after finishing his food. The table held their breaths.

"Yes?" said Umid, stunned. Memory of the previous hours, when Edjer had berated him and Niobe, was still strong.

"I need to see the prisoner…"

Niobe placed her chalice down, disappointed.

"On the morrow, I can go," suggested Edjer, "We cannot wait."

Niobe's head sank into her chalice. She drank honey mead. The drink did not numb her as fast as she wanted.

"He is in the Guardsmen dungeons," replied Umid, nervously.

Habiel flinched as Khalil turned. Umid met their gaze and held it. The table shifted between stares at Umid and Edjer. The Arms of the King, nor any of *The Children,* wished to go to the dreaded place. Death awaited those who entered.

A strong silence held. Edjer struggled to filter his anger. Veins flared near his temples and pulsated down to his neck. He spoke tightly, controlling himself: "I will go."

"Edjer, no!" said Habiel, loud enough for the other tables. Conversations briefly paused. They all turned and stopped. None removed their hand out of range of the dagger strapped to their thighs.

"Cordial, remain cordial. You all represent the kingdom," added Jabez. Drunkenness freed his tongue from restraint. Conversations resumed.

Edjer turned to Habiel, utilizing a look to tell him not to worry.

"I will go early. If the King allows."

"Then I will send the order with an attendant when we return," said Umid. His nerves were noticeable.

The love Edjer had for all *The Children,* Umid had for Edjer. He held onto hope their love could be repaired. *If only he knew.*

It was the flimsy belief of a brother's love holding the monarchy up on itself.

"Righteous, the honorable *Prince Edjer,*" sneered Niobe.

The table felt the shift.

"Only a fool believes in honor." declared Edjer.

She finished her wine. Niobe pushed away her empty plate before she spoke. "The great recluse returns from exile. How is it you do not believe in honor? I say you lie… *brother.*"

"Attempts to stay moral are dishonorable, are they not?"

She laughed: "Moral? What morality remains? It died with her..." Umid tried at placing his hand over Niobe's. She batted it away: "Oh, you now wish to be King..." She had reached the apex of her frustration.

Edjer froze at her boldness. "We agree upon this."

Umid feared the coming words. Manissa's hand slowly slipped down from the table.

"Dear Manissa, sister, do not interrupt our Prince Edjer. Tonight is not the night for knives," said Niobe. Her eyes had not moved from Edjer's as she spoke. Manissa, disappointed, retreated her hands back to the table.

"Continue, *Prince.*"

"I have not much to say," He spoke softly; the other tables did not hear him. "We do not care for honor Niobe, you and me. We go for the eyes; we rip off the ears of our enemies. We take the genitals to end bloodlines, we wish for heads to dispel ideas. We are beyond honor. To fight with honor is a waste of time. It is dishonorable to our intentions."

"Oh, tonight we have found common ground, dear brother." Niobe goaded him further.

Between them, platters of empty loins of meat were left. The jugs of honey wine and ale were nearly empty. Niobe poured into Edjer's chalice.

"We agree Edjer, there is nothing left for us." She raised her drink. They took part in the custom of clashing chalices before her question: "Then what, Edjer, compels you to serve? Have you forgiven your kin?"

All eyes veered to Edjer. He drank his chalice in peace, holding his composure as best he could. Niobe knew she was close.

"Do you wish for Umid to see the truth? Is this your reason?"

Umid's gaze remained plastered on Edjer: "Answer her question, brother?"

Edjer looked into his chalice. "There is no world where I can offer you my forgiveness."

Umid froze in grief, as a boy learning of heartbreak.

Niobe had succeeded. "I ask for none either way."

"Then you have yet to understand the truth of my anger, and of those in this room."

"Demetrius, let us depart," interjected Jabez. His jug was empty.

The politicians at the table understood the misstep Edjer made. Testing a brother was no crime. Testing a king's rule required a head.

"We will walk with you, Uncle," said Umid, stammering.

Umid cleared his throat before he rose from his seat. The room stood for him. Formality was a sin to *The Children*. The affront to King Umid shared they would forever remain loyal to Edjer.

They waited for the royals along with Tomias and Demetrius to leave before sitting.

"You cannot enter those dungeons," warned Habiel.

"You are all prepared if I am to be killed. You know to flee immediately."

Manissa nodded in affirmation, then Khalil. "Death is escapable here, Edjer."

"It is never too far. We face a genuine threat, and it keeps them distracted. But I am sure they will make it an accident to avoid panic."

"How must we proceed?" asked Habiel.

"My life is mine to consider. We will protect them. After the Ceremony, my blessing is yours. Leave if you wish, but know now, we owe our people."

They paused, thinking. Family was never so easily separated.

Outside, similar conversations took place.

"Umid, you must be aware of what it will cost us if we allow Edjer to live."

Niobe spoke in front of the drunken Jabez and King Umid. Jabez had asked Demetrius and Tomias to bring the carriage. They had moments before they could not speak freely.

"Niobe, Niobe," mumbled Jabez, smiling. His teeth were stained with the honey and ale of the indulgent night. He was finally numb again.

"You fool, even you saw your nephew."

"I told him the truth. He should not fear death. He should not, Umid."

King Umid watched silently while Niobe and Jabez needlessly argued in front of the compound. The sky was clear, the stars and moon lit the dark blue night. The front of the compound was gated to stop intruders from peering in. Predators lay on both sides. Their voices needed to stay low.

"Stop." Umid demanded time to process. "Nothing will be done. Tomias tells me Edjer wants to return to his home. We best not aggravate him. A king does not kill his own brother."

"*Aggravate?* Love, you are a King. It is you he should not aggravate."

He attempted a yell in a muffled voice: "You aggravate me, now. Mind your tongue." His finger pressed the tip of her nose. She stopped. Niobe feared Edjer more than ever. She waited for Umid to remove his finger from her face.

"He will not return to you."

Umid struck her with the back of his hand. She was knocked off her base for a moment.

Instinct required action. From the blow's force knocking her, she was brought low, allowing her to dig into the dagger in her waist.

She swiftly placed her knife under his chin. Her response was spontaneous and much too quick to take back.

"You become bold in anger. Sheath your knife before someone sees."

Her eyes squinted. An animal appeared from dormancy. She needed to exhale to remember where she stood. Umid knew better to antagonize one of his kin in this state.

Niobe's eyes slowly widened. The knife found her waist as the animal within sheathed itself under her skin. Jabez feared the spectacle.

Rarely did one lose control.

"He submits. I see it, Niobe." Umid talked slowly as she controlled the pace of her breath. "Give me time. We will be free of him."

Umid had asked too much of Niobe to come to the compound. Niobe had screamed the loudest when the flower was etched into her hand. She would never submit to pain again.

Similarly regretful was Jabez. That night, Demetrius sluggishly brought him through the palace doors. They swayed as their feet met the stairs. Demetrius had drunk a reasonable fill, but his master was far gone. Jabez, in his palatial black, and Demetrius in his Arms of the King garbs, brushed against the castle walls.

Both laughed as they woke the attendants walking up the steps. "A prince knows better," said Demetrius, softly laughing.

The bald African man was strong enough to carry the meek Jabez to his room. However, playful activities like their quest to bed allowed Jabez momentary joy.

Usually, Demetrius escorted him from brothels. But since they had drunk and ate together, he allowed Jabez a moment for joy. The old man thoroughly enjoyed the trek.

When they found the room, the pain returned.

Jabez's room was smaller than the King's chambers. There was a fireplace of its own, with a lit candlelight on a stand near the mattress. There was a main bed, and another for Demetrius in the corner. Someone needed to be present when Jabez would scream in the night, crying for his son who had died in battle, for a love he had lost years ago.

Demetrius softly laid his master down in his rightful quarter. The candles were near their end as the fire withered away.

A sword hung above Jabez's bed, his son's sword. It was prostrated downward, like the Perfugan sigil.

After laying his master down, Demetrius removed Jabez's robes. His gaze became colder as the robes were taken off.

When Demetrius began to pull away, Jabez grabbed his arm, looking up to his servant.

"Was my mistake noticed?" asked Jabez.

"Prince, please, do not entertain the thought. We understand…"

Jabez closed his eyes in shame. Tears began to cover his face. "I – I am – I feel…." He paused. "I wish to hear it tonight."

Demetrius turned. "No, master, this is not a good night."

"No!" screamed Jabez. His tears softly left his chin.

"I wish to hear the story. Allow me this. I wish to hear it tonight."

Demetrius owed Jabez a payment of life. On the battlefield years ago, Demetrius had nearly died. A man had cut his chest, and the finishing blow was near. Jonathan, son of Jabez, took the blow for Demetrius after he found his comrade on the ground. He had given Demetrius time to take his weapon and kill the enemy, seconds Demetrius had needed to survive.

"Tell me, Demetrius," said Jabez, staring into the empty air.

Jabez looked over and brought his hand to Demetrius' palm. Chilled, his servant knelt by his bed.

"Tell me how my son died with honor."

FIFTEEN

800 days until the Ceremony.

Perfuga, it is the name of our great Kingdom, derived from the old language. It means, *Fugitive.*

I do not know how much more of history I can believe. Old kings had rebranded our home as a place of hope. But much is lost in translation.

I have thought of an unspoken question, was Perfuga a good place?

There was no place crueler. A good kingdom is at best, amoral. And Perfuga was indeed without morals. Perfugan royals understood that for a land to be great, it must stand on two principles: loyalty of commoners, and continuation of blood.

Like Perfugan royals fiddled with people, they fiddled with my brothers and sisters.

Perfuga only fought in wars it could win. No kingdom could chip away at its legacy after the Great War. It had funded the futile fighting, enriching both sides with weapons and provisions. There were two walled cities before the Great War, only two, where now Perfuga finishes the construction of the seventh. War will always be profitable.

But the best of its decisions was taking in two boys with heroic attributes, Edjer and Umid.

All of Perfuga joyfully accepted the royal adoption of Umid and Edjer. The continuation of blood through my heroic brothers would guarantee Perfuga immortality.

With this, Perfuga built a fantasy for refugees. It had two refugee princes and opportunities for those who wished to work.

Good and evil are nothing to a kingdom. I ask, what history do you know, that you can genuinely believe? I was raised in the palace. You did not see royals instruct Guards to hold down young girls to have their arms branded. *The Children* did not ask to be ordained as instruments.

Heed these words. A kingdom can only be deemed holy by nostalgic commoners. Kingdoms will either weaken and be destroyed, or they will grow stronger and purge their people if they do not improve. Heed the words.

Written by Tomias, the Royal Scribe
Letter to Native Quarter Senators

———

Amorality is a disease of no morals. Commoners debate the validity of the Cities of Mammon, yet it is the brothels and keeps in our Capital that flourish most. One should not judge. My own addictions have grown here, especially to wine. I have no tongue to taste but I am cursed with a mind and heart that feels.

My lust to forget comes from our journey with *The Children*. You and Khalil were our best hunters, while King Umid was the best tracker among us.

Us boys were always slow to eliminate our prey. You all taught me to hunt, but it was Niobe and Asiya who taught me to kill. It was unjust to subjugate the Royal Concubines to their position, but understand, the reports royals were given, exemplified excellence. Lady Asiya, Queen Niobe, and Headmistress Manissa were the best of the killers. They learned death in its rawest form during our journey.

The women we traveled with, decided upon *necessity*.

I know what I have seen in palaces now brother, you must not trust any politician or king.

Written by Tomias, The Royal Scribe
Letter to Edjer in Exile

—

The Children were not accepted by commoners in the beginning. All we wanted was a home, and food. The lands we crossed were much harsher than tribulations in Perfuga as a youth, but what was done to us was a crime.

The palace was opened for my kin and I to study and live in. It was not immediate; we were housed outside of the palace as the rooms were prepared. The best sleep we received were those initial nights. When we found the palatial beds, however, nightmares persisted.

It did not feel right living as we did when we lost so many.

What skills we learned along our path were harnessed and compartmentalized in Perfuga, with other, more dangerous talents. Knowing how to kill is easy, learning the will to do so is harder. Most of this, we learned from nature. We learned survival and brutality. We learned camaraderie. When a jaguar's hunger is at its peak, formations are taught instinctively to those who wish to survive.

Many fell on the initial trek to Perfuga, but after the first few, we learned a connection must be sought between us to live.

Bonds formed in pain, as we watched many die. Some fell from hunger, others from disease. But most fell in the nights, peacefully, from fear. It is no easy sight to see a child lose their sanity. For those who survived, there is a bond of love between us. It is a bond of understanding. We know the trust and faith we had in one another. We quantify our titles to one another as 'brother' and 'sister' because it is the only way to translate a connection we cannot define.

It takes an amoral place to break such a thing.

Perfuga twisted our loyalty into servitude. It was brilliant.

Through its manipulation, we inherited many of Perfuga's misfortunes. Today, I can say, Perfuga broke us. It separated the men and women, making sure none would be betrothed.

I do not expect it to be long before Perfuga will be empty of Royal Concubines, of the Arms of the King.

Written by Tomias, the Royal Scribe
Message to Jabez

—

The Royal Concubines.

To most, they are a myth. Perfugans dream of them. In our soldiers' songs, valiant efforts are rewarded in the pillage of the Concubines' sanctimonious bodies.

The only one seen by commoners is the future Queen, Niobe. If you did not fear her as we learned to as pupils, you would be captivated by her beauty, her beautiful brown skin, the piercing eyes of a speeding cheetah.

Perfuga did not truly know what they offered. They were marked out of lust. Perfugans saw it as an honor, but to us, it was primitive.

The artists worked on each girl through the night to perfect its shade. The stem loops around their hands to the midpoint of their forearms. The flower is beautiful, pure in its making. It is purple, with a mixture of black and green shadings, and dark borders to exemplify the conjoining of the purple and green in the plant, with four petals, equal in size.

The women were instructed to never be taken by another or be seen outside of the palace. When they leave, it must be on assignment, and they must leave covered. Their dresses allow for the flower to be shown yet hides the blade in their thigh.

Perfugan royals built them a separate area to train, to live, like the compound given to the Arms of the King.

In the nights, during the strenuous days, Perfugan royals would enter their chambers and discuss what ailed them. I would ask, when I saw the women, what were their perversions? What ugly responses I heard.

But the women know how to survive. They started to manipulate the royals into leaving them to pursue arts within the palace, to learn and read. Yet, the decree held that no man touches the women, under any circumstances, withholding them from love. Guards were executed for simple jokes at their expense.

Despite the injustice done to *The Children*, it was peaceful in the palace then. Umid and Edjer represented Perfuga. All knew Umid to be the next king, but all feared Edjer in battle. Men fought with Edjer once and remained loyal to him for an eternity. He was ferocious, for the protection of those who earned it. Edjer won the wars, and Umid, the glory, as the next in line.

The royals favored Umid not only for his appearance, having white Perfugan skin, but for his obeisance. They allowed Umid a choice of woman from the Concubines and began the formal courtship of Niobe and Umid.

But every individual needs their compass, a muse for their heart in difficult matters. And Umid's ascension worsened everything.

Umid and Edjer mobilized quickly to take control of the armies and instill peace. This was the beginning of strife between my two brothers.

Up to that moment, Edjer had visited Umid in the palace every day. He followed his dutiful responsibilities to sit in the Inner Council. Edjer even began training to become Leader of the Armies.

The plan had been to give Edjer control of all our soldiers, as well as the Arms of the King. Edjer successfully completed the training. Yet, he was unfulfilled. Everyone knew.

So, Edjer returned to his origins, the class where all *The Children* were taught. The new Headmistress Lady Asiya, one of the Royal Concubines, had just started. She was the only one of us from Edjer's homeland. I believe Edjer's decision to stop attending Council meetings coincided with Lady Asiya's classes. He would sit and watch where the royals once observed us. Lady Asiya had been the first Headmistress after the original attendants.

His visits became a regular occurrence. In time, he began helping Lady Asiya, speaking to the children, following them into the fields outside their Capital borders. Lady Asiya became the muse Edjer needed to remember life.

There are conflicting stories, but this comes to you as a Royal Scribe's Deduction.

I saw his eyes.

Lady Asiya had listened to all his worries and sins. When he spoke to her from the heart, he need not translate. I saw them in the garden, and I never thought anything of it. We all saw, and we let them be. We could not fathom the consequences. Understand, Umid and Edjer do not speak of this. Jabez, in all the wine I give him, fears speaking on the topic itself.

You must remember, amidst a stalemate, a few Nation-States asked to be inducted into the larger kingdoms for protection.

Umid sent, for two years, *The Children* to the lands we were native to. He sent us out with gold, silver, crops of fruit and vegetables, with books and art unknown to the world so the Nation-States would join Perfuga.

We were sent out and lived with our people for two years. Lady Asiya and Edjer, you see, were alone. Of the forty-one of us, twenty-two were sent out. The others went in groups of no less than three or four.

We were all successful in obtaining fealty, except Lady Asiya and Edjer. Still, we did not see a problem. When we returned to Perfuga, the celebrations were vast. We brought with us ambassadors to live in the Capital, as they still do with you.

You might not understand what I speak of when I talk of one's eyes. We know each other far too well. On our pilgrimage, when one's eyes shifted too quickly in the desert, or in the humid jungles, it meant danger loomed. Pupils guide us far better than bodily movements.

We looked at one another when we saw Edjer and Asiya interact. Even in the end, they had sworn there had been nothing.

The following year, conflicts over debts rose to new heights. Umid was not ready to rule, nor did he believe he was. We expected more time to pass before Umid faced a dilemma like this.

Many challenged him. Edjer was swift in ending any debate. Umid appointed his own Inner Council, keeping his father's men and adding Niobe and Alcaeus.

All was well, but he waited to appoint Edjer, Leader of the Armies. Edjer did not complain. We, too, waited. I deduce Umid wished for the truth of Edjer's dealings with Lady Asiya.

This is where conflicting stories take shape.

I believe Umid confronted his brother, and Edjer denied any wrongdoing. What Edjer would say, Umid believed. But I know of Umid's second weakness, Niobe. Surely, she warned Umid of the heart's ability. She forced his hand in announcing Edjer would keep his birthright, becoming the leader of the Arms of the King while the Royal Guards and soldiers remained with Umid.

Edjer continued his duty, and in the eyes of King Umid, he still could do no wrong. Edjer swore he never bedded Asiya; he swore to Umid. And Umid believed him. Umid was too preoccupied with enemies that forced him into conflicts over debts to bother. There was no time to investigate his greatest warrior.

For a brief while, peace, and more importantly, continuity prevailed.

In the eye of this stalemate, there was a winter in which a storm came upon the Capital. It lasted three days, with heavy rain and winds that shook the banners in the palace. All were given a curfew for the safety of the people.

On one of the nights, reports were shared that a messenger came to the palace and walked into the King's chambers. No one saw a face. The messenger was covered by a black hooded cloak.

None know what was said.

The Royal Concubines panicked as Lady Asiya was nowhere to be found in the morning. Edjer, too, was summoned to the King's Chambers. It is said Niobe and Edjer share scars from the fierce fight that occurred that morning. None can speak of it. We are curious, still, about that winter night.

Lady Asiya was said to be taken to the Dungeons where she was executed by the Royal Guards. It is a decision *The Children* know to be made by Niobe and Umid. No matter the charge, no matter the conviction, a sacred rule was broken. A life, survived through the agonizing path blazed by us children, cannot be taken by our own kin.

It is sacrilegious.

The fate of Umid and Niobe is written by the hands of warriors. Whatever the charge, the order of death without consultation of the rest is treasonous to the family. Treason can only be met with death.

The conflict arises in a clouded picture of events one can only imagine. It is difficult to rationalize their decision, but I dine with the killers each night in the castle. These days, despicable acts are not beyond Niobe and Umid.

We did not care if relations were had or not. We are a family, and understand that, this is my opinion, we are the Royal Family. Our kin hold the crown and the scepter, the swords that guard the gates.

If our brother did commit the crime, he and Asiya should have been forgiven. Umid does not have the right to kill one of us. He may be a king, but not to his kin.

Upon her death, Edjer was exiled for nearly ending Niobe's life. He numbed himself in blinding conquests for years after what he did to Niobe. Like family must do, our brothers helped him out of his dark desire to kill. We brought him back, but the remnants of his soul died with Asiya in those dungeons.

My drunken courage allowed me to ask what truly happened. Jabez feared the question. He simply said, "There are two principles a king must follow. Subjects may act as they wish if we do not threaten the tenets: the continuation of one's rule, and the loyalty of his subjects." Terror entered his voice when he spoke: "You all are too unfamiliar to royalty. When others report to the king what he knows to be true, yet himself hides, he must act. There is a Royal Decree, but he knows he cannot kill Edjer. How can he end whispers of weakness without killing him? He was forced to end the source of doubt."

I leave you with this. A year after Asiya's death, Jabez once came to me stumbling like never before. His tongue was loose, extremely belligerent. We all mourned, but internally, we await the order we remain patient for today. Jabez speaks in many tongues, but when he sits with me, he uses the old language. He said the words clearly, *Interfectorum Regum,* The Killer of Kings. Jabez did not stop there. He uttered this after: *He will kill us all.*

Tomias, The Royal Scribe
Letter to the Native Quarter Senators

SIXTEEN

18 days until the Ceremony.

Edjer waited, fiddling with his fingers on the cement table. He attempted to control his breath, relieved he did not have to go to the dungeons. He closed his eyes, alone, thinking of what Umid wished to protect him from. Umid had waited days to comply. He had asked Edjer to sit alone with the man in the Inner Council Room. What horror must have passed for Edjer to be asked to stay away?

The dungeons must still hold remnants of the travesty.

Royal Guards knocked before bringing in the prisoner. They quickly left the two alone.

Edjer found the man beaten, chains on his hands and legs. The prisoner resembled a northerner, with sharp features of those from the Bear Kingdom. Edjer quietly assessed as the prisoner bowed in his presence.

"Be seated," ordered Edjer.

Edjer's anger fluctuated whilst he interviewed the prisoner. Still, after beatings and mutilations from Royal Guards, the prisoner reiterated the same message.

Traitors; a threat; plots; protect yourself. While the prisoner pleaded his innocence and desire to sell information, his interrogator was lost in thought.

Edjer heard the prisoner's words but could not stop thinking of the dungeons.

He had only been there once in his life, to execute a prisoner. It had been his first rite of passage as a Perfugan soldier.

Edjer recalled that the underground contraption held eight cells. Wooden bars, thick as a loaf of bread, kept hope out of the souls of men and women imprisoned. The blood of past prisoners still stained the walls, uncleaned to instill fear.

He had to leave the past alone: "Where are you from?"

"I am a Northerner—"

"I expected as such. I had been told, but your features differ from your own people," added Edjer.

The prisoner smiled, as if for the first time in a while.

"My diet. I live in the Bear Kingdom."

Edjer winced. "The Bear? Have you told the Royal Guards?"

The prisoner tightened: "Yes, Prince. From the beginning. I told them of my station."

"Your station?" asked Edjer.

"I am the servant of Prince Lomotos of the Bear Kingdom."

A chill ran through Edjer's back. "Can you remember the faces of these guards you told?"

The prisoner helplessly gasped. Tears began to fall from his eyes: "Prince, I am unable to remember my own mother's face in my current station... I had only wished to sell my secrets."

Edjer closed his eyes in frustration. The prisoner scoffed.

"This is the confirmation you need...Information flows from your kingdom."

"How long?" Edjer asked.

"I do not know. Years maybe, Prince Edjer...I can only speak to their manner. They are confident beyond doubt."

SEVENTEEN

12 days until the Ceremony.

The Senators did not expect Prince Edjer.

The Hall of Healers had been a project Asiya had desperately wished to complete when she and Edjer had returned from their Nation-State. Lady Asiya had been ashamed her brothers and sisters had returned with ambassadors and promises of fealty to Perfuga. Choosing to appease Perfuga with a gesture, she and Edjer had built a stead in the Native Quarter capable of feeding the growing refugee pool. They had stocked supplies for the adapting refugees, medicine for healers, and provisions for the hungry. Since Asiya's death, Edjer had routinely sent the necessary materials, but had never entered again.

The facility had turned into a meeting place for inhabitants to express discontent to Senators representing the Native Quarter. The Native Senators, on this day, utilized it to hear Myawi's pleas.

Looking around, Edjer recognized the Hall of Healers had lost its initial fervor as a place of resources. Lady Asiya's death and his absence had much removed the feeling of community.

The Hall was still well-stocked and managed by the same people Edjer and Asiya had left it to. The walls inside were beige. Paintings and refugee art covered the building. Migrants from the

Nation-States, as well as those from the Bear and the Tiger remained there in the Capital to avoid working in the Cities of Mammon.

In the middle of the main room, seated at a concrete table, five senators, with Myawi and Edjer, argued for fifteen thousand citizens.

"Myawi, we do not have the same faith in Perfuga as you do."

Edjer continued to look around, nostalgic. He was captivated by the banners. There was a reason his Nation-State was not represented. He and Asiya had begged the leaders to renege on their declaration to enter a pact with Perfuga. Both had pleaded that the outside world did not know the truth about the freedom Perfuga offered.

"The King demands unity. If not for posterity, King Umid wishes it only for the Ceremony."

The Native Quarter Senators had one man speak, the oldest of the refugees.

"This meeting of Senators before his Ceremony is foolish. For false unity, Umid will bend to any demands."

Myawi's frustration grew: "Dare I ask, what does this matter have to do with you?"

The Senator clamored, "What do you think they will plead for, Myawi?"

He continued: "In one lifetime, one, *we* have grown in wealth and power in the Capital; even in Umid's perverse cities. We have senators in his chambers, and ambassadors for our mother nations. They will demand Umid limit us."

"What can Umid do to guarantee your attendance?" asked Myawi.

Edjer did not move as the men argued. His eyes were glued to the walls. The compounds and structures of Perfuga whispered death to his ears.

"Let us break for refreshments, Myawi. Senators, I will be at this meeting and the Ceremony. You disrespect your journey to

Perfuga by bowing to those who fear you." Edjer spoke slowly, attempting to tune out the warnings.

"Let us break," repeated Edjer.

Edjer rose and was off to the kitchen. He pushed through heavy doors to reach the back room where four women sat. They were discussing a gossip of note, laughing on a wooden table with their tea before he entered.

They slowly quieted upon seeing him, before rising, "My Prince."

"Those who know not to bow to me do not heed my words."

He sat next to them, in need of refreshment. Two women prepared food behind Edjer by order of the eldest. The women were sluggish in movement, comfortable with his presence.

"The Prince returns." The oldest woman watched him closely.

He leaned his elbows against the table before covering his face with his hands. "This was meant to be a place of hope."

"Sweet Edjer, that peace has long left us."

The rest of the kingdom had been told Asiya fell ill and died from the disease of the lungs, under the guise of the harsh storm. The ones who wished to live believed the fable.

"Has the King not killed you yet, boy?" asked one of the women.

His eyes grew wide. "Rumors travel to the Native Quarter?"

"We have just escaped instability. You must not blame us if we are afraid of its return."

"The people are right to be anxious, I do not know of the future."

"We have survived for years. If our generation must die, it is in the blood of our children to survive."

The eldest woman analyzed Edjer with her piercing eyes. His rough hands did not move from the table. She watched his indifference, the stress on his face, the grief. Edjer had become so much like Jabez.

"What do you ask of me?" inquired Edjer.

"Every one of us wishes for you to take the crown," said one of the women.

"Treason."

All laughed before the eldest spoke again: "Where was the honor for Asiya?"

Names of the dead whispered with freedom provide a gateway for ghosts. Many alluded to her in his presence, but her name was rarely shouted.

"What do you know of it?"

"A King may lie, but lovers do not. Women know the eyes of lovers, boy."

Edjer did not respond. He awaited his food.

"You are no longer the one from the stories, Edjer. You reek of fright and dread. Where is the man that killed legions of men with his brothers on his back?" continued the woman.

He was defenseless against the attacks. They had always been blunt; a cadre of sisters he sought for advice. They were truthful, and in a time of lies, he needed to be reminded of his place.

"What did I tell you, years ago, about the fabled *Two-Headed Beast*?" asked the oldest woman.

"Two brothers seeking immense power came upon a golden chalice..." began the woman.

"Please..." whispered Edjer. Behind the doors, Myawi listened.

"You must hear it; I told you of this when she passed. The brothers had been given the chalice and told to spill thine own blood and mix. If they wanted the power they desired, they had to drink.

"Oh, you were fools, so quick to fill yourself with what Perfuga wanted you to ingest."

His eyes watered.

"The sweet, golden chalice was drunk in darkness. It is said, within a fortnight, the two brothers awoke and found themselves bound as one. The warrior was given fire to spew at enemies, and the ruler, wings to fly."

The other woman in the room interjected: "Perfuga does not wish to speak the truth of where the beast originates."

The oldest continued: "Indeed," she paused, "The beast guards the lands with immense power. They forget their past form. They guard what lands they remember as theirs, with fire. They pull others from their own fuming destruction, masking themselves as heroes. It is insanity, their pursuit to be saviors of kingdoms. All the while, they are the ones burning the lands they wish to protect. They have soared too high in the sky to see where their might has landed."

Edjer remembered the story, the dormant rage he buried deep within.

"I never told you the ending. But let me tell you now, you are surrounded by death. The curse of the story does not leave you ... The creature flies down, wondering why they have received no call. They come down to see all the land, burnt. The two heads look at one another, one blamed for the fire, the other blamed for flying too high. They battle each other, connected, until life leaves their shared body."

Edjer lowered his hands. He looked at the women: "You wish me to kill the King?"

"The time has passed. The beast has long killed itself."

Myawi did not wish to hear more. "*My Prince,* we must continue our talks."

"I will meet you in the Hall. Leave me."

Myawi looked at the women. They awaited his leave as if they were his superior. Myawi was terrified as he left, of both the women, and his Prince Edjer. He bowed, "As you wish."

EIGHTEEN

10 days until the Ceremony.

Jabez hated mornings. He would arise to see a tired Demetrius resting. To him, Demetrius was a good soldier, a good leader of men. He was loyal. Before Habiel took Demetrius' post, Demetrius was a lieutenant for the Arms of the King. Those in the palace knew his talents were wasted on Jabez's protection.

Demetrius was from Ambassa, the same land as Tomias. It was a land where the debt of a life was paid in servitude. This was the only way he could repay Jabez's son. And yet, Jabez was ashamed of what he stole Demetrius from.

Jabez looked out his palace window with a blank stare. The flame of his candle burned near the bottom of its stick. It danced to the beat of the air flowing in.

He waited for Demetrius to wake from his slumber. The previous night, Jabez had gone too far with his trip to the brothels. He had struck the keeper of an inn asking him to pay for his night's revelry. Whether Jabez had dropped his coins, or left the pouch in his keep, he could not recall. He had joked about his debt, and told the innkeeper, regardless, he would return soon.

Striking the boy for doubting him, the keeper had sent word to the palace for Demetrius.

Only in the brothels did Demetrius leave Prince Jabez alone.

Jabez adored Demetrius, aware that squires and servants would kill a legion of men for Demetrius' position. He followed Jabez wherever duty took him. But like no other, he spoke to Jabez as a man, no different than he would a commoner.

Every morning, it seemed, Jabez examined the son he inherited from a sacrifice. But this morning diverted Jabez's attention from Demetrius. In his hand, a note was crumpled.

The room's walls held a cream color against the morning shine. Near the window, two chairs were placed against a stump. Jabez traded glances between the window, and Demetrius. He wanted his servant's ears.

"I feel your eyes, Jabez," said Demetrius. He lay on his side, covered in sheets.

"I require advice."

Demetrius arose from bed in a long-sleeved undergarment. "A moment, Prince." Barefoot, he and Jabez met at the table by the window.

Jabez began, "Early in the mornings, the sun overlooks our kingdom before her citizens wake."

"It is because hope has left. The sun may return in the summer," said Demetrius.

"Demetrius, you do not wish revenge for my son?"

The question stole the joy from the morning. Demetrius was slow to his words, "An action of war, Prince."

"If I identified his killer, would you not take his life?"

"I would not. Actions of soldiers are guiltless in war."

"An honorable platitude. Who is to blame for my son's death?"

Demetrius was quick in reply: "The kings that sent him to war."

A pleasant sound came from Jabez in agreement.

"Edjer sends news."

"What does my brother say?" asked Demetrius.

"The kings of the Northern Kingdom, the Bear, and the Nation-States approach. Our ambassadors and spies tell us they have embarked."

"Umid is risking too much today."

"You all underestimate Umid."

"You are sure?" asked Demetrius.

Jabez was sincere in his reply, "The people adore you *Children,* in all we turned you into."

Demetrius dimmed. "If they knew us, like you do, would they kill us or love us?"

"Of that, I do not know. You were forged by the air breathed in the wilderness."

Demetrius turned away. Jabez looked at his crumpled message.

"Edjer shares what he and Debyendu spoke of. We are not to trust royals a part of any delegations. They conspire against us..."

"Do you not trust Edjer's words?" asked Demetrius.

"A widowed man trusts no one...But, I fear the gazelle has given the lions entry."

Demetrius exhaled. With his hands, he brushed his graying beard, then to his bald head. He began to dress in his robes.

"I have hunted lions before, sire."

NINETEEN

10 days until the Ceremony.

Lomotos' sword was not known for its make. The lives he took awarded him and his sword illustrious notoriety. Yet, his past losses forced him into brooding thought. On horseback, he was to guide six hundred men to Perfuga for the Ceremony.

Before his journey began, he sat in his chambers, inhaling the scent of fornication. In his bed, an attendant to his estate. Her clear, white skin meshed with the cotton sheets of his bed. Lomotos smiled, eyeing the slight curvature of her hips under his sheets. He heard footsteps outside his door, stealing him from the memory of his creative tactics in bed.

The room had a mirror atop his desk. Beside his workstation, a compact fire pit warmed the room. Books rested on his table while shelves by his open windows held a cascade of journals and stories.

Lomotos covered his hairy body with a hunter green robe, pulling his long, brunette hair over the neckline. He knew the footsteps of his older brother. Lomotos met Semjaza at the door.

"Tell the attendant to leave," ordered Semjaza.

"Let her sleep, brother. She took more than she could handle," said Lomotos, smiling.

Semjaza ignored him. He walked over to the bed, kneeling by the girl's head. He marveled at her beauty in the sunlight. Semjaza stayed on his knees, holding his own weight in silence. He removed the hair covering her face, brushing his hands against her soft cheeks. Lomotos grimaced watching his brother's ploy.

"My dear, please wake."

Her eyes took seconds to adjust. Semjaza grabbed her garments from below the bed, brushing her skin whilst resting his hands on her pillow. She panicked, separated by mere hairs from a royal.

"Leave us."

She rose from the pillow. Her breasts hardened from the chill of Semjaza's eyes. The woman quickly darted out of bed.

"If I see you with Lomotos again, you will not see another day."

She left. Lomotos shared a smile on her way out.

"Your obsession with purity will swell our balls."

Semjaza took a seat where the woman lied.

"You confine me to my estate with that woman prisoner, and you ask me not to bed my attendants?"

Semjaza's face shot up: "You did not rape her Lomotos?"

"No, brother, I did not *bed* our prisoner. You think me an animal."

"Lomotos, our people now arise from mornings in comfort. Purity of their royals gives them confidence, men to strive towards. Our soldiers train harder. Citizens believe in their work. Do the reports you read differ?"

"No, brother. It is a tough ask for those who have only known loss in war."

"Where is our prisoner?" asked Semjaza.

"The attendants bathe her as we speak. She will meet us after she is clean."

Semjaza nodded. His plans moved accordingly. He closed his eyes to see what came next in his head.

"What of Perfuga today, brother?" inquired Lomotos.

"The spies speak of an assembly of Senators. There is strife Umid wishes to hide from his visitors."

"He's a fool."

"Your own folly should be punished, Lomotos. You have made mistakes of your own."

"I am rash, it is a problem of mine," confessed Lomotos.

"Our traitor sits in their dungeons. We do not know what he speaks of. Your mistakes cost us more than you know. We cannot surprise Edjer, now."

Lomotos scoffed, "They cannot imagine what is to come. We can deal with the traitor."

"Do not underestimate him," snapped Semjaza.

Lomotos clenched his jaws. He tightened his hands as he put on his armor. They were to ride out to meet their brother Azazel with the army.

"Your ideas are nothing without approval from the general of the army. You have planned well, but the men will fight where I dictate."

Semjaza laughed at the brotherly competition.

"You laugh, but your plan for retribution is simply a strategy without my soldiers and our harlot queen," continued Lomotos.

"All of you could not find your mouths if I dropped the sweetest of cakes in your laps."

Lomotos knew the words were true.

"I asked for my direct orders to be followed. If you would have sent the message to Debyendu instead of King Akshat, we could have surrounded Perfuga."

"An error on my part. I believed the king to rule the people."

"You, of all, know better," said Semjaza, his eyes to the fire. He saw their path in the smoke leaving the room. "Too many fear Edjer and his men."

Lomotos looked at his brother. "In a fight, each side has a chance."

"You rob a kingdom of their hope, their king of his confidence, you can pick them off, Lomotos. There will not be a war, we will pillage."

Lomotos nodded in agreement.

An attendant ran to his door. She yelled from behind the wooden barriers, "She's ready, my Princes."

TWENTY

10 days until the Ceremony.

The wooden table was fresh, pristine. Rising above the steps of an elevated platform, six chairs were prepped for the Inner Council. The seats overlooked hundreds of senators.

The chamber of the Senate was a massive, domed facility. Paintings of great warriors covered the chamber. The senatorial seats resembled steps on a staircase, with the leading members in the front and the others in the ascending rows.

Golden robes were given to the supposed neutral Senators. The garments fell below their knees, while their hands were free of sleeves.

The chamber was across from the royal palace. They utilized only half of the building for the meeting of senators, where the other half was being readied for the Ceremony.

Jabez examined the politicians. Those without demands sat patiently awaiting. He saw the senators with Alcaeus in the front preparing. His eyes perused the space, before he looked at the top row of senators, the senators of the Native Quarter along with ambassadors of the adopted Nation-States. They awaited the promise of the Prince of Death.

Two Royal Guards swung the door open for the royals. Four more Royal Guards escorted Queen Niobe and King Umid through. All rose at sight of them.

"Senators, arise, O arise. King of Perfuga, Father of the Adopted States, with the Queen and Mother of All Concubines. Heed your Royals."

Each man bowed their head as Umid passed, only rising once he glided out of view with Niobe.

The two royals sat in the middle, with Myawi to their right, and Jabez and Alcaeus to their left. The processions quieted to a sheering stillness. A seat was unoccupied at the corner of the table.

Edjer, everywhere he went, brought uncertainty. Whispers of plans and rumors resumed when the lost Prince did not arrive behind his brother. Umid could only look at the door, waiting.

There was no support for Edjer in the Senate. He did not resemble a native, nor did he respect politics like Umid. The ambassadors of the Nation-States and Senators of the Native Quarter wanted more from him, as did the commoners who wished him to be king. The Senators adopted Niobe's desire to end his sway over the people they serve.

Edjer lingered in the royal garden before the meeting. In recent days, he felt the weight of the past. Edjer believed dread to follow each additional breath he took.

Time he took to live felt as if he gave strength to death, like death would not be his alone to suffer. The feeling came and went since he spoke with the prisoner.

Decades ago, on the mountain range, when the little girl Sevina had fallen to her death, his own feet had lost grip on the ground. When his brothers had lifted him, they had thrown Edjer atop the rocky ledge in one final push. On all fours, he had landed on the thin trail. The leap to life brought him in front of a girl, the first moment he had locked eyes with the girl from his lands, Lady Asiya. She was just Asiya then. She had picked his bloodied hands from the rocks, bringing him to his feet. They had all continued, but he could never forget the safety of her hazel eyes, surpassing in power the sudden grief of the sister he had just lost.

Asiya's eyes, they had been the color of the mountain's clay, after the rain had ruined their path.

Edjer wished, in every living moment, Asiya would have agreed to stay in their homeland during their visit to their Nation-State. He had never wanted to return to Perfuga. His request had been a betrayal to *The Children*. However, she had refused, and they had never discussed the topic again.

There was no one he could confide in without exposing himself. He was a soldier who broke rules and lied. His station had saved him from punishment, along with the love of a brother. Asiya's death may have come from Niobe's hand, but he knew his own acts of love had condemned her.

He walked into the Senate chambers ashamed of himself. None rose, nor was he announced. He would still be the warrior guarding their gates, winning wars, and for that, the people adored him. He motioned to the last seat with a blank face. For a brief time, he attempted to be the Edjer they feared. The Prince of Death.

—

"Tribesmen and their Governor wish to have your ear, King Umid."

Alcaeus gave them the floor. A governor and an elder from a village town rose from the first row of seats. They were in commoners' clothes.

"My King, we swear to you, we wish you well," began the Governor. "We are all foreigners in any case," he uttered.

The Senators rumbled in displeasing whispers to the theatrical beginning. Citizens of the Native Quarter watched their neighbors. Content with the interruption, the comment held weight.

Edjer watched with indifference. He looked out at the excess of it all. Hundreds of senators. They were all below their eye-level from his view, except for those he had promised.

The Native Quarter Senators were glued to Edjer's every movement.

"Begin your claims."

"My King, we must begin with the taxes. You tax our villages the way you tax the citizens of Mammon. The opportunities offered throughout your kingdom are not indiscriminately shared. These wars are paid for by the work of babes, even our slaves."

"We wish to remedy the problem, Governor," added Umid.

Edjer moved to look at the other Inner Council members.

"The Ceremony, yes. The proceedings may not cure the unfair tax laws."

The Senators were patient. The invitation for the Governor to speak was a ploy to see where they could push the King.

"Continue."

"The Cities of Mammon are not like the villages and towns of trade. We do not have the immense wealth and resources these places of per—these places do."

"These places of *perversions*. Do you think they take home what they work?" asked Umid.

"I do not—"

"Do you think only the men work in these walled cities?"

"No, my Kin—"

"With better output, and a workforce as grateful and as obedient, I do not think I should tax these citizens at all, would you not?" Umid went silent for a moment. "I'll ponder the idea."

The Governor looked up in silence. "But my King, the tax—"

"Avoid talk of taxes. People of Mammon work their children from four, and mothers when they do not hold babes. There is work in your villages, so work! Do not speak of taxes."

"As you wish," uttered the Governor. "We wish to speak on the debts of the Ceremony."

Umid became furious: "What is this? My Senators, we have enemies approaching. Do not dodge topics, speak freely!"

"We wish to inquire what promises will be made to the kingdoms," answered the Governor.

"To what end," replied Umid. The Governor was hesitant.

Umid continued further: "Will you judge the decisions of the Inner Council? Do you all wish to enter the small chamber and decide policy?"

"Hear their words." Edjer sparked the movement of heads. All quieted their whispers and watched Edjer. Umid turned as well, shocked.

Umid caught himself from stumbling: "Continue."

"We simply wish to know what will be promised to prepare for any rise in taxes."

"I understand the burden. The rates are high for you, but we take three coins for every five from Mammon. You must see yourself lucky. Propaganda that you pay the same is false." He caught them by surprise. "The kingdoms will be offered to take a quarter off their total if they repay in three years. After the payment, all taxes will fall to the old rate."

Nearly all were satisfied by Umid's words.

"It is favorable, we do not wish to anger you, King Umid," said the Governor.

"What if they wish to fight again, my King?" uttered the elder statesman. The Governor turned to the man. He was veering away from the given script.

"I will send the Prince you all fear." He received brisk laughter from the Senators. "We will survive. They do not wish for war, and I expect a good deal to be struck."

"Yes, my King."

The Governor looked up. A feeling came over him, of pride, a devilish eagerness. His question also detoured: "Will the borders remain open in another war?"

"The borders will never close."

"What happens when the King can no longer fill the Cities of Mammon with his refugees? Will more quarters for *Natives* be built?" The Governor was bold.

Silence. Each man wished an answer from the King.

"Do they hurt your villages or towns; I am curious?" asked Edjer.

"They do not Prince, they simply take wealth that citizens should hold."

Agreements came in shuffles and whispers. The Native Senators tightened. They had somewhat expected this.

"The Native Quarter sits above the sewer lines of the city. When we came, you dared not approach." Edjer's words found no defense.

He continued: "Mammon's cities numbered two. There are seven today. If refugees did not come, it would be you who would leave to avoid the hardships of working in those mines."

"Discord grows in our villages and towns. Factions hoard in fear. Many leave our villages to Mammon in search of treasure. They do not return because of the distractions," retorted the Governor.

"More loot for you to find in your own lands. The Native Quarter does not discriminate. I have heard many of you refuse business with them. Why do you avoid where money is near? If you toiled as much, you would understand the pleasure Cities of Mammon offer in return." Umid wished to retract from cruelty. "The Cities of Mammon commit no more crimes than the villages and towns. The Native Quarter itself is nearly without crime. What do you wish to say, Governor?"

The Governor was tired of impotence. This was his time. "Who is who? King Umid, do you keep track of who comes to your lands? There is no protection for us. Who can tell if a spy enters? The threat terrifies my family, my children."

"Myawi, are you a spy?" asked Umid.

"No, my King."

"Senator Musay are you a spy?" asked Umid to one of the oldest Native Senators.

"I am a loyal citizen," said Musay, loudly, boldly.

"Governor, hear me well. Other kingdoms fail because their kings practice too much of these silly games our ancestors did not. Open your business to the Native Quarter. The Cities of Mammon mean nothing to you. Citizens of those walled cities will know nothing but work. They submit to its safety."

The elder statesman backed down to his seat while the Governor stayed upright in defiance on the front steps of the Senate seats.

"Be seated," ordered Umid. The Governor stood still. Umid laughed off the disobedience. "I have given you an order. Be seated."

The Governor remained stoic.

"I am ordering you. Be seated. Now!"

Nothing. Umid's frustration rose as did the anxiety of every individual in the room. Umid looked around as all eyes befell him. What he feared most was before him.

Defiance.

"Guards! If this man does not sit – execute him!"

Alcaeus buckled. He spoke up from the table: "Elius, sit."

"Guards!" The weary Royal Guards were slow to draw their swords.

Death rose from its seat.

"Anyone that strikes the man will draw his sword upon me!" declared Edjer.

The Royal Guards stopped at once. Umid turned towards his brother. He watched Edjer descend to the Governor.

Edjer looked as if he levitated. He walked to the man with respect.

"I understand my perspective differs from yours. But I have seen cruelty in its rawest form, Governor. I have seen the mutilations of innocence in war, and I have seen it done on my orders. Those who do not understand violence or the weight of words deal in ultimatum as a weapon. It is beyond a last resort. I grant you my respect for you stand now valiantly. This shall be whispered to many. But please, be seated."

Tears rolled from the Governor's eyes. He was as afraid of dying in that moment, as he was giving up: "I would rather be martyred than to fail my people."

A sword was unsheathed, that which held death's whisper as its tune. "You know well as I, death by this sword knows no martyrdom. You will be lost to death's abyss as all the rest."

The Governor was frozen in place. As soon as Edjer's sword rose, the man took his seat. The chamber was still as Edjer returned to his seat.

Throughout the rest of the in-house proceedings, details of the Ceremony were discussed. The traveling royals were to stay in the palace while their attendants were to rest in nearby inns. A curfew was agreed upon. Details were hashed out, but no one forgot the sound of Edjer's sword.

Before Edjer left the proceedings, Umid grabbed his hand across the long table.

"Brother."

Edjer turned as Umid continued: "I wish to call a meeting today. Please, join us before the enemies enter. We must discuss."

TWENTY-ONE

10 days until the Ceremony.

Edjer sat opposite Umid. They took the head seats in the council chambers. He had told Umid he would not eat but discuss policy. Attendants still brought refreshments, warm brews, and wine for Jabez and the royals.

Edjer refocused: "May we begin?"

"Share with the Council the preparations."

"My men will roam the city, occupying the inns, keeps, and brothels during the Ceremony. They will watch all the advisors and servants of the visiting kingdoms. If any messages are sent, or if they wish to attack, they will be intercepted."

"And in the palace?" asked Myawi.

"I have advised more Royal Guards to walk the grounds. The royals and their families will remain here." He stalled for a moment, eyeing them all. "Khalil will lead the palace security. The Concubines, they are to be openly armed and will do the same."

"The Concubines have agreed," added Niobe.

"I ask that your spies and soldiers report any activities they find suspicious, regardless of scale. We fear our enemies have knowledge of our kingdom in full."

"How so?" asked Myawi.

"I am sure, they are or have been given information from a Royal Guard, or a spy in the city."

"A traitor?" asked Alcaeus.

"To have kings ready to attack, it is a fear of mine that many within wish to see our demise," answered Edjer, patiently.

"Does this come from the prisoner in the dungeons?" asked Umid.

"He goes on of reports given by the Bear commanders. They anchor these rumblings of conflict, of that, I have no doubt. The man speaks of their confidence, *I believe him.*"

"He could take you on a chase not of your own volition?"

"The kings are comfortable encroaching on your lands, providing you a welcoming face in your own home. To be confident as to walk into a foreign land, they are sure of success. *I believe him.*"

Umid nodded, ashamed he was the last to understand the danger.

"Habiel will remain in the dungeons. The cells must be manned. They will come for the traitor. He may know more than he can recall. To be this bold, they will want him dead. The man they send will be the one we interrogate."

"I will place Guards with Habiel. The soldiers will be under him."

Edjer bowed to his brother's command before continuing. He cleared his throat.

"The Arms of the King and the Concubines will also be placed in your senate chambers for the proceedings. They will hide as attendants to oppose an unlikely direct threat. I ask that you not share this information. Their identity must remain a secret."

As he ended the request, an attendant came into the room. She strutted to Umid's side before whispering a message to him. She quickly departed.

"Any more brother?" asked Umid. Edjer shook his head.

"Leave me with Edjer. We will dine in the commons." Umid put his hand on Niobe's. "Stay." The others left. Myawi embraced Edjer as did Jabez on their leave. Demetrius gave his brother a nod on the way out.

"What do you seek, brother?" Umid watched Edjer. "I wish to reward your recent efforts; we have not seen you in the palace this often as of late."

Edjer lowered his head in shame: "No reward is needed."

"Niobe reminds me we must discuss the future, beyond the proceedings."

"Tomias must have shared my demands for the afterlife."

Niobe chuckled in surprise. She was comfortable that he knew the threat he truly was.

"Brother…" Umid hesitated, "I carry no ill will towards you."

"And I…"

Silence. "It is not ill will that provides a dilemma."

"…it is not my intention," replied Edjer. He mumbled at first. His composure faded with every memory that flooded him. Sevina. Lady Asiya.

"Niobe and I act as this kingdom's rulers. We have since we were given these roles."

"Mm," whispered Edjer.

"Niobe and I have chosen to send you to your home nation. It will be shared as your decision following the Ceremony."

"You mustn't tell the others," hammered Niobe. She did not look at him when she spoke, instead searching for the stars through the open windows.

"You will be allowed to live your days away…free. If you choose to stay, I cannot have people undermine the crown we have been given."

Edjer did not speak.

"We will discuss when we conclude the accords. The decision is yours. If you stay, brother, the knife will not appear from behind."

When Edjer had failed to withhold his love from Asiya, this was the expectation. He could not answer. He simply nodded and bowed, a shell of himself.

"The first of them have entered our kingdom. The Northerners have crossed the border. They will be here in days."

"I will be ready," mumbled Edjer, leaving his brother's chambers. He left his disappointment in the palace, where he was subdued and betrayed long ago.

Niobe needed Edjer off the grounds before she conversed with Umid.

"Will you be able to do it, if he does not wish to leave?"

"Let us eat."

"Wait, Umid." Her voice was stunted by doubt. "We cannot...we cannot hesitate."

"I should have let him do as he pleased."

She grabbed her chalice. It was now wine.

"You *are* a foreigner with the *Crown*. We made the right decision." She lied to ease his mind.

Edjer was dangerous in his inspiration of doubt. Whether insecurity, or truth, it was a threatening power to make royalty hesitate.

"I arrived as a foreigner with a family, and rule as an outcast with a Crown."

"You are not alone. You will never be alone."

King Umid grabbed her hands. She held him throughout their quiet dinner.

Umid eyed a candle on his return from the dizzying meal with his council. Lazily, Niobe continued to drink wine. Umid lowered his head and pressed it against the crown of hers. He loved her, but he knew she could not comprehend this feeling of hurt. Umid had expected her to understand his reservations, the love of brothers. Edjer and he had led a pilgrimage of children for a new life. When they had arrived, they had been told to prostrate in front of the Perfugan royals and beg. Umid refused, but Edjer reminded him of those they had guided, *The Children* who had barely made the crossing, on their last breaths. Edjer had known the truth about Perfuga the moment he and Umid were told to beg as a slave. It was submission. The act of begging, Edjer had made a show for the rulers, crying. He had led Umid in pleading for mercy, for their brothers and sisters, and for Umid himself. Edjer had always protected Umid. When he had a chance to repay his brother, King Umid fell mightily short, ripping out the heart of the man he loved.

Necessity. It dictated a king's actions, but what of a brother?

Umid, in the night, lying awake with a bare Niobe, took her chalice and drank from her cup, numbing the shame.

TWENTY-TWO

1000 days until the Ceremony.

Slave, servant, and soldier. Those words mean nothing to a commoner. They are oaths of an order unbeknownst to most. It is a blessing to claim ignorance on the matter.

A constant in all kingdoms is the trueness of children, the will of a child. Babes are troubled by the simplest matters. Many children carry insight we wish we retained from our youths. As a child, one is inoculated against pollution.

On our path to Perfuga, traders and merchants were long gone. Danger came in the form of deserters of war and desperate, unclaimed citizens desiring coin. The journey saw us lose brothers and sisters to bandits along the way. They first started with the girls to trade to fleeing merchants. There were no women on those roads that did not see men pillage their bodies. Soon after, they wanted the boys. Bandits and thieves wished to induct others into their groups or sell slaves of their own. Journeying in this treacherous time, we had to become disciplined with a weapon. We nearly became the same animals we fought.

Our youth was stolen from us. I believe, as I write now, children see angels, the omens in the sky, messages in the water. They are communicated to, across distant lands, by the mystical.

They can feel the air, messages of the moving clouds, answers within a soul. I implore you to watch a child's actions when they are alone.

We had lost our maps one day when we had to cross a ravine. Two years of our journey, we were blinded. Instead, it was a conversation with stars, with dense sea beds of dirt providing clues of our location.

Survival became innate.

Yet, the closer we were to Perfuga, the sloppier we became. We ignored signs of drying terrain, and tasteless dirt nearby. We had begun envisioning a dinner prepared for us.

The White Desert is a well-known land between the Bear and Perfuga. It signals a breakage between the kingdoms. It is said the terrain to the east and west of the path is too rugged to cross. We learned too harshly the truth of the matter.

Our journey had led us to the White Desert. The sand was beautiful, a pasty color that hides the sand's power to suffocate journeymen. We were devastated, especially those who had not seen the map. The Desert felt like an impediment of divinity.

The days were endlessly hot, paired with a crushing breeze in the night. Insanity in the beginning of the journey had been born out of anxiety and fear. What stormed our camp in the desert was terrifying in its potency, an all-different lunacy. Many would flee, in the dead of night, and talk angrily with their departed mothers and fathers. We would find many of them face down in the sand, days later. Those who had succumbed to hunger had believed the gods told them to put a dagger into their stomachs before desperation took them. Drops of blood in a backdrop of nature's clear white hue is not an easy painting to replicate. Khalil constantly attempts to draw the brother he had lost to insanity in the plain sands.

The older ones had attempted to calm the ruinous mood, but never could.

But Demetrius had counted one-hundred and three days. The sands of this desert reflect the beauty of clear skies. A divine trick.

Niobe and Edjer were instrumental in guiding us out. They were as lost as us, but they continued as they always did, with little ones on their backs.

My own sanity returned the day we escaped the White Desert.

Tomias, The Royal Scribe
Letter to the Senators of The Children's Journey

TWENTY-THREE

3 days until the Ceremony.

The noise of the bouncing carriage paled compared to the regiment of soldiers traveling in the rear. For days, the Bear Kingdom had marched with hundreds of soldiers.

Lomotos had fallen into spells of sleep. His head bounced with the carriage.

Semjaza had refused to sleep on the path to his brother Azazel. Throughout his trip, the soft, hunter green pillows in the carriage had felt as if they were baiting him to sleep. His mind welcomed the discomfort.

He closely watched his prisoner. She was shackled, bound by her feet and arms. Her eyes had never left the open neck of the snoring Lomotos. Semjaza would not sleep whilst she sat awake, enjoying the dangerous distraction she provided.

She was cleaned and prepared to go before others as if to a ball. Semjaza wished to dress her in holistic white, but her bandages were unable to contain the bleeding. Her wrists seized gorging blood from the deep wounds, but the slashes on her back still leaked droplets of life onto her clothes. The woman was breathtaking, even as she bore marks of torture. Attendants and nurses hid her wounds well, clearing her once dirtied and smoke-stained face from months spent in captivity. On the surface, her hair fell with elegance on her back. The sparkling dress would leave onlookers stunned, with a view of her neck and collarbone. The short sleeves left her skin shining from her biceps to her forearms.

Semjaza took his eyes off his prisoner to open a wooden covering. He looked outside, finding the end of the beginning. He kicked his brother's heels to wake him.

"We are passing the White Desert."

Lomotos, triggered by the rough touch, closed his mouth, rubbing his hands on his rugged beard.

"We are close to Azazel," shared Semjaza.

Lomotos reasserted himself with the living. He found their prisoner's eyes stuck on him.

"She watches me the whole journey, brother?"

"She still has hope she will find me asleep. I do not doubt she has found a way to escape her chains. The soldiers behind us force her obedience."

Lomotos leaned in close to her face. "I see what Semjaza sees, now." He stroked her face, "You are remarkable."

Since her capture, she had never engaged in conversation, nothing but the falling of her head while whispering the words, *afghar li.* She wished she had been heard, truly. The woman knew the others were not prepared.

"Careful, brother."

The chains on her hands and feet were secured to the wall, utilizing an amenity used by many on the love carriage.

Her desire to loosen her chains and slit his throat was strong. She desperately wanted to end her impotence. The soldiers were lazy in securing her restraints, ignoring the weight she had lost from hanging over the fires for months at a time. But to what end? She would need to battle the six hundred soldiers outside and find a horse despite her immobile feet. Death awaited her with the most grueling of circumstances. The recent years of her life had found her surrendering to the world's spin.

The carriage stopped abruptly to the noise of another nearby party. Semjaza and Lomotos were quick to walk out and greet their brother. King Azazel and Queen Liliah of the Bear waited at a table in an older outpost.

The trade routes were filled with hundreds on the path to Perfuga, for riches to be made during the Ceremony. Opportunists and politicians, with their commodities, children, and servants, ventured to Perfuga for the promised peace and their own hand in profit. The cloudy day made it look as if gray waves danced along the white sands.

The sun shone upon the desert, a day's journey away from Perfuga if one knew the correct route; otherwise, the dry oasis swallowed you whole.

On an empty, patchy field at the desert borders, hundreds of soldiers traveling with Semjaza began disembarking.

They awaited their orders.

"Azazel, I apologize for our late travels, we should have arrived at daybreak."

The brothers embraced Azazel, a strong one to mask their anxiety.

Discussions between the royals held up travelers waiting behind the hundreds of soldiers. This was the final marker Umid had told the Bear they could not pass with their men.

"The road?" asked Azazel.

"Good. It was quiet. Secure." Semjaza was unafraid, but his concerns rose as the proximity to Perfuga shortened.

"We need to be quick and dismount the men," added Lomotos.

"He is right, Azazel. We hold up merchants. A curious eye can ruin us," Queen Liliah.

Her words brought a sober response from Semjaza. "She is right."

"We must kill the traitor," declared Lomotos. He stuffed his face with wine and bread to replenish.

Liliah intruded: "Who will do it?"

"An agreement has been made."

"They are not fools, Semjaza. They may ensnare you," said Liliah.

"Neither am I, my Queen."

They ate and discussed amid nature's peace.

"What news, brother?" asked Azazel.

"King Akshat warns us of Debyendu. He has been asking his spies about our plans. Akshat asks for no harm to be done to his brother."

"How will we combat the agitator?" asked Liliah.

"We will comply. We wish for friends, not enemies," replied Semjaza.

Azazel nodded before ordering them: "...Bring the prisoner."

Lomotos walked to the carriage and retrieved her. She was unable to properly walk with her sandals, familiarizing herself with her bandaged and blistered feet. Semjaza brought a chair, and in the spirit of neutrality of the routes, the royal family ate with her.

"Eat, my lady," ordered Azazel. She watched the royals around her before doing so.

"She eats, without force, a miracle has come to us already," joked Lomotos.

Azazel raised his hand at his brother. The jokes ceased. The royals ended their meals prematurely to watch the woman. Her dark pigmentation was elegant, pleasant in the bright sun as her skin absorbed the rays. The opulence of her silk dress masked her strength, her intelligence, a knowledge of elemental signs. On her wrist, a marking of defense. She only missed the knife in her thigh. Niobe had stolen hers when she had been disowned from the family, from her kingdom. The purple flower sprouted in open defiance of the life she was subjugated to. She had been a soldier of Perfuga, a servant to her family, finally a slave as a concubine.

"We do not attack for riches, or minerals, my dear," began Azazel.

"I will rob Perfuga of the hope that it is stolen. Our blood funded the Great War that brought Perfuga riches. Even now, Perfuga outlasts its deserved penance. No more.

"An animal can be distracted and lured. A creature, a warrior out of love—"

"…A warrior out of love can be forged into a being, able to expand into an inexpugnable unit." The prisoner's words were the first sounds outside of prayers and whispers over tortuous fires. They were all impressed.

"Lady…lady—?"

"Lady Asiya," shared Semjaza.

"Lady Asiya, you are well informed."

She no longer responded, expecting the death she had awaited. Asiya did not know how she would be welcomed by Perfuga. She expected to be paraded; her capture was for a spectacle.

"Perfuga's hope lies in your former lover, my dear. I must apologize…I have become like those who I despised most."

She pointed for the wine, with Semjaza catching her grip before she went further. He was patient, and careful not to antagonize.

"Let her go," pleaded Azazel. He poured her wine and fed her, continuing to rationalize his use of her.

—

Edjer sat in the compound's library, waiting. Across from him, Myawi and Habiel ate. Tables away, Khalil painted, choosing to instead complete the image he had tried a lifetime to master.

The compound was empty. Many of the men had already gone patrolling. The Northern Kingdom had arrived, as did the Far East Empire and Nation-States.

Edjer had wished to discuss the preparations before the last of the conspirators arrived, but he dared not bother Khalil, finding an elusive comfort in Khalil's portrayal of the empty and dangerous, White Desert.

An artist with steady hands, Khalil painted on a smooth white canvas. The slight touch of brown with the white paint formed the White Desert against an evening, falling sun. An orange sky highlighted the droplets of blood he painted on the desert sands. In it, Khalil's last strokes focused on a dagger left stabbed in the sand next to a lifeless body. He never kept the paintings, burning the canvases at his perceived failure.

Khalil burned this one again before he sat next to Edjer.

"Habiel finds that he is not allowed to guard the prisoner, Myawi."

"It is delicate. The Guards have heard Edjer's report to Umid that they are not to be trusted," shared Myawi.

"The feeling is shared," said Khalil.

"Umid has agreed, why do we have a problem?" asked Edjer.

"I will go, Edjer," assured Habiel. His voice was confident.

"We have no time for their reservations. Habiel, if they stop you, subdue them, do not kill them," ordered Edjer.

Myawi was silent. The blur between foes and allies began to simmer into one. "I will handle it…Why are you convinced they will come for the prisoner?"

"We of all, Myawi, know the price we would pay for a silent slumber." He paused. "They are too close to leave it to chance. It worsens their need to kill. They will come."

Khalil spoke as he poured into his cup. "We need to protect the royals."

"He is right. If Jabez, Niobe, and Umid were to fall, it would devastate Perfuga."

"And you?" asked Habiel. Edjer ignored the question.

"Jabez, Umid, and Niobe must always be protected. The only ones to guard them should be the Arms and the *women*." Edjer knew only his own could do so.

The burden fell on Edjer as the dire reality of the threats was finally felt. The proximity of enemies brought the inescapable feeling of an impending attack. In the Capital, a skirmish had already occurred between Royal Guards and the Far East soldiers stemming from the most recent of wars. A Northerner was also beaten and robbed after a visit to the brothel, but it was said the man refused to pay a Perfugan whore a Northern rate. Edjer expected this; he knew petty clashes would end quickly. The real fight did not begin until Semjaza and his brothers arrived.

Prince Debyendu of the Far East Empire had recently warned Edjer: *You are in the grasp of their claws, hugged by the Bear on all sides*. To him, the preparations would not be enough. The protection he ordered was not for stopping an attack, he hoped to withstand one. He knew it to be a matter of survival.

TWENTY-FOUR

Day of the Ceremony.

Banners and flags of enemies and allies danced alike.

Candles lit up five tables for the five powers in attendance. The last of the delegations had arrived as Edjer watched the banners of all the kingdoms placed together.

Whilst he eyed the sigils, each kingdom had entered with ministers to bless the proceedings. The Nation-States and the Far East Empire had their ceremonial proceedings facilitated by priests and shamans.

At the Bear table, a whole other proceeding. A man with a flute played a low tune for Semjaza and the rest of his family. The melodic tone was carried through the room unbothered by the smoky visage.

The Prince of Death watched all the rulers and their traditions closely. His gaze stopped on Semjaza. Their eyes met, briefly, before Semjaza veered.

The proceedings were to be contentious. Blood of lost kin whetted the swords between the different enemies.

Edjer finally took his seat beside Jabez.

As Perfugan royals were the last to be announced, all rose.

The beginning of the Ceremony was signaled.

Jabez whispered to Edjer before the politicking began: "The dead are at peace. They have witnessed the beginning and end of the solstice. It is the living who lingers amongst the den of demons."

TWENTY-FIVE

5 days since the Ceremony began.

"You have been given the privilege of visitors as of late," shared Manissa.

The students were seated in a square formation. Niobe watched the end of the classroom lessons from the door to the inner halls.

She forced a smile for the orphan students.

The games were nearly to begin.

In the middle, surrounded by their peers' eager faces, the mute girl and the Arabian boy who had met Edjer stood alone. In their hands, blunt-tipped, wooden swords.

They were the last of the day's tournament. Boys and girls like these, like Edjer and Niobe before them, had to find a way to connect with their teachers.

The fighting returned a memory to Niobe of her only loss as a child, in a marvelous fight with Edjer that had seen her leave bloodied and bruised. She rooted for the mute girl, wishing to see the wooden sword shift, like a paintbrush, the way she had wielded it once.

"Embrace first, Liku and Daveed."

They bowed to one another.

"Ready?" asked Manissa.

Daveed was confident: "Ready." Liku made the hand movements, patient: "*Ready.*"

"Begin," ordered Manissa.

Niobe hid her terror. The swords moved too fast, as swift as *The Children* who had fought long ago. Daveed was impatient, swinging wildly, hoping to end the fight quickly. They were no older than seven, eight years old. But they were disciplined. Daveed's swinging was clamorous at times, but he had power, the power Niobe had seen in Edjer and Khalil.

Liku maintained a slow breath though, moving without striking. She dodged the blows and maneuvered in the space allotted between the boxed children.

As expected, Daveed began to show signs of fatigue. The wooden sword was light, smacking the ground sluggishly after his misses. Liku dodged all his attacks. Daveed nearly hit her, before slowing to a standstill, forfeiting his efforts to just watch her. He smiled. He looked down to his twin brother, Aman, and the other member of their group, Isaias. They were always the last four, and the winners of the tournaments.

"Hit me!" yelled Daveed. Liku smiled at his composure failing. She hid her own fatigue well.

Daveed returned, wishing to land a great blow. He was met with Liku's sword. He bounced the deflection into another blow. She made sure to find his weapon again. The other children swayed to avoid getting hit. He was unprepared for her control, the quickness. She was able to smack his calf before escaping to the edge.

Daveed felt the bruise begin to swell. He hobbled near the opposite end of the square. They were in the thick of the decisive battle, both growing nervous, anxious even, the longer the fight went on. Liku had spent too much time dodging him. She knew a blow would bring her down, but she used that against Daveed. He came and came, and she deflected and took wins in the smaller blows. His calves, forearms, and ribs took repeated beatings.

Daveed knew what he had to do to win. He forced himself forward and was able to elbow her in the chest. She countered with tiny blows knowing he wanted to grab her. She followed with an elbow to his damaged ribs to escape.

"Take him now!" screamed Niobe. The memory of her own loss compelled her to speak.

Liku looked at Niobe and then entered another bout of swordplay. Daveed attempted to strike her as hard as he could in the stomach, knowing she would block him. Liku stopped his advance, grabbing his hands, but he brought his strong grip on his sword up to her chin, knocking her out of balance. He did not stop. Daveed persisted in grabbing her while she struggled to calibrate, and before long, he brought Liku to the ground. He put his sword around her body to end her resistance.

A yield or a Headmistress's decision finished the battle. None were known to give their hand, but Manissa had seen enough.

"It is done, Daveed." The two rose and embraced. Manissa handed them a cloth.

Niobe's claps ended the silence. She walked to them and instructed the children to squeeze together. The four strongest: Liku and Daveed, Aman and Isaias, sat together in the back while the others were glued to Niobe's feet.

Manissa had tempered the intrusions of visiting royals like Semjaza and Debyendu over the last few days, but Niobe's, she had no patience for. Manissa took a knee behind Liku and Daveed, tending to their wounds.

"The small tournaments were always an interesting game. The older you are, the better the fight." Niobe looked at the four in the back. "Not many know what children are capable of."

Manissa refused to acknowledge her; she continued tending to the two children.

"I wish to tell you a proverb, a favorite of mine," began Niobe.

"My teacher once told us of a great dinner held by a King centuries ago. He had called all of the kingdoms together for a great evening. He had awarded three, two men and a woman, who wished for a higher post, a chance to plead to him in front of his guests.

"The king had given them an easy question to answer. Who, or what, is mightiest of all?

"The first man told the king; wine is greatest of all. He shared that with wine, we are all rich and we are all poor. We are one. We falter, we love, then we fight. This prince was given applause.

"The second man told the guests; a king is greatest of all. He spoke with confidence. He declared that a ruler commands us, and we fulfill the order's desire. If it be to war, to kill, to aid, or to burn, the deed will be done and be done so in glory of a king's blessing. Is it not the greatest of crimes to disobey a king? This prince was given louder applause.

"The last of them, the woman, the king found her daring. She saw the queen, and said, a queen is greatest of them all. We are all born from a woman are we not? She shared that women give us life, and the quality of the life is dependent on the queen's happiness. The garments made, jewels stolen and killed over, are they not to be given to the woman, the queen of a king? She argued a woman is a man's love, greater than that of any mother or father. He will forget them for his woman, becoming one with her. The woman had even walked to the king and queen, and asked, if the queen had stopped smiling, would not the king's pursuit of happiness end? Would he not work endlessly to see her smiles return? Is not the woman the greatest of these? The woman was given the greatest applause."

Umid and Edjer watched from the door. The rest of the Inner Council waited at the steps. Niobe captivated the children enough to attract the attention of the royals.

"Finish the story, my Queen?" asked a student from the back. Manissa's gaze slowly shifted, towards Liku and Daveed, then to the voice next to them.

A boy, Isaias, wished to hear more.

"I am sorry, I—"

Niobe was taken aback seeing the African boy. She did not know what he meant.

"There is more to it, my Queen," added Isaias. Manissa put her hand on his shoulder. She wished to warn him of the danger of provoking Niobe.

"I am sorry. I was not told of what remains."

"The other option," said Edjer. Niobe turned towards his voice.

"It is written, in the library," started Isaias. "The woman awaited their applause to die down. She was offered the glory of the kings, but she wished to say more."

Isaias looked at her with confidence. "She declared to the king; all are wicked under the sun. Like I have seduced you and your queen with my words, what if it be my plan to destroy you now.

"The woman shared that we all desire one commodity that we both fear and love, truth. It is hidden by the creatures of earth and blessed from the heavens. Truth has no side in the fight of animals and men, no desire for an outcome. The strength of kings is measured by its presence in their kingdom."

Isaias looked into Manissa's fearful eyes before he finished: "She is strength, she is power and majesty, for all of time. This woman was found to be the smartest of them: the one who had bravely tricked the king and his queen."

Niobe curiosity peaked. She asked her question: "And what was her reward?"

The voice came from behind her, "'Ask what you wish, even beyond what is written, and we will give it to you, for you have been found the wisest. You shall sit next to me and be called my Kinsman.'" Edjer's voice captured the awe of the students.

"Let us go, Niobe. We must be on our way," said King Umid. He turned to Manissa: "Watch yourselves on your trips to the fields. Messengers and traders are filing in by the caravans." She nodded as he left.

The royals walked to the Senate Chambers together, quietly.

Five sets of stools and stumps were placed in front of scribes recording information for their kingdoms. On the other side of the chamber, tables hosted the delegations: Perfuga, The Far East Empire, Nation-States, Northern Kingdom, and the Bear Kingdom.

Immediately, processions began as Umid entered. Attendants, hiding tattoos of flowers beneath their garments, provided refreshments to the kingdoms. Pompous royals sat behind the Northern side, while the roughness of the Nation-States proved true by their commoner garments. Debyendu, along with Semjaza and the Bear, were clean and poised. Candles and papers sat at the tables, with royal spreads of fruits and cheeses, encompassing the materials needed to end the gridlock holding the proceedings prisoner.

"Assurances need to be made," argued the Northern King. His accent was rough, one borne of the arduous seas he fished in.

"Of what nature?" replied Umid.

"If we agree to cut the debt, we need assurance no side deals will be made?" The Northern King looked at Debyendu.

Semjaza was disappointed his ally could not stop jabbering about Debyendu. He had sent messages to the others that Debyendu had been compromised.

Umid replied, "We must agree, first. Most of you do not wish to barter the last quarter even after I generously forgive a quarter already. You wish to remove half?"

"You still take half in gold and demand more? The debts were to be paid over ten years," interjected Azazel.

The others voiced agreement in nods and hums.

"You have already wished to test our might in war," added Umid. He had given them days to rest, but the arguments were stuck in the same place.

"I offer a counter." The Northern King raised his voice.

"Speak it."

"None wishes to see war again; we have lost enough sons from war and daughters from grief. We have agreed to remove a quarter.

Then if this be true, I offer to pay what you ask for in two years, as discussed. Of that, the payment will be half gold, and the other half grain. What say you?"

Umid looked down at his table for clarification. The offer seemed favorable, yet he wondered if his people would accept, if the amount would allow for a decrease in the taxes his citizens had complained about. Before he could assess, the others spoke.

"We can agree," said the delegation of Nation-States.

"We can find agreement if the proper scales are given for payment by grain," said the Bear. "But we agree."

"Wonderful, and you Debyendu? If your king were here, he would agree…" pestered the Northern King.

Umid remembered Edjer's words, *they are confident.*

"Speak freely my friend. We search for peace, don't we? It is the Northerners, I am told, that are the conniving type. It seems the talks suffer from a side deal of another party," accused Debyendu.

Edjer watched Semjaza become still while Lomotos stiffened. Silence befell the chamber hall.

Umid witnessed treachery firsthand. Entities were at play, working as one, but the terror of the idea became apparent. Kings plotted against him. After only five days, the talks felt as if an end neared, too quick for his comfort. He fought to bring peace, but he and Edjer felt the snakes beneath them.

"King Umid, the deal in front of us, it is good. The Far East Empire can agree if Perfuga can meet the terms."

Umid looked, again, down the table to his Inner Council. Edjer felt as though the sudden agreement had triggered the beginning.

"I require days to draft a schedule of payment, and securities for those who wish to renege on their word. I will come to you in a week's time with a draft to be agreed upon," declared Umid.

Universal mumbling. Whispers between the royal families and delegations pestered away at Umid's composure.

"The Northerners agree."

"As do the States."

"The Bear is content."

Debyendu bowed his head. The large circle swallowed Perfuga by surprise. Umid expected hours of debate, another month before terms were to be scrolled.

"Please, enjoy the Capital and palatial grounds. We will send messengers."

The Inner Council watched the invited royals walk out of the chamber. Servants and attendants broke into the open circle between the tables. One of the Concubines, with her gloved hands, walked past the rest to report what she had heard before the discussions began.

"Umid, the Bear talked of a report sent by a messenger this morning. Their soldiers guard a prisoner."

Umid's interest sparked, "What of the prisoner?"

"Nothing. They ceased talking when I neared. Prince Semjaza knows we listen; I am sure of it."

"It matters not. The others will slip," added Niobe from behind.

Another man, a false servant, member of the Arms of the King, walked towards the table. "The Nation-States do not expect to remain long. They whisper to each other of buying from the markets on the morrow. They prepare for a departure."

Umid looked down at Edjer. Prince Edjer listened but did not look at his brothers and sisters. He was focused on Debyendu's table. There was paper where Debyendu sat, a folded messenger's scroll. The red of the Far East's tiger sealed the words.

Edjer went and grabbed the message.

"Umid, Debyendu wishes to meet in your chambers."

TWENTY-SIX

5 days since the Ceremony began.

Semjaza leaned against the door to listen, for assurance of privacy. Inside their room, Liliah and Azazel sat on opposite sides of the bed. Lomotos sat by a desk where the representative of the Nation-States sat with him.

The Northern King smiled as Semjaza moved from the door. They were floors up, far from the eyes of Perfuga, but the locale did not calm his fears.

"Let us get on with it," proclaimed the Northern King.

"We must. We surely have been seen by one of the servants," replied Semjaza.

"It matters not. To their eyes, we are discussing the deal we have posed."

"In Azazel's chambers…?" asked Liliah. Her tone insulted the Northern King.

Too close to the plan's execution, how could they not begin to fear others' eyes?

"The unit we dispatched entered the gates yesterday. They await my order in one of the inns," announced Semjaza.

"How many?" asked the Northerner.

"Four," replied Semjaza.

"Then we must prepare to leave?" said the Northern King. He himself did not know if the words were a declaration or question.

"I am," interrupted the representative of the Nation-States. The African man was dressed in black robes, older in age. He was bold, even though he held the least power.

"Wait, we must wait," ordered Semjaza.

The others were puzzled. "What is the problem?" asked Lomotos.

Semjaza walked to Liliah's side of the bed. He lowered his head to look into her eyes. "Liliah, please answer me truthfully. Lady Asiya has yet to outrightly say the words." He paused. "Is what your spy spoke, the truth?"

Liliah looked up to him, smiling confidently. "Yes."

Semjaza grabbed her chin. He examined her eyes, the confident smile on her face.

"You, yourself, say you have seen the one we seek. Send the soldiers." The Northern King dispatched his own orders.

"Wait." Semjaza released his hands. He spoke to Liliah, "I want to see the spy."

"You cannot, Semjaza," added Lomotos. He rose from his seat.

"I require it. I have my reasons."

Liliah was not afraid: "It will be tough. But we must visit the brothel together, then." He nodded to her words.

"...we cannot be here when *it* happens. Do you succumb to fear now, Prince Semjaza?" asked the Northern King.

"Mind your tongue!" interjected Lomotos

"Lomotos..." whispered Azazel, attempting to calm his brother.

The room quieted. Revelations had fallen into Liliah's hands some time ago. Umid's hope of peace had been tarnished from its inception as the kingdoms long planned their revenge.

"You should all be scared. We are surrounded by the most dangerous killers. We have lost to them before." Semjaza looked to his comrades until he found the Northern King. "Do you not see the Prince? Edjer watches with intention. He knows. My friend, you speak of not being afraid. Then we have become allies with a fool."

The Northern King stepped forward to confront Semjaza, but Lomotos was too quick. He unsheathed his colossal sword. The sound of his pure metal finding freedom stalled the Northerner's pride.

"The Prince knows we plot," declared the African man. "He speaks truth."

"We have paid the right men, given the right men passage into the kingdom," added the Northern King.

"You are correct. But I require patience."

Semjaza's words smoothed over the tension. He walked to the fireplace to watch the flames dance to the free Perfugan air before he robbed the kingdom of its hope.

The representative of the Nation-States was the first to speak: "I will give you your time. Do not hesitate."

"I will not." Semjaza paused. "Within days, the prisoner will die first." He then walked to the representative at the desk: "A man's sleep before he gambles is precious, is it not?"

"It is. It keeps his sanity protected."

—

Edjer waited. He calmly sat in the Inner Council room.

Niobe paced around the cement table. She walked with angst, anticipating the news Debyendu wished to discuss.

"Will the others not be joining us?" asked Edjer. His voice was calm, as was his manner and movements.

"Myawi is with the Royal Guards patrolling the city. I have asked Alcaeus to employ the Senators to write out our agreement."

"And Jabez?"

"Confined to the Palace. He is surely drinking in the cellars with our hopeless scribe," answered Umid.

Edjer's hands were clasped on the table, waiting. Niobe's pacing stole Umid's attention.

"Niobe, please, sit."

"He keeps a king waiting. This itself is heresy," uttered Niobe.

"The King grows in worry from his general's false patience and wife's anxiety," quickly quipped Umid, "Please, sit."

Niobe walked from across the chamber, striding against the fading light to sit.

"I hear footsteps," said Edjer. Moments later, the door opened to an attendant. Niobe waved her off, demanding the guest.

"I mustn't stay long," declared Debyendu, as he walked in.

"We have waited," replied Niobe.

"I must be sure not to be seen. You have housed your enemies in your own home, King Umid."

"What news, Debyendu? What of your secret message?"

"I have been watching their soldiers at your trade post, King Umid. They mimic patterns and behaviors of foreign traders and merchants. It seems a unit of their own have become the men they seek."

"We watch the soldiers. We did not see any leave their detachment," said Niobe.

"My lady, a unit of four killed merchants and took up their identities. Four of the Bear soldiers are in your Capital."

Umid and Niobe shared a displeasing look of concern.

"Where are they now?" asked Umid.

"Even I do not have the resources to watch your crowded Capital. They are in, I am sure."

Debyendu was careful to stand amongst the presence of Perfugan royals as he spoke. He watched Umid and Niobe discuss while Edjer examined him.

To Prince Edjer, panic was worthless. *Survival.*

"If you are able to identify them in our walls, could you remove them?" asked Niobe.

"Remove them, my lady?"

"Kill them, can you kill them?" repeated Niobe.

Debyendu stopped short of laughing as he smiled, "With what men?"

Niobe retorted, "I am sure you did not come without soldiers of your own."

Debyendu smiled: "I am no longer, then, acting as a supplier of information. I am now another pair of hands that move to the Perfugan King's demands. Am I not?"

Niobe and Umid looked at him with contempt. They knew his plea. "Go on."

"If this be the case, in which I fight for the Perfugans, whom I have just bled against in war, I wish payment for my own people."

Umid looked at Debyendu shift in the darkness. The Prince of the Far East Empire slowly moved to sit. The chair screeched on the hardened floors.

"We will only pay a quarter of the debt. And we will pay that in gold, I assure you."

Umid and Niobe rapidly discussed the deal in glances. Edjer was silent watching the game be played.

"We would need payment within the change of season," replied Umid.

"It will be done, regardless of outcome."

The words were the ones Edjer wished most for Umid and Niobe to hear. Survival was the only chance against the threat surrounding their periphery.

"What do you presume is the reason for the soldiers?" inquired Niobe.

"It is simple, an assassination."

Umid sprang up at the word. "Of whom?"

"Prince Edjer."

Umid froze.

"Continue," affirmed Niobe, breaking the silence.

Debyendu continued, "They cannot kill Prince Edjer outright. An attempt itself would do the opposite of what they desire. Anyone with spies here knows Edjer is not one with the royal family." The sentiments froze Niobe and Umid.

"You dance with words," said Umid.

"It is truth, however. If they kill him, morale would be lost in Perfuga. It is the reason you did not announce his exile... It is imperative those Bear soldiers are found and killed."

Self-interest stole his remarks. The Far East Empire would perish if Northerners and the Bear were to ever hold power as the Perfugans did.

"We will mobilize the Arms and Guards to find the intruders," said Umid.

"No," interjected Edjer. "You will tip your hand."

"He is right. They will be hiding the soldiers properly. They have two kings and leaders of Nation-States on their side. They will know how to prepare."

Umid removed himself from the table. He walked, frustrated, replicating his lover's pacing. "What stops me from killing my enemies, all of them? They are in my kingdom, as close as they will ever be. What stops me now!?"

"You must wait to act. Killing all your enemies will unite others in war against you. There is a time for everything. You have paid me. Now I am at your service. Let us act accordingly."

Debyendu left after obtaining King Umid's blessings. He had already begun searching for the soldiers days prior, for his own kingdom's livelihood was at stake; the Tiger's Paw had always been a master negotiator.

The three siblings stayed. "Edjer, can you locate the soldiers before Debyendu?"

Edjer did not reply. He was growing tired of the palace. Promises of a return to exile seemed a fantasy, distorting the image of paradise he once thought possible.

"Umid, it does not matter. Soldiers are meant to kill. The Bear will kill one of us or Jabez. We need protection here," begged Niobe.

Umid pleaded to Edjer to return to the castle for his own safety, for the days felt like a prelude to catastrophe. But Edjer was steadfast and echoed he could not. Niobe supported Edjer in this, convincing herself, death by her hand or another, if a threat solely existed tied to Edjer's death, Perfuga would survive the dark times.

She did not know what awaited.

TWENTY-SEVEN

8 days since the Ceremony began.

The dungeons were a disgusting reminder. Habiel detested the assignment, but knew trust was essential to the role required.

For days, he had sat at the opposite end of the dungeon, facing two Royal Guards he shared his duties with. He had always leaned on thick wooden bars and looked at the empty cells. The cell on his end, with old stains of blood on the cemented floors, had once been his sister's. The time he spent watching, visualizing Lady Asiya's demise, had felt like its own prison.

The dungeon was unkempt and unclean. A pungent smell of excrement humidified the heavy air. Leaves and sewage accompanied the dirt on the cold floors.

A hollow hallway, from end to end, was encapsulated by cells on both sides. Habiel had watched rotating shifts of foolish and diligent Royal Guards enter to observe the prisoner. When they had bored him, he would turn and watch Asiya's old quarters. Caged windows at the top of each cell shared the hour of the day. Sunlight, moonlight, a prisoner of such a contraption would not care and neither had Habiel. The great lieutenant had become a babysitter for his sister's blood.

Umid had promised Habiel the late watch would be with men he trusted most. King Umid had sworn Habiel would be able to rest in those moments if he wished.

Habiel had not left the prison since the Ceremony began. He refused to leave a task unfinished. There were always Royal Guards he trusted, those he had fought with before, and also others he had not find worthy of trust. The ones he had shared battle with came often in the night.

And on this night, he had begun to watch without worry.

Two Royal Guards, posted on stools across the dim hallway, began their shift with erratic laughter. They spoke loudly, surely indulging in wine before entering the dungeons for their watch.

The ends of the halls, above both Habiel and the guards, held torches illuminating their faces.

Habiel had seen these two over the first few days of the Ceremony. His distrust of the Royal Guards in the beginning had started to fade as days passed without an incident. The sluggish men displeased Habiel, but they were harmless, instead enjoying humor-filled stories. He slowly began to fade, knowing his sister would haunt his dreams again.

"Lieutenant, join us, please! We will fight sleep together!"

A Royal Guard yelled at him from across the dungeons. A lonely walk in darkness was the only way Habiel could find a seat amongst them.

"A man alone dreams of darkness! Come! Sit with us!"

The yells across the way echoed in the prison.

Habiel's steps trumped the dead leaves on the way to the Royal Guard. His fearless trek ended near their stools. They waited for him under the light of a torch's fire. Habiel had been unable to see how entrenched in the comical talks the prisoner was.

"We do not have wine, but we share stories with our traitor friend," said the first Guard. The second let loose with endless laughter.

"The opposite side did not share in the warmth," replied Habiel softly, smiling.

"Warmth is not a commonality, lieutenant. It demands to be found and shared," said the first Guard.

"A scientist and a storyteller," said his partner, continuing in laughter.

The prisoner had recovered from the beatings. Bruises cleared. He wrapped his arms around one of the bars on his cell door as he leaned closer, hoping to engage more with the men.

Habiel sat with them and began to fall into a slumber immediately. The two Royal Guards looked at one another, smiling.

"Lieutenant, would you like to hear a story?"

"Of?" Habiel's quick reply was shared with closed eyes.

"You have heard the one of a King, a Foreigner and the Prisoners?"

The prisoner in the cage laughed. Habiel sat unamused.

"It is a true story," said the second Guard.

"Continue," ordered Habiel. He was careful to place one hand on his knee, and the other, out of sight. He clutched the dagger given to him as a child, tightly, in the back of his waistline.

"There was once a wise king, a patient one. The city was on fire after the death of his son, amid war with his neighbors—"

"There are striking similarities."

"Please, lieutenant, a coincidence."

"Continue, at your own risk," said Habiel.

"The wise king, he had lost his son. And the city had loved the young prince. He had championed himself as the people's savior. He was their voice. As the city descended into chaos from the news, people began to loot.

"You see, the king himself loved his son dearly."

Habiel was pleased with the beginning.

"The king filled his prison with all the looters, thieves, bandits, and killers. His own search for his son's murderers packed his dungeons. It was said the boy was killed on the Kings road.

"Even as war was at hand, and with the distrust of his citizens, the king decided to listen to all his prisoners' pleas, remembering how much his son had preached peace. There was especially one he wished to hear from, a foreigner who had witnessed his son's death and was found scavenging the desecration."

Habiel was interested in where the outcome would take him.

"This southerner sat in the cell and told the other prisoners who he was. They begged him to go last to not anger the king before their plea to the ruler. He agreed, and one by one, as the city burned, the prisoners went in and were pardoned by the king. When it came time for the foreigner, nothing went as expected.

"He sat the prisoner down and asked him, 'What happened to my boy?' The prisoner told the king his son was ambushed on the road. He told the king he had followed the prince to steal gold, for it was rumored the prince traveled with jewels to sue for peace with their enemies. He told the king he had found no jewels when he came to the body. He said it was an ambush, and that his son died with honor."

Habiel began chuckling, "Did the king have the prince killed?"

"The lieutenant has a warrior's patience," uttered the prisoner. The Royal Guards laughed. Something dark lingered in their extended chuckle.

Habiel felt uneasy but could not understand why.

"No, lieutenant, the merciful king was much more foolish. He told the foreigner he had pardoned all the other prisoners on that day under one stipulation. You see, the foreigner, he was a former citizen of the land the king was fighting. Opportunity fell at the king's feet.

"The king rambled to the man, confessions he would never utter to another soul. You speak truth in that the king's men killed the prince, but you insinuate jealousy. The prince was a servant of the people, in full. He was their *slave*, willingly. The prince had known losses in the war would see them become a conquered land, and most of the king's men had begun to refuse conscription. The prince had believed if a royal were to die, the people would be united in a fight.

"The prince and the king had plotted a death for the better of the kingdom. A ruse. And yet, he had not gained the favor of his people. A thief's hand, however, was brought to the king now. A foreign thief from an enemy land. Before the king slit the foreigner's throat, he told him, 'You will win me a kingdom boy, the way my son planned. You will be the righteous hand that is taken for a merciful cause. You will be the man that killed my son.'"

Habiel laughed at the end, one he did not expect. He asked, "And how was the story told to you soldiers?"

"Thieves and bandits plague the roads," replied the Royal Guard. The butt of his dagger was quick to strike Habiel's chin.

Habiel was knocked off-guard, but he instinctively clutched his weapon. He fought, but the limited lighting hid the other hand of his enemy holding a push knife. The Royal Guard struck Habiel's abdomen with succession and inflicted successive fatal blows.

Habiel's blood profusely poured out, but adrenaline sprung him to action. His dagger was much too big to need more than one stroke. From liver to sternum, with a push deep into the Guard's body, Habiel snatched the life of one of the men.

After the first Guard dropped, the second one turned once he finished his task of eliminating the prisoner. The Guard found his partner had instantly been killed by Habiel.

Flames from the torch enlightened Habiel to the devastating blows he took to the gut. A plethora of minuscule wounds oozed with blood, but even with injury, he was formidable.

The second Guard ran towards the other end to escape.

Habiel attempted to follow and shuddered, fearful of an inability to walk. He experienced glimpses of freedom from the other side beginning to show itself, but he was condemned to one last objective. The dark hallway was cluttered by the footsteps of a coward running for his life.

Habiel grabbed the blade of his sizable weapon and flung with his remaining strength. The Guard's body struck the cement floors.

Habiel similarly took a slow descent to the ground.

He left the living creating his own stains of death on the prison walls.

TWENTY-EIGHT

15 days since the Ceremony began.

Prince Edjer sat in the courtyard, shaded by the first tree ever planted. He listened to Manissa's grief in the timid sound of her lessons.

His own grief eluded him. Edjer was caught in a limbo of his own creation the more he searched. Whilst Umid panicked in the tower, Edjer was frozen in the garden like thorns on roses.

Habiel's death made him think of Asiya. He remembered catching her after one of the classes, walking the children through the Capital. Edjer had stopped her and asked her to sit, too timid to speak his feelings outright. He had waited for her to sit as the bravest man of all the known kingdoms found true terror.

Finally, the memory ran its course. Edjer landed on the thought of Habiel's senseless death.

Tomias' steps dragged on his entrance to the courtyard. He rushed to Edjer. *"We need you to go up to him Edjer, you have sat here long enough!"*

Edjer did not move as he said, "Sit down, Tomias. Calm yourself. The rest of the palace cannot know."

"We need to go up to Umid."

"Umid panics because what he feared happened. He was told of his Guards, and now, he panics to hide his own failure. What he feared is in front of him, worse than he expected."

"He needs you. He crumbles in front of his own council and the foreigner Debyendu."

Edjer brushed his face, "The memory will not leave our ally."

"You waste your words on me. Edjer, you must go to him."

"Let him continue. The damage is done. We must wait for him to calm."

Tomias needed Edjer's confidence to feel reassured. He turned to Edjer, *"What would you do?"*

"He must maintain composure in front of his men."

"What would you do, Edjer?"

"He is right to let the Concubines bury Habiel in secret. No one must know of the deaths. His Ceremony would be in jeopardy."

Tomias moved his attention away from Edjer.

"We learned of a plot with years of preparation, within days of an ill-fated accords. We were not unified to start. It was never prevention, Tomias.

"Has he prepared his deal for the royals? He must reconvene."

Tomias nodded before moving hands, *"He wants time, for Habiel."*

"The day is lost like our brother. The royals will surely know the prisoner's dead. Umid should have kept guards in the cells."

Tomias placed his arms on his legs. He was out of words for Edjer.

"We have the advantage in one way. The death was not clean. They do not know what happened. If they are sloppy, we have a chance."

"What must come next?"

"What the King demands," swiftly replied Edjer. Tomias' disgruntled look stole the expression from his face.

"Tomias." Edjer turned to him, avoiding the flowers. "What do you want from me?!" His voice rose. Attendants turned to Edjer. His eyes squinted as the animal within showed itself.

Rarely do they lose composure.

"I once knew the urgency of the living."

Slowly, Edjer calmed before he let it out.

"Tomias, we were raised knowing the showers of wind, and the pillows of petals. Do none of you feel the scars as you bathe?"

"Umid asks us in the palace to be in attendance at Habiel's end."

Silence. Even Manissa's lessons stalled to hear Edjer's words.

"We do what the King demands, Tomias...Only for him to betray us, later."

They walked into the palace, first passing Manissa's classroom. The children were not immune to Edjer's presence and turned to try and see his reddened eyes. They were too late. Edjer was swallowed by the inner halls.

TWENTY-NINE

15 days since the Ceremony began.

"These alleyways can force a man to lose his urges."

"Umid wishes to hide the deeds of his politicians and servants. It serves us well," whispered Semjaza.

Liliah and Semjaza strolled through the streets of Perfuga's Capital under the cover of night. The pair utilized hunter green hooded cloaks to stay hidden.

Semjaza had always detested the times he had to rely on Liliah. She led him through the mysterious Perfugan streets, towards the brothel they desired. She was comfortable navigating through the blackness.

But something began to happen. Semjaza found himself rationalizing her life the longer he was alone with her.

"How much further?"

Her quick pace, turning and twisting, was a game to her as she attempted to lose him the deeper they ventured into the city.

Finally, Liliah abruptly stopped near a narrow alleyway. He trailed her impatiently, stopping once his feet bumped her heels, triggering her smile. The two remained hooded until the door opened. Liliah shared a glimpse of her face. She was greeted like a queen by the brutes standing guard. They embraced her with a bear hug of their own. Liliah whispered to them before she looked back to Semjaza. The guards at the door were slow to acknowledge him, unaware how to greet a prince in the clandestine ambience.

Of the two guards, the larger one separated from the door once the royals walked inside. He followed them from behind through a hallway full of thick doors on both sides. The chips and cracks of the boarded walkway creaked to their steps.

An opening at the top of each door was closed but sounds from lovers and fornicators slithered into Semjaza's ears. At the end of the hallway, he heard steps push towards one of the doors. Semjaza paused immediately. The slit opened, providing a square view of a man's eye and the surrounding skin.

"Water! Water," pleaded the man, joyfully. Women laughed behind him, and moaned, as the lover wasted precious minutes in an ask for replenishment.

"Prince," sternly warned the guard. Liliah, in the darkness of the unlit hallway, studied his fear closely.

Semjaza walked to them, lost as a boy in a blacksmith's shop.

The imperial room was readied for them at the end of the twisting path, the biggest room offered by the brothel.

A room with two beds, and opulent bed frames fit for royals; Perfugan armor and banners basked the room in decoration. A padded sofa was placed in the middle, spiraling about under a fluorescent umbrella. A fire was lit near the top of the umbrella itself, where the coverings sprouted.

Semjaza walked to a stand near the beds to take part in refreshments. Liliah whispered an order to the guard before the man left the royals. He closed the door and ran off.

Semjaza knew the room to be soundproof, but the outside steps could still be heard. He marveled at the ingenuity.

"You seem pleased, Prince."

Semjaza ignored her as he inspected the beds. He took a seat on the sofa.

"A profitable establishment. Surely, it is used by politicians."

"Prince Jabez himself," she added.

Semjaza watched her worth to his kingdom rise. He nodded to his Queen.

"I was once a worker of this establishment, before Umid ascended," continued Liliah. "It did not look as it does now."

The arrangement of the padded seats allowed her to sit on the opposite side of Semjaza. They both looked out into the empty space in front of them.

"I own this establishment," she said, in a low voice.

Semjaza chuckled. "A secret should not be shared."

"I am speaking with the ruler of my lands. Owners of brothels hold many secrets. She breathes indispensable air."

"Mm," replied Semjaza. He was content she could not see how impressed he was.

He took a sip of his water before speaking: "A secret requires the tongue of the talebearer and the ear of his comrade."

Semjaza did not hear her creep against the soft cushions. She was within arms distance before he could put down his chalice.

Liliah shared a slow whisper, "May we then strike a bargain? A tongue for an ear?"

She leapt towards him. Her teeth held a grip on his ear as her tongue pressed against it. Semjaza was not immune to the touch, but he hid his insatiable desire.

He spoke without stopping her advance, "A bargain is struck."

Semjaza turned and violently grabbed her with his heavy hands. He dropped his chalice without a care for the room. She eyed him as he placed his nose nearly against hers. They looked at one another under the fire. He judged her in his decisive look.

She was not afraid of him. He slowly let go without indulging.

"Your talents are best used on my meek brother."

"Pursuit for purity will kill you. You will stumble if you do not indulge."

"How many have you spoken those words to before killing them?"

Liliah laughed, "Kingdoms indulge. I own a brothel in every Capital. My commerce of choice is pleasure."

Prince Semjaza snickered at the queen. He watched the flame dance in Jabez's favorite room. He wished he could see Jabez in the act to confirm what he had been told.

"Tell me of the girl," ordered Semjaza.

"She came to me three years ago with a story. She knew of my new role, and she traveled to me. Deliah is her name.

"She swore Jabez would confess when the potions entered his body. One day, he told her of the great lie hidden from the Prince of Death. He spoke of a sin which he wished to be cleansed of. She confirmed her information after many nights with him. He indulges in these potions to sleep…"

Semjaza exhaled as the pieces fit together. He heard steps. "Open it."

A petite girl of a youthful age, no more than twenty, entered. She was Arabian, a confident woman with black hair and a smile to compliment fit her keen sense of awareness.

Deliah looked around and immediately went to pour herself a drink. She did not acknowledge the royals in the room. Her worth was known to her; men had paid ransoms for minutes of her time.

"You risk too much," uttered Deliah.

Semjaza was astonished by her boisterous attitude.

"My dear, time is precious." He looked over to Liliah. Liliah pulled a pouch out from behind her.

Deliah took the payment with her free hand. She walked to where Semjaza sat and pulled a cushion out, where her gold was stashed.

"When did Jabez last speak to you?" asked Semjaza.

"His taste for the potions steals his consciousness. We no longer talk," answered Deliah.

"Does he know…of his own confessions?"

"There were times I believed he was aware. He speaks… to free himself. When he talks of Prince Edjer, especially. But I do not believe he gives me a thought outside these doors," said Deliah. She continued to drink amongst her royal counterparts.

"Mm," sounded Semjaza. A brief pause took sway in the room.

Deliah began to relax, even chuckling, "My Prince, Jabez wishes to die but is too much a coward to take his own life. He believes this a shame he must endure."

Semjaza was given the needed end of a satisfactory trip. He learned what he came for.

"I require an ear, Liliah."

Deliah did not see Queen Liliah plunge a pocket dagger into her neck. A secret he paid for remained his.

—

Perilous days forced Edjer to remain attentive. Torches connected to the corners of the hallway lit the empty palace courtyard. The fires were still, as was the wind.

Umid had ordered Edjer to remain in the castle. The decision left Edjer lonelier than years spent in dutiful exile. His eyes remained on the fire trapped inside the torches. The once peaceful garden courtyard had become his prison.

He heard something lingering.

"You do not fear me. You approach without your guards," said Edjer softly.

From the hallway opposite the garden, Niobe appeared on the dirt path. She walked along the edge, unafraid to eye him down.

"They are not worth much these days." Niobe stopped when she reached his feet. "Do you await the children?"

Edjer, slow to find her face, was puzzled, "Are they not in their chambers?"

"Manissa ignores my warnings. She takes her time returning from the fields."

"They are beautiful as the seasons change. I try to remember them."

Edjer rose to her presence. They began their silent walk to the Inner Council room.

"The wines of thine, are of mine own…" whispered Jabez in tune. His mind bowed to the easy touch of flavored wine.

Feet shuffled behind the door to Umid's chambers. Umid prepared for the gloomy news. His rewritten terms were a day away from an introduction into his Ceremony.

Descending the steps to his chamber door, Umid spoke: "Be seated."

He took the seat at the end of the table, facing them. Jabez and Niobe sat on each side closest to him, and at the opposite end, Edjer.

"We rested last on the topic of expulsion," uttered Niobe.

Umid sighed.

Jabez fluttered his eyes. A sly chuckle could not be contained.

"Uncle, control yourself," ordered Umid.

"Expulsion is impossible," added Edjer.

"Yes. Without an agreement, we will all be at war." Niobe needed to remind Umid of the people's impatience.

Niobe added: "Killing the wrong people would create a conflict worse than war. They wish to prolong the conference if they have yet to attack. Let it be their doom. It gives us time to find Semjaza's soldiers."

An empty silence emerged. Umid looked disappointed. Habiel's death weighed heavily on him. He found Edjer looking towards dead space.

"What have you, brother? What takes your attention from these matters?"

"The past speaks today." Edjer slowly began to recognize where he was. "We must begin to prepare for what is to come. We can continue the search for the soldiers, as we do now. But you must know, they have already beaten us."

"You do not wish to defend Perfuga!" King Umid's frustration came out. Silence was returned.

"Edjer, look upon your King!"

The Prince of Death obeyed. Umid was at his end.

"You see my eyes, do you not? How can I turn to my servants, and give them my back to dress me, when my own brother cannot be trusted?!"

"Umid…" quietly interjected Niobe.

"Do not interrupt me!"

Edjer returned a stoic look.

"Before we became Prince, and King, do you remember the royals discussing their desires for you?" asked Edjer.

"They wished for me to attack the Bear when the time was right. And you fought it," replied Umid. He leaned on his cemented table, calming his anger.

"They wished for you to fight our *enemies*. I warned you; you had no reason to."

"And they told you to watch your tongue."

"An opportunity to take me aside presented itself when we finished dinner. One of the royals told me, a boy of seventeen, the only reason for my station was because of you. The only reason a home for my sisters and brothers existed was because of the heir that presented himself when we begged for a home.

"Oh, I was quick to reply to him. I was not afraid to look into his eyes."

Edjer remembered the moment. Darkness took hold of him. All were entrapped in the death he could wield in both words and gaze. "I warned him. If a hair were pricked from your head, if you were hurt by their plots, I would be slow in how I would slice his neck open. I promised him brother; I would watch as they all grasped for air to call the Guards I would kill outside their doors.

"A mistake on my part." He snickered at his misstep. "They beat me in the end. I had yet to find out they had molded you already … in their image."

Speaking the truth, Edjer had finally found the grief for Habiel he had been searching for.

"The brother I defended punished me for taking part in my own love. You believe my disobedience was done to undermine you, when I proved I would die lifetimes over for you. I threatened rulers for a brother who murdered my own heart."

Edjer was slow to retrieve his dagger, the weapon given to all *The Children*. Niobe's eyes grew once she saw the weapon in his hands.

"Edjer!" called out Niobe. Her hands raced to grip her own dagger.

He placed his dagger steadily on the table before he left his seat.

"I will serve you till the end of your Ceremony, and I will go to die in my home. It truly is all a fable; the stories they tell of us."

They watched him leave. Jabez began to chuckle. The whites of his eyes swelled as he looked to the ceiling.

Niobe and Umid shared fearful glances before looking at the end of the table. Even Kiliea, in her righteous defiance, had not left her inheritance. She had taken the dagger with her. Umid and Niobe were petrified at Edjer's forfeiture.

"King Umid?" pleaded Jabez. His laughs turned to cries.

"I have seen it in as many dreams as nightmares," Jabez continued, manic, talking in tune. "He will kill us all. Our days decrease in number for he will rightfully end us. I have seen it!"

Umid's anger festered. He rose from his seat with impatience, "Bring Demetrius in and take this drunkard from me!"

Niobe walked towards the door, but she could not pass Edjer's weapon. She grabbed the knife, afraid, remembering her own blunder with Edjer when she had rid the kingdom of Asiya. Her own dagger had struck deep into Edjer's stomach.

When grabbing his weapon, she felt the same pain she had faced when she had taken Asiya's.

Then, Niobe did what she had always done: continue. She yelled as she cleared the table, "Demetrius, come retrieve the fool!"

THIRTY

16 days since the Ceremony began.

"How does Perfuga conclude this to be the scale of grain to gold?" began Umid. "We cut your debt by a quarter without hesitation. Have we not been patient? The terms dictate half gold, and the other half grain."

Northern protest was Semjaza's tool to exacerbate Umid.

"Gold may have a different meaning in Perfuga, but you would have us empty our storages to feed your people."

"Be calm, we do not act as rulers," declared Debyendu.

"If—if, I change the time of repayment for the gold, I want the scale for grain and food to match what our senators created." Umid wished for an end to the farce.

The Northern King betrayed his orders. He looked to Semjaza for approval. Edjer clocked his mistake.

Semjaza's fist clenched underneath the table. With confirmation, days away from providing the deathly blow, Semjaza and his comrades were too close to fail. Semjaza felt the gaze, but he did not look.

"We can proceed with terms," slowly declared the Northern King.

"The Nation-States can provide the gold in five years' time, and no less. Grain will be given immediately, if the others agree?"

Azazel shared, "The Bear will require more time for gold, but grain, we can agree."

Debyendu followed, "Gold is not a problem, but grain, we will need a year. Due to our wetlands, King Umid."

Silence. No one cared for these details.

Night befell the Capital, and more than half a day was spent on Umid's terms. His people were growing impatient, bent up with rage as foreigners reveled in their brothels and inns.

"We will disband for two days. The final terms for repayment will be set and we will agree. This dance is at an end," warned Umid.

Umid rose at once. He stood frozen, watching all the others, especially Semjaza. Others rose once he exited the chambers.

The Northerners rushed out.

Representatives of the Nation-States and the Far East Empire walked out together to their nightly stations. Lomotos and Azazel led the Bear representatives behind them.

They left Debyendu, and the seated Semjaza, to speak.

"A beautiful chamber is it not?" asked Debyendu.

Semjaza looked upon the marvelous building, with banners the size of buildings lying on the walls. Then he looked behind him to the Senate seats.

"Beyond doubt," answered Semjaza.

Debyendu shared a contentious grin.

Semjaza attached himself to the hip of his adversary whilst filing out of the hall. "Perfuga is wise to award the powerless with a prison of their own making."

"False power to the powerless is the meaning of distribution."

"Ah, with that I must agree."

A brief silence took hold as they left the building together. They walked deeper into the city.

"I was given reports, the brother of the king rules the people."

"My messengers share a similar note."

"My fingers maintain a soft grasp of power, while yours, an approach of directness was never my flavor." Debyendu hoped to goad Semjaza.

"A strong grip allows one to yield it indiscriminately," shared Semjaza.

"Is it better to brandish a weapon or conceal it?"

"You are truly a warrior. I am merely a strategist."

Debyendu chuckled: "Do not deceive me."

Both the Princes quietly walked towards the inns. Royals like Debyendu and Semjaza slept in the palace, but their advisors took up in the inns. And so, the royals had found their nightly routines to consist of discussions in the crowded inns before finding their beds.

"I have never deceived you, Debyendu." Semjaza's white robes brushed slightly below his knees as he kept his pace stagnant. He held his composure against his half-truths.

"You approach a powerless king before that of the kingdom's ruler?"

Semjaza smirked: "You know better than I, orders can be misheard."

"How would your people act if they knew their ruler frequented brothels?" asked Debyendu.

The Tiger encroached on the Bear.

"You are mistaken. To defile one's body is the greatest mistake of all," replied Semjaza.

"Whispers tell of the Bear renting a whore for the duration of his stay. It seems you wish to take all of Perfuga's top commodities."

Semjaza fancied a laugh without exposing his intentions. "Your brother warned you not to meddle in affairs not of your own. You are without immunity, *Prince*."

Debyendu came closer to what he desired. "I wish to be made aware. Of everything."

The two men stopped.

"I do not aspire to be in your position. Royals can be bought now, even by other rulers."

"And the Bear dares to kill enemies in foreign dungeons," replied Debyendu.

Semjaza played the insult off with a smile, "Orders can be misheard ..."

Debyendu took time to understand, hearing the words. *He did not mean to kill Habiel.*

"I am not cruel, Debyendu. I wish to make up for the mistakes of my past, for your sister."

Debyendu became a slave to his own game. He found himself lost in his enemies' words.

"My rash actions caused the Great War, and the Perfugans took advantage. I do not wish to kill them, when I can *steal* what is theirs. Do not interfere. Your brother is with me."

Steal, the word awakened Debyendu from a trance.

"You will not believe me, but my brothers and I, we loved your sister," added Semjaza.

"Efforts you make to help Perfugans make no difference. You will return with no debt, as promised to your brother if our union holds. It will be the end of my search for forgiveness."

Their walk ended outside the inn where Debyendu's servants stayed.

"A meeting, Debyendu, I wish for a meeting."

"With whom?"

Semjaza looked at Debyendu, finding an opportunity. "We miss a voice in our open discussions. We second sons are the keepers of our kingdoms. We must meet in a place of Edjer's choosing. His safety is promised if mine is as well."

Debyendu was too in shock to give an answer. Semjaza left him with the request.

Semjaza looked at the inn's doors before walking way. He had wisely hidden his secret unit of four soldiers where Debyendu's advisors stayed. He had walked away from their conversation more confident than ever before.

Orders had been given to the Arms of the King to patrol the many motels, to find the enemy soldiers. Tafari, in his servant clothes, brushed past Debyendu, catching the Tiger's Paw on his ghostly walk to his servants' room.

Survival had been the philosophy and goal of rulers in all lands, both past and future. Debyendu ached to know who he could trust to survive what was to come.

THIRTY-ONE

18 days since the Ceremony began.

Another of Khalil's paintings rested on an easel, of a soft, brownish color. The landscape piece conveyed the emotion many of *The Children* had felt in the White Desert. Insanity had brewed strongest in the last obstacle to Perfuga.

Edjer was alone in the hall, at the end of a table, waiting. He had not returned to the compound in some time.

He looked at the scarlet paint, the droplets of blood.

Why keep this one, wondered Edjer. He stared into the painting. The lifeless body of Khalil's brother lay flat in the sand, knowing the boy had dreamt of a heaven he had hoped existed.

His visitors dragged their feet as the princes strode through the empty hall.

"The abode of the Arms of the King," announced Debyendu.

Semjaza marveled at the compound.

"Sit," suggested Edjer. His guests sat in front of him, purposely placing their hands on the table. Prince Edjer mirrored them.

"You are true to your reputation; you do not speak to enemies with hands on your blade."

Semjaza's words took Edjer's attention from the painting, resting in the shadows, behind his two visitors.

"What would be accomplished?" asked Edjer.

"An end of an enemy?"

"Then two of your kin would take your place."

The response garnered Semjaza's admiration. They sat quietly as the light of the late afternoon sluggishly dimmed.

Edjer left for another table. No fires were lit for fear of the smoke giving warning of a meeting. He brought them refreshments, warm teas he brewed. Edjer placed a ceramic cup in front of them and poured. Debyendu and Semjaza did not hesitate, nor were they afraid to drink.

"It is a sin to kill guests in your home; an old notion my father spoke of."

"The Perfugan royals?" inquired Semjaza.

"No. My father was a servant to a sea merchant many moons before I came here."

"Was he religious?"

"He was."

"I have yet to understand its purpose. Prostitutes are given forgiveness before soldiers and kings in most ideologies."

"Where lies the problem?" inquired Edjer.

"Submission. I have submitted to the rule of law already. No man can serve two masters."

"Submission is half of it. Kings do not care for religion for they have the power to create their own divinity...I have no desire to rule, Prince. Politics, I leave to you both." Edjer put his tea down, "I have seen purity in its rawest form. The swaying of dying weeds in savannahs, a love for nature's stillness. This all once appeared to me in dreams, but I lose my childhood to an unwanted awareness. I forget the dreams I once had."

"Yet, you have what neither of us hold. The people's love," declared Semjaza.

"I serve the Perfugan people until I am freed. While they have my talents, I do not bow to their requests. I need no divinity to tell me of what is temporary and what is eternal."

Semjaza was astonished at Prince Edjer. He knew then, Edjer was what he needed him to be for his plans to work.

"I am not a cruel man," proclaimed Semjaza.

Edjer's glare keyed in on the painting posted in the shadows.

"No man understands cruelty until his rage is triggered. You cannot know your own cruelty until the moment the decision to do so is in your hands."

Edjer poured another cup of tea for his guests as another chilling silence took the room.

Semjaza looked deeper into Edjer, until Edjer looked back at him. They held each other's eyes in pure quiet. Prince Semjaza then saw something beneath Edjer. Blackness. Not just his skin. Nor his eyes. It was Death itself.

"I thank you for this meeting," said Semjaza, placing his hand out. Edjer, confused, took his forearm with a slow grab of force, and looked up at him.

"Umid is my King, and I shall protect him," decreed Edjer.

Semjaza was stoic, nodding to Edjer as they released from one another. Before leaving, Semjaza stole a glance at the painting he had observed Edjer eyeing. He smiled after catching sight of the canvas.

Debyendu waited until he heard the doors close.

"You reek of mortality."

"Semjaza no longer fears me."

"No. More than ever he is filled with terror. You underestimate yourself. The Prince of Death truly exists."

Edjer began drinking his tea, "So many stories of myself, my brothers, and sisters. It has all been lost to fable. People know nothing."

An unending silence filled the room.

"Many speak of a lost sister. We hold similar grief," stated Debyendu.

"If you believe so, you could not imagine mine," responded Edjer in a whisper.

Debyendu fidgeted, itching to speak: "If I recall, the last I saw you, I claimed I had a story for you?"

"You did," replied Edjer, sipping his tea.

"A young princess was once tasked with uplifting her brother, the king, and giving the world a peace they would speak ages about. She was to be betrothed to a rival. Worried, she had only asked for one thing in return," Debyendu paused to smile, "She had wanted to tour all the kingdoms. See the world for all its mishaps and perfections. She wanted to know the world she was giving peace to. Kingdom to kingdom, she was basked in honor and gifts.

"She brought a flower from her homeland to each kingdom. One she took care of until she had met each set of royals. There was a prince in which she had gifted a certain flower, a purple one, *the Persian shield* called Strobilanthes Dyeriana. She had stayed in this kingdom an extra year, alone, claiming she had wished to learn of their histories. Unbeknownst, she had fallen in love with a prince. And him with her."

Edjer watched as Prince Debyendu wiped his eyes.

He continued after he cleared his throat: "When it was time for her to be betrothed to her brothers' rivals, the old courtship was too strong to wither. A letter between her lover and the princess had been intercepted on the eve of her betrothal. Ruthlessly, the rivals had executed the princess.

"Hiding the shame of her affair, both the Tiger and the Bear fell upon each other in a battle for pride, both wishing the true culprit of Perfuga to enter. Choosing to abstain, the Great War went for years as men died without purpose. Perfuga's personal apology came in a promise to loan gold for the fight. Only after did all the kingdoms learn of Perfuga's treachery. Perfuga had weakened us by prolonging our fight, giving both sides gold and weapons..."

Edjer watched closely for any lies. Yet, he could not find one.

"It is indeed an interesting story," shared Edjer.

"How linked we all are, Prince Edjer. The man you call Uncle, began the Great War we all fear will return today. Jabez had made the mistake of thinking a courtship could last with my sister, Amala."

Edjer tightened. He had no response.

"How close you are to her, yourself. Do you know what they call her now, Amala?"

"The Angel of Death," replied Edjer.

"Hmm... a desecration of time. What history can you trust?"

"You can trust your people." Edjer was strong in his sentiments.

Debyendu laughed until he began to stammer. Warm tears fell from his eyes.

"Edjer?" A nod was returned. "I ask again, would you leave Perfuga?"

"Once this is over, I have been ordered to a permanent exile. Whether a knife will follow, I do not know."

Debyendu's eyes widened. He failed to keep his composure, but his agenda did not stop.

"Leave now, then, find peace. What more must you lose?"

"What is a dream accomplished awake? Death will take me before I leave, it is of nature's doing."

"We would accept you," pleaded Debyendu.

"None could—"

Debyendu found deep sadness the longer he looked upon Edjer, both bonded in unspoken grief. *She would have admired him,* he thought. Politics moved aside in a search for clarity. "The sins of old rulers mean nothing. The past remains a cage."

"Yet here we live. Fighting our generation's fight. The Angel of Death, Prince of Death; the people desire to know death. War is its agent, and each generation will call upon it. Amala was not to blame. If others pray for me, I pray they ask that I am not, myself, responsible... for death."

"You must know, freedom is in reach," suggested Debyendu.

"A man responsible for his people does not run away," declared Edjer, "What was free, lied in a field, proclaiming she would be mine. Freedom is offered in a few moments of one's life, Debyendu. Mine was robbed from me. I have made sacrifices. And the last one, more than ever, I could not withstand. Debyendu, I have cheated fate."

Debyendu stood as he spoke: "Then – destroy your enemies."

THIRTY-TWO

5500 days until the Ceremony.

Your tribe is the one who molds you into a man and woman, into soldiers, killers, protectors. The warrior within is rarely found just in the trainings of a father or mother; a soldier's passion to love, to kill, without hesitation, are birthed from the tribe that instills conviction in a child.

On one occasion, Khalil roamed the marketplaces, with Kiliea by his side. They had found another young group of our brothers and sisters playing with kids in the marketplace, being taken advantage of. Immediately, Khalil and Kiliea warned the merchants and their children to end the unfair match. A fight broke out. After their return to the palace, the rest of us were enraged. We, *The Children*, all went out to hurt those kids, and we did.

The owners in the marketplace were ordered to provide the kids who led the fight against Khalil and Kiliea. Balance was ours that day. Everyone watched the beating Edjer and Niobe gave them. Then, my brother and sister inflicted pain upon the merchants.

The next morning, when the palace found out, Myawi and Jabez were ordered to train us.

The Children were reshaped.

The strength in our bones was like that of lions. People cannot understand this evolution, as we were hunted by jaguars, snakes, demons if you believe me, for years. Our bodies were prepared for a fight. We could only imagine the reports shared by attendants and soldiers who trained us, by you and Myawi. We would catch Perfugan royals on occasion, marveling at our training, clapping, astonished at the feat of teens.

Truly, I can tell you, we were taught to respect royal orders. We believed it to be an honor at first: Arms of the King and Royal Concubines.

We were just children.

But Edjer knew something was wrong. Our sisters had told him Perfugan soldiers had held them down as they were marked as Royal Concubines. They began being groomed by Perfugan royalty for their perversions. And likewise, we were beginning to hear of our own campaigns to come.

Edjer had snuck into the Native Quarter and told the elder refugees what had been done. They had instructed Edjer to bring his brothers and sisters one by one, in small groups if he could. A great dishonor had been done to *The Children*.

Edjer had been told not to alert the rest of us as to what was happening. Perfugan royalty was turning us into slaves, but the Native Quarter elders hoped to provide us with something to end our powerlessness.

The first of those Edjer brought to the Native Quarter: Niobe, with Kiliea, and Khalil.

Group by group, he guided us through the alleyways, into the Native Quarter. Always did he wait for nightfall to steal us from our beds.

I remember the night I was picked to go. It is the day I can always recall vividly. Edjer had begged for silence. We slithered through the Capital as you royals slept.

A premier blacksmith shop had sat at the corner of the Native Quarter.

I remember hearing the metal clash, forming the sly weapon I hold now beneath my clothes. An inscription is branded into the dagger my brothers and sisters keep in our packs, our waists, even hidden in our legs.

The inscription is in the tongue most spoken between us, Harabic.

Altawazun lays mufrada, walakin 'iidha kan min haqika, fakhtarh bihikmatin.

Balance is not singular, but if it be yours, choose wisely.

The elders, four women who take care of new refugees in the Native Quarter, whispered our names and birthplaces as they handed us the finished piece. They had warned us of the day we would know of our bondage to Perfuga, and the bloodshed that would occur.

A dagger with a black grip, the length of a soldier's forearm and the width of a scroll, kill who you must for your family, the women had declared. We immediately toyed with the weapon. Some of us were swift, like a hawk, twisting and turning the dagger, while others, the force they struck with was abnormal, animalistic. Silent ones learned to throw the weapon.

An inheritance was given to us. We never separate from our weapon. It is a symbol of our bondage to Perfuga. And our freedom to come.

We are sure you did not know what we were training to become. But we beg you now, allow us to open a compound for the Arms of the King, in the Native Quarter. The women are lost to the palace. We cannot stay and watch this any longer.

Free us, Jabez.

Tomias, The Royal Scribe
A Plea to Prince Jabez

THIRTY-THREE

20 days since the Ceremony began.

The Inner Council awaited Jabez in silence. Every other member was present. He was stumbled through the halls while Demetrius stoically held him up.

"A king mustn't see me as I am," uttered Jabez.

Demetrius pulled him up the last steps. With his cloak, he wiped Jabez's perspiration. Demetrius tried to give strength to the tired man.

"Family is family, sire," added Demetrius. He opened the doors.

"Demetrius, you may stay today," exclaimed Niobe.

Elsewhere, another struggled with what had been perceived as a mundane task.

Tafari ran from his post with news he desperately needed to share. Many roamed the streets, seeking vendors from all the kingdoms. He slowed remembering the Capital was ridden with spies and enemies.

Perfuga was surrounded. But Tafari had aid in his news. He maintained a walking stride, as the eyes began to fall on the young man. Edjer had given him orders to sneak into the rooms inside the inn he had watched, especially of the esteemed guests. Edjer's instincts had proven right.

Tafari's anxiety rose, fearing the gazes.

Whilst the mind of the pup stressed, Prince Edjer had news of his own.

"I met with Semjaza and Debyendu," uttered Edjer to the Inner Council. Only Jabez turned.

"Speak up, *brother,* we hope to have misheard," ordered Umid.

"I met with Semjaza and Debyendu," repeated Edjer.

Niobe was the only to not succumb to shock, "What was said?"

"Call in the rest of the army clearing the Far East Empire. Call reserves from the walled cities. Semjaza means to embarrass you. It is a fight for the status we hold."

"The armies cannot get here within a fortnight," said Umid, stumbling in his brother's rigid answers. "We have 400 Royal Guards and the Arms of the King."

"The Concubines as well," interjected Niobe.

"It is a display, Semjaza seeks. He wishes to *steal* the hope within Perfuga. Look amongst the table.

"Before the Great War, the kingdoms were alike. When was Perfuga understood to be a haven? When was pride strongest? Among us now, there are only two born of this land. The moment *we* entered Perfuga was when she first was believed to be a land of endless milk and honey. If Semjaza wishes to steal hope, it is *us* he comes for."

Frozen looks stole the faces of Umid and Niobe, his brother Demetrius.

"Kiliea, Kiliea!'" yelled Niobe.

"I retrieved her in the night. She is in the compound," answered Edjer

Umid asked, "What must we do next?"

"Kiliea will be brought to the palace. *All of us* must remain within these walls. You must issue a banishment, quietly, of your attendants and Royal Guards tonight before the royals of the other kingdoms return. We will take Semjaza. We must kill the Bear royals."

All looked at Edjer with shock.

Edjer looked towards Demetrius, whispering, "A sword will be required in your hand." A nod in compliance was returned.

"Umid, the men in the castle are not to be trusted, nor are the servants. They are compromised. We must remain with our sisters, under a shared roof," concluded Edjer.

Knocks on the door took their gazes hostage for a beat. As if an enemy stormed the gates, Edjer rushed to the entryway. He found his man.

"Tafari, why do you leave your post?" inquired Edjer. Walking in, the boy fell into the arms of his superior.

"Forgive me, I ran once I reached the palace walls."

Tafari bowed and kept his head lowered for his breaths. His exhales worsened their resolve.

"Tafari," attempted Edjer again.

"General, I found them."

Umid rose from his seat.

"Who, Tafari?" asked Umid.

"Sire, I saw each room in the inn. They are in the motel with the Far East Empire. The Bear soldiers, sir."

"What proof do you have?" asked Edjer.

"General, I did as I was told. I found soldiers' packs. Underneath their beds, they hid swords, daggers, bows. I took this as well."

Tafari handed Edjer a hooded cloak, hunter green, with the roaring sigil of a Silver Bear. Edjer handed the cloak to his brother. Umid weakened to its sight.

"Take the Guards and kill the men!" roared Alcaeus.

Niobe scoffed: "The Royal Guards cannot be trusted, Alcaeus. The bushel is rotten. We cannot be rash."

"How long since you took this?" asked Umid,

"I came here right away, sire," answered Tafari.

Umid moved closer to Edjer, his head near the ear of his brother. "We need to kill them, quickly, and quietly," suggested Umid.

Edjer walked to Demetrius, "Do you still train?"

"When Jabez takes long to wake in the mornings, I do."

"We need to capture one, we can kill the rest. Tafari, return to the motel now, and leave this where you found it."

Edjer returned the cloak to Tafari.

"Alcaeus, Myawi, stay with Jabez. Uncle, they must remain in your room until we deem it safe," ordered Edjer.

An immediate response returned from Jabez, "As you wish."

Alcaeus and Myawi followed Jabez to his chambers, leaving *The Children* together.

"Where is Tomias?" asked Edjer.

"He sits in his chambers."

"Umid, send written orders to him to bring all of *us* together in our sisters' hall. You must now assume all those around you wish your demise. No servants, or attendants can be trusted."

"And you?" asked Umid.

"Demetrius and I will take one of these soldiers and kill the others. It will give us a chance."

"Take Khalil."

"No, Khalil has been seen in the palace. He will help you empty the halls."

"Alcaeus cannot leave the palace," added Niobe.

Edjer turned to Niobe, "Do not allow him to send a message to any senators." Then he gave one last order to Niobe: "You must protect him." They looked at Umid together.

She was discomforted by his order, but this was it. It was time. Niobe deemed the order necessary. "I will."

Edjer looked at Umid before he left with Demetrius. A game of Death awaited.

The inn was quite empty. Before they were to take on the soldiers, they observed. Finding empty hallways on each floor, Edjer had to be silent to complete the objective.

They regrouped on the first floor.

"Tafari will stay behind me," ordered Edjer.

"General, what is your order?"

Demetrius removed the dagger hidden in his leg.

"We need to take one of them."

Tafari nodded. He removed a knife of his own from his waist as they ascended to the third floor. It was smaller than *The Children's*, but nonetheless, capable of killing.

"Quietly, Demetrius. The Bear delegation is in the next inn."

Demetrius nodded. "We must be quick."

Their faces were covered. Edjer was dressed as a servant. He and Demetrius wore loose garments riddled with stains of dirt from the royal gardens. They covered their faces like foreign traders, knowing the status of servitude did not turn heads of curious men.

Slowly, Demetrius walked down the empty hallway. The hall was lit with candles, the walkway clear with opened windows on both ends.

"Now, Demetrius," ordered Edjer, from the edge of the hall.

Demetrius knocked on the door. He returned his weapon to his thigh.

"Linens, sir?" asked Demetrius.

The man at the door was similar in size to Demetrius. He was tall, and bulky. Demetrius was able to look past and find another man on one of the four cots. The suite was enormous. A problem existed in an open window. The neighboring inn where Semjaza and Lomotos discussed with their politicians, sat within range. A yell would alert the royals. Their intrusion would mean Edjer and Demetrius' death.

"Yes, more linens and refreshments," replied the man.

The door shut after Demetrius' acknowledgement of the request. He walked to Edjer.

"Only two soldiers."

"Just two?"

"He is of some size. The other is much smaller. We must take him. There may be more, but I could not see."

Edjer and Demetrius met with Tafari at the edge of the floor.

"I suspect the other two will return. But we must go now. We cannot risk waiting."

"Where are the linens?" asked Demetrius.

"Behind the keeper's stand," answered Tafari. Demetrius ran down the steps.

"Tafari, you will not go in with us. Wait by the stairs. If the others return or if one tries to escape, it is on you to kill them."

"Yes, General."

On Demetrius' return, Tafari moved into position.

Demetrius clamped down on the linens with both of his hands. Between the white sheets, he placed his dagger inside. Behind him, Edjer knelt, hidden by Demetrius' stature. Edjer had his sword drawn. His hand was on Demetrius' shoulder when the knock finally came.

The first soldier, the large one, went down without a fuss. Demetrius struck his dagger into his gut and with ease, twisted the blade and glided the weapon up. Edjer leapt in and began the struggle of taking the second soldier captive.

Their enemy was well-trained. The man drew a sword from underneath his bed once his comrade fell.

Edjer and Demetrius began crowding the man into a corner.

"Alive, Demetrius," repeated Edjer.

Demetrius went forward first. The soldier was too preoccupied with his own adrenaline to call for aid.

Demetrius saw openings for a kill but detracted. The man swung violently to keep them at a distance.

The sound of commotion concerned Tafari in the hall. The door to the room was open, and loud noises would soon cause others to file into the hallway. Worsening the circumstances, Tafari heard steps creak from the bottom floor of the quiet hotel.

In the room, the soldier's negligent swinging wounded Demetrius' arm, causing him to bleed through his garments. Demetrius' patience wore thin.

False confidence boosted the man's belief he could defeat Edjer and Demetrius.

The man continued, understanding they wished to capture him. He foolishly tried to escape to the door. A kick from Edjer took his legs. Demetrius struck the man, forcing him to fall. But he quickly rose to his feet.

"Edjer," uttered Demetrius.

The soldier swung his sword as he moved to another corner. He was becoming rabid.

In the halls, the stairs creaked louder as a conversation played out beneath Tafari's feet. Voices grew in volume.

The man made one last play and rushed at Demetrius. He felt that if he could get the large man on the ground, he could kill Demetrius, the bigger problem. The man did not know who the shrouded faces were. His decision to bring Demetrius down was the end, as Demetrius allowed the man's weight to fall onto him. Demetrius wrapped the soldier's body with his hands and took the man's weight with his hips. He hurled the man's body down to the wooden floors, with a devastating sound resounding through the inn.

The soldier survived the fall and removed a dagger from his waist. His goal to stab Demetrius' neck was ended by Edjer's blade. Edjer was swift, taking the man's hand before Demetrius acted on instinct and stuck his own dagger through the man's neck.

Drenched in blood, the brothers heard a whisper from the hall, "Edjer..."

Demetrius waited atop the soldier with his hand over his captive's mouth. Edjer crept his head out to the hallway and saw Tafari outside the door.

"Men approach," continued Tafari.

The low whisper heightened Edjer's nerves. Problems lied in front of him: two dying soldiers with no information, and two others approaching. Tafari had left his post to warn them. Edjer's handprints, the markings of his boots, blood was everywhere.

Edjer saw the two soldiers catch sight of him from the top of the staircase.

The soldier in front grabbed his comrade and took off.

"Go, Tafari!" ordered Edjer.

Tafari ran towards the men with his blade drawn. The chase was meaningless. Seconds between them and the soldiers at the stairs were too far to reconcile. Edjer swore loudly in frustration.

"Edjer!" shouted Demetrius.

Edjer ran to his brother's voice.

"The man lives," whispered Demetrius.

The second soldier who had taken effort to kill, he was gone. But the first; the man had a few moments before death.

"Speak if you wish to live," warned Edjer, kneeling beside him. His urgency was well hidden in a calm voice.

"...what life exists is gone," said the soldier. He struggled to breathe, let alone speak.

"It can go in peace or difficulty. Speak," ordered Edjer.

"To what?"

"What do your superiors seek?"

Laughing, the dying soldier spoke, "An end to the Perfugan dream. You are *liars*."

"Details! These threats mean nothing!" threatened Edjer.

"What unsaid plans would surprise you. The matter would be better if you experienced the true failure of your kin. Your country has always seen their greatest warrior, an enemy."

The man coughed up the blood engulfing his mouth, showering Edjer.

Prince Edjer recoiled his head back and found his prisoner had lost strength following cryptic last words, "The heir will die by the failures of his fathers."

Demetrius wiped Edjer's face of his enemy's blood and began covering his own wound on his bicep.

Edjer shut his eyes and rested his weight on his knees. Tafari ran down the hall with his heavy footsteps.

"Edjer, I could not reach them."

"Never leave your post boy. There is always reason for an order," said Demetrius sternly.

Tafari closed the door behind him to find a mess. Blood covered the room. The perspiration of the living and dead became vapor amidst the rare sunshine emanating through the window.

Edjer sat, baking in the rays as he planned his next move.

The scales had tipped towards the enemies of Perfuga.

"They have warned Lomotos and Semjaza by now. If they have not come, they fear we hold the soldiers hostage," Edjer paused to think for a moment, "Soldiers and spies will surround the building. They will require a spectacle," concluded Edjer. He looked at Demetrius.

They understood one another.

"Does the task disgust you brother?" inquired Demetrius.

They unsheathed their weapons and began. Edjer started on one of the dead men while Demetrius on the other.

"Tafari, grab your dagger, and bring me the linens by your feet."

The men began cutting away at their enemies. They painted the room with the dead.

When they left the hotel, nightfall had taken the Perfugan Capital. The markets were closing, and the people were rushing home before the curfew.

Edjer guided a hooded Tafari. Both of their clothes were bloodied. Behind him, Demetrius held the disfigured bodies of the soldiers in a sack made from linens.

To commoners, they were butchers. To the spies watching the motel, Perfugans held a dead soldier's remains and a prisoner in their grasp. Their enemies would see a captured comrade with knowledge of the Bear plot in Edjer's hands.

The spies surrounding Edjer and Demetrius began to fade into the crowds of departing citizens. Perception would spread the misinformation Edjer desired Semjaza to hear.

"Do not stop Tafari, we will be at the palace in minutes."

———

"Keep the hood on you," suggested Edjer.

They walked into the palace to find the halls emptied. Within minutes Semjaza would return and enter his room.

Khalil welcomed them into the garden after hearing the doors close.

"Khalil, go inside," ordered Edjer.

Edjer was cautious. He wanted to wait until he was safely past the garden and in the halls. Every piece of Tafari's skin was covered to not give any indication of a false prisoner. They freed Tafari from the discomfort once they reached the inner workings of the palace.

"The others?" asked Edjer.

"With the women," replied Khalil.

"Alcaeus and Myawi?"

"They remain confined to Jabez's quarters. He entertains with his hidden wine."

Demetrius, holding the bloodied sack of his enemies, laughed at his master's ingenuity.

Tafari removed his coverings. His eyes adjusted to the dim palace, "General, what must we do next?"

"Take the sack from Demetrius and burn it in the kitchen. The castle is empty but beware of the returning royals. I have another task for you," said Edjer.

Tafari took the linens from Demetrius. "Yes, General?"

"Take Khalil. Retrieve my sister from the compound."

Edjer's orders were stern. Khalil went off as the bloodied brothers moved through the palace on their own.

"Do you believe your games worked?" asked Demetrius.

"There was no success found today, Demetrius. We did what we were able to."

Blood dripping from their garments left the floors marked. A palace, once a slave to their games, was chillingly mute. The cold steps of Demetrius and Edjer continued until they reached the Hall of Concubines.

Together as one, *The Children* looked at the entrance. They were shocked to see their blood-stained brothers push the heavy doors open.

Edjer and Demetrius hesitated at the sight of their kin.

Rows of pools with the clearest, steaming blue waters were lined up against one another. They were aligned against the far wall opposite the door.

The room itself was dark; light came from lamps with meek flames, as well as the reflection of the pools. Cobblestone walkways were tarnished by the droplets of blood falling from Demetrius and Edjer. The two stained everything they touched.

"Are you wounded?" asked Niobe. She and Umid appeared amidst the clutter of siblings. The two men shook their heads, no.

Slowly, Edjer and Demetrius removed their clothing and fell into the warmed pools.

Both eyed the bottom floor of the water, beds of hot rocks steaming the baths.

Niobe retrieved their garments and burned them in a fire brewing near the doors. The others watched, powerless. She returned and knelt by the pool to find Umid horrified. Blood levitated from his brothers' rough skin. All were frozen in sight of what they believed to be a butcher-like massacre.

"What events have passed?" asked Umid.

"We killed two of the soldiers, but the rest escaped our grasp."

Umid turned away in horror.

"Is everyone in the palace?" asked Edjer.

"Manissa tests my patience with the children outside the Capital," said Niobe.

"Khalil will return with Tafari from the compound soon. Alcaeus?"

Niobe scoffed, "The fool wished to send messages with the leaving attendants. I intercepted them."

The doors crept open to an outsider accompanied by expected guests. Tafari walked behind Kiliea and Khalil, through *The Children* who were no longer children. Kiliea was slow to smile at the kin she had once left.

Niobe left the water instantly seeing the girl she had fed, carried, and protected. She nearly stumbled on the cobblestones. She walked straight to Kiliea, stopping in front of her. Niobe awaited a response, finding Kiliea frozen. After a beat, an embrace made them one, after years of displacement. Niobe held her tightly, hoarsely exhaling.

Niobe moved from her to readjust to the responsibilities of the crown, wiping tears from her eyes. She returned to the water. Khalil followed behind her, with Tafari steadily trailing.

"We await Manissa," said Khalil softly.

"The royals?" asked the bare Edjer, still in the water.

"They…" began Tafari, "…just have returned to the palace. They are flustered."

"Good. We need our weapons. We must take Semjaza now," replied Edjer, washing his body of the blood of his enemies.

Edjer was the first to leave the water cleaned. He was bare; a nasty scar on his stomach was visible. Niobe froze at the sight of her own work.

All watched as Edjer put his new garments and linens on, the robes of the Arms of the King.

Within seconds, Demetrius followed.

"They will act within the morrow," declared Edjer.

"Did the soldiers reveal anything?" asked Umid. Edjer ignored him. Outside the pool, Edjer and Demetrius whispered to one another.

Then, Edjer shared his orders. "Khalil, take Kiliea and Tafari, and a few others. I need to know which royals are here."

"I must go with them, Edjer, it is my duty," said Demetrius.

"You will go with them, then, brother."

Umid's patience was tested by the control Edjer wielded.

"I will go with them as well," announced Niobe. "I am a foreigner here."

"Go," whispered Edjer.

Umid was at his end, "What did the soldiers reveal?!"

King Umid's outburst angered the others. Umid locked eyes with Edjer.

"Calm yourself. The soldier was clear. *The heir will die by the failure of his fathers.*"

Niobe twitched, ignoring the premonitory warning. She took Umid's arm to comfort his fears.

"We must protect our own royals in the palace," warned Umid.

"We will."

Umid scoffed, "You too, brother, are a royal."

The statement left Edjer trapped, mesmerized by a single recurring thought of the past days. Enemies desired him. But, to what outcome? He had been the subject of their interest from the beginning.

The thought had left him wondering about his enemies' intentions, sparking him into action days prior.

I am nothing, I have been nothing, thought Edjer.

He was not able to shake the inlaid threat shared by Semjaza. *I am not a cruel man.*

"What more can happen to me, Umid?"

"Your death, by a foreign kingdom, you underestimate your meaning to the people. A foreigner would force our hand into another Great War."

The others looked at Edjer, the Prince of Death. They froze at Umid's exclamation. His brothers and sisters would commit their own exacting vengeance. Grips on the knives tightened, and the eagerness of their reunion dissipated.

"Let it be," declared Edjer.

THIRTY-FOUR

20 days since the Ceremony began.

Manissa was alone in the fields with her children. Two Royal Guards were all that protected them in the darkness. Never was there anything to fear in the routine trips to the fields with the palatial students.

The orphans gathered around Manissa for the lessons.

"Do you all wish to stay here, longer into the night?"

They nodded. The guards held lamps with a faint light. Around them, nothing.

Manissa marvelously eyed the sky, "We are fortunate recent clouds leave us with the shine of stars. Look out and slowly close your eyes.

"A story will come to you. An imagination is formed in solitude. Give yourself time. What dreams may come to little orphans; I am well aware."

A group of four moved farther away from the rest of the children. They welcomed the soft flower beds beneath them.

Manissa awaited them to fall into their angelic visions before she returned to hers.

A ways away, a kingdom began its fall. The students were immune to the burden.

Young Isaias, the one who had challenged Niobe, took time to settle in, moving the fallen weeds away from where he wished to lie.

THIRTY-FIVE

20 days since the Ceremony began.

"Fools, we were fools to believe you!"

"Quiet, the others may hear us!" ordered Lomotos.

The Northern King lowered his voice in Semjaza's quarters. The plotters were entrenched in dire worry. Returning to an empty palace, they wondered if their heads would be taken before the morning came.

"Calm yourself, you are a king," suggested Semjaza.

"We are surrounded! The king unites his family in the hall of their pleasuring women! They stand united!"

"Semjaza, the Northerner speaks truth. Your soldiers were taken this afternoon. Our spies, as well as yours, have seen it." The representative of the Nation-States did not wish to understate the urgency.

"We expected resistance, it is their nature," assured Semjaza.

The Northern King approached the bed where Semjaza sat: "You fool, this is no resistance. We entered into this agreement to disunify their people, their family. We have failed."

"We do not fail. You act as a commoner. Resistance was expected. They are dangerous." Semjaza was patient, strong, like a king.

The Northern ruler's snicker was met with a strong reprieve from Lomotos.

"Do not antagonize those unafraid to die," warned Lomotos quietly.

"Nothing has changed. We will begin tonight." Semjaza wished to avoid the panic of infighting.

"We must then prepare to leave?" asked the Northern King.

"We leave tonight. And be discreet. If they kill us in the palace they would begin a war. Do not engage them."

Semjaza's orders brought comfort. The play was in motion.

"We must not all file out together," added Semjaza, "Lomotos and I will take the last leave. Begin your departure and send word to the inns for the rest of your men to follow."

The two surviving soldiers from the inn were prepared outside the Capital walls for a last attempt at success. For days, they had located their target and watched him. It was time.

"Do not be in Perfuga by sunrise."

Semjaza watched the royals hurry out.

"Are the soldiers ready?" asked Lomotos.

A deep exhale left Semjaza. He was not immune to the anxiety.

"We need to leave," replied Semjaza. He covered his face with his hands.

"If the teacher returns and we remain, they will pick us apart by our limbs," warned Lomotos.

Semjaza laughed at the realistic threats: "I am aware, Lomotos."

"You stake our livelihood on this plan, Semjaza. I ask, do you believe this will divide them?"

Semjaza rose. He looked into his brother's eyes, taking his hand. The pain was shared, "Would you not kill me if I had done what Umid has?"

"Without hesitation. His brothers and sisters hold my worry."

"They follow their Prince of Death, Lomotos. They are one in him. He is a good man who must fall."

THIRTY-SIX

20 days, leading into the 21st, since the Ceremony began.

When is a dream not a dream?

In the comfort of nature, the mind can wonder and create. Imaginations may grow, as dreams take shape.

In the plush fields, Manissa's students looked to the sky. They had been instructed to return to the palace before dark, but rarely did Manissa take the students away from the peaceful bliss of the stars' shine. The fields had once provided the same peace for her and *The Children*.

The students were scattered. Two guards patrolled where Manissa was unable to see. Thirty students all lay flat on the ground. They all faced the same starry sky.

The boy, Isaias, welcomed the peace of the swaying fields. He lay alone; his eyes closed.

Visions he did not understand came to him. At the age of eight, he was smarter than most. An orphan since birth, he excelled under Manissa's instruction. Her training, however, could not prepare him for this.

These visions were bigger than life. At least they seemed to be. He had no understanding of meditation, of sleep, of dreams. No anxiety had yet entrenched him that he struggled to conquer. Isaias submerged into the chilling earth bed, forgoing resistance. He allowed the visions to take shape.

He felt as if he transitioned to another side of himself.

Isaias saw fields in the daylight yet did not know where he was. He found two lovers walking in the field, but their faces were not clear to him.

Isaias watched how the woman's touch changed the man. Against a radiant and hazy purple sunset, the man held her tight.

They were all alone. Isaias was an uninvited surveyor.

The woman motioned through the fields, knowing the man's eyes followed her closely. Isaias felt the man's pain the further she walked.

He found himself thrust into another dream. This time, he saw the woman speaking directly at him.

Lady Asiya.

"The serpent is shapeless, my dear boy. He can appear to you in many forms, and he will appear to you in your weakest time. The slithering snake is blamed for our natural faults.

"It will attack your loved ones to spite you. Tales of the wicked will seem unreal, but you know nothing of cruelty until you have done cruel things yourself. Work done to keep the heart pure is harder than conceding to natural evil.

"The serpent will appear to you in all paths. Fear must not dictate your action. Do not let the heart speak for you so quickly.

"False honor runs through the veins of men when the snake's venom colonizes the host. There is honor to be had in a mind aware of all that slithers after surviving evil's initial bite."

The dreams ended abruptly.

Isaias woke up confused. He wondered if the orphans around him saw the same woman in their dreams. He remained flat in the dark field, catching his breath. Since the Ceremony began, his holistic fantasies had altered.

He looked around the fields for his friends. They were still dreaming, entrapped by their visions.

Isaias rose from the ground, looking around for Manissa. He had questions. The boy scoffed at the Royal Guards fighting sleep as he walked past them. He kicked one on his boot to wake him, but the guard did not move.

The initial jump of a racing primate could snatch a child in a blink.

Two silent soldiers finally completed their dispatched objective. Dragging Isaias from the rest of the children, the kidnappers held his mouth shut. They would not survive if Manissa had even heard a sound. A cloth was placed over Isaias' mouth. Away from the guards and the menacing Headmistress, the Bear soldiers crept away.

Before leaving, one of the men completed a crucial detail of Semjaza's plan. He grabbed a scroll from his pouch. He stabbed the scroll with a dagger into the ground, holding a message in place for when Manissa would know true fear.

THIRTY-SEVEN

21 days since the Ceremony began.

Screams echoed through the palace. Her children trailed her. She continued screaming as she entered. The orphans mirrored her. Tears had been shed for their missing brother.

The sealed doors of the Hall of Concubines kept the noise away.

But Kiliea, Khalil, and Niobe ran to Manissa at the opening to the inner hall.

"My children!" roared Manissa. "They have taken my student!"

Kiliea moved the torch in her hand, lighting the children's faces. Raw untapped rage covered their faces. Isaias' three companions, the twins and Liku, were voiceless while others cried. They kept their tears. They wanted the lives of the kidnappers.

"Stall your cries, Manissa. Our enemies are in these halls," ordered Niobe.

"You witch, why do they still live?" replied Manissa. Her face tightened as she leaned forward. Khalil was quick to come between them.

Kiliea continued to track the children with her fire. Her walk through the students flooded memories of the lengths she had gone, the life she had endured. The pain would never end.

"Calm yourself. What happened?" asked Khalil. He wiped the tears from Manissa's eyes as her rage chilled. She slowly tamed the animal inside her, an animal that lay beneath all *The Children*.

Manissa handed him the scroll. The hunter green Bear seal was broken.

"'I demand the Arms of the King in the White Desert. We will await.'"

Khalil read the words in confusion. He handed the note to the curious Niobe.

Another's steps came crashing down the upper floors, dashing through the hall.

"My Queen, where is Edjer?" asked the running Tafari.

"What happened?" she asked.

Tafari paced himself. He looked at the broken Manissa, and the tearful pupils. His news mattered.

"The royals have left! Their rooms are empty," said Tafari. Slowly, a thought came to him: "Where is the General?" None answered him.

Niobe sprung into awareness. She had ignored a premonitory thought earlier. She read the note again. Leaving Tafari, a daunting conclusion came to her. *The boy,* she remembered. She recalled Umid's remarks to Edjer: *Your death, by a foreign kingdom, you underestimate your meaning to the people. A foreigner would force our hand into another Great War.*

"No, no, no," whispered Niobe. Devastation flooded in, "Give me the torch!"

Kiliea surrendered her flame.

Niobe raced through the children with the fire. *If he wishes to steal our hope, it is us he comes for.* The words echoed in her mind. She watched their faces intently, searching. *The heir will die by the failure of his fathers.* She knew him by name, but his face was distinct. He had spoken so confidently to her. He had always looked like his mother.

Edjer was nowhere to be found. He had led a few of his brothers to the armory, but he had not returned in some time. Niobe had only minutes before he did. Niobe's face lowered in shame for a moment. A shriek, then a yell, escaped from her. Terror spread through her body. She had believed her sins, forgotten. The orphanage was to be a haven for him.

Niobe gritted her teeth. She placed the flame near the last child, the girl warrior Liku, finding the child battle-ready, filled with hate.

The others: Tafari, Manissa, and Khalil, they watched Niobe lose herself. She murmured in worry of the fate destined for her and Perfuga. When her heart finally steadied, she wielded her power.

"Instruct all the Royal Guards to return," said Niobe to Tafari, "They must retrieve Umid from the Concubines."

"Niobe," interjected Khalil. She turned; the stare of a lioness ended his hesitation.

"Do not allow the Concubines to leave the halls. Order the Arms of the King to their compound. No weapons will be allowed in the palace. Find him. Bring Edjer here before sunup!"

"Niobe," whispered Khalil again.

"Khalil, who do you serve!" asked Niobe.

"Do not play, witch! Children's lives hang in the balance!" thundered Manissa. Khalil held Manissa before she struck Niobe.

The students watched *The Children* splinter.

Niobe bypassed Manissa. "Children, return to your quarters. Do not leave the palace."

The students did not flinch, eyeing Manissa. The Headmistress recognized the ruthlessness of her sister. Bloodshed did not scare Niobe.

"Go!" ordered Manissa. The students quickly departed.

"I am calling an immediate council meeting," said Niobe.

She paused, thinking of her coming confessions. "I must tell you a story first ... then I will ask you to betray *him*," whispered Niobe, requiring aid from Khalil.

Niobe took the last living lieutenant of the Arms of the King aside. She spoke to him in private. And like hers had, his heart broke. Tears left his eyes before he complied, hoping for an end capable of appeasing the family.

"Khalil! What has she done?!" screamed Manissa. Khalil took Manissa away with him.

Niobe and Kiliea were alone in the palace halls. She looked at Niobe, petrified, "What — did you do?"

Niobe could not look Kiliea in her eyes, "Before the end of the day, we will mourn either Perfuga's King or its greatest warrior."

THIRTY-EIGHT

21 days since the Ceremony began.

Niobe stood alone in the Council Room. She fearfully awaited execution of her orders. She watched as the sun began to overtake the uneasy night.

She needed time.

From where she stood, the door behind her cast a large shadow. A king's chambers were sacred, for its secrets bore heavy. Umid had deferred to her for many of his decisive measures, but behind those doors, rulers had suffered the consequences of those decisions alone.

Jabez was brought into the Inner Council room by Demetrius. He looked stronger, as Myawi and Alcaeus sluggishly followed behind him. Duty had cured Jabez. But Alcaeus and Myawi, they slowly came to their senses as they fell into their seats.

Niobe focused on Jabez. Not many knew, but he and Umid had helped her hide Perfuga's greatest sin.

"Take part in the refreshments. Clear your minds," ordered Niobe, sternly.

"Demetrius, leave us," continued Niobe.

"He will not. I have been told the royals are gone. If the moment comes for my death, I wish him nearby," confidently said Jabez.

"Are your loyalties to your King or Edjer?" she asked Demetrius.

The room's occupants sharpened to the question. Alcaeus and Myawi quickly turned. Demetrius tightened his posture, "My loyalty lies with my master."

"What has happened?" asked Jabez.

Niobe walked over to him. She handed him the note from the Bear.

He read and asked, "What is this?"

"Await the King," whispered Niobe.

Demetrius was a piece of the Arms of the King. He would go if the men went. Jabez's voice sharpened, "What is this Niobe?!"

Demetrius sat in the chair near the window. He did not like Jabez's tone, "Master."

"Demetrius, you do not involve in these matters!" ordered Jabez, "Niobe, tell me!?"

Silence. Then, Niobe spoke: "They have taken the boy."

Prince Jabez's face sank. Feelings in his legs dissipated. His words were chopped in his reply, "Wh…which boy?"

"The orphanage."

"Niobe!" fluttered Jabez in fear. "He will kill us."

"Calm yourself."

"Do not speak of calm!" exclaimed Jabez. His fiery response shook the room. He rose from his seat.

"Demetrius, please, leave the palace, now, please," pleaded Jabez. His voice was vulnerable, dropping as if pleading for his own life. He walked to Demetrius.

"Jabez," called Niobe.

"Master, what is wrong?" inquired Demetrius.

"Never mind this, leave the palace. Leave before your brother returns. Leave!"

"Jabez?" Demetrius had never seen desperation of this magnitude.

"Please, Demetrius, you need not stay!" he begged.

Jabez put his hands on Demetrius, caressing his servant's face. He wished not to lose another son, but his requests were met with silence. His soul departed once he heard the doors open behind him.

"Why do your yells plague the halls?" asked Umid, walking into the room.

"Shut the doors," said Niobe.

Jabez's face fell in defeat. Umid watched Myawi and Alcaeus rise while Jabez and Niobe ignored him. He saw the tears on his Uncle's face.

Niobe herself refused to look at Umid.

"Your yells mirror Manissa's cries. What has happened?" inquired Umid, taking his seat at the cement table.

The sun finally held over the night. Light came through the open windows. Jabez struggled to sit, leaving Niobe standing alone amongst the men. She walked over to King Umid and handed him the note.

"The royals left the palace in the night. We did not see them," shared Niobe.

"What is this?" asked Umid.

"The Bear, they took a boy from Manissa's group. They left this note."

"'I demand the Arms of the King in the White Desert. We will await.'" Umid was as puzzled as each reader had been. The sinners had left the transgressions of the past alone, thinking themselves absolved.

"The details elude me, Niobe."

"Umid, have you forgotten?" replied Niobe, hiding a slow onslaught of tears.

Umid eyed the note. The heat from the sunshine lay directly on him. He saw its seal, the dim words inked in red. It had long been written beforehand.

His head turned from the note, slowly, to his lover. She could not face him. Umid shifted his gaze towards Jabez, lost in thought.

"Which boy?" asked Umid, rising from his seat.

"Umid, control yourself," grittily uttered Niobe, her hand over her mouth.

"No! Who could know, Niobe? Who could know?! What is this?!" Umid yelled in Niobe's ear, then to Jabez.

"We must plan and prepare. He will come," said Niobe.

"Quiet!" Umid calmed himself. "Where is Edjer?"

No one knew, "He has been ordered to the castle. I asked the Royal Guards to bring him here before the information reached him."

"Oh, Niobe, what would he do with it?!" Jabez's interruption grounded them. "He will kill us."

Myawi was the first to speak up for he and Alcaeus, "You call advisors in, but you do not wish to share information."

"Hold your tongue!" yelled Umid, using all his power.

"Umid, please sit," whispered Niobe.

Ignoring her, he walked towards the steps of his chamber. Stumbling, he stopped before reaching the door.

Umid turned away from them before speaking, "One of you broke our promise. We were never to speak of it."

"Another lives," answered Jabez.

"No, no! It is not possible," stressed Niobe. The thought brought a sharp pain to her gut.

"I called the meeting. We are displaced into a grave storm. Our enemies hold hostage a..." She stopped, looking at Alcaeus and Myawi.

"Niobe, please," warned Umid. He did not turn, focused on watching the door to his quarters.

"You all remember the sister lost, As—Asiya. To the people, she had died from—"

"Sickness," interrupted Alcaeus. He shuffled his feet, watching her intently.

Niobe looked towards Demetrius. He looked back at her with a childlike innocence.

"Yes. Some believed she took the affection of our brother, Edjer. She was fair in his presence.

"A courtship grew, but we let it be. They were family, and we knew more about one another than a man can know his own lover or child—We let it be."

Demetrius knew she spoke the truth.

"Umid's ascension meant we — we were no longer brothers and sisters to anyone. We had asked, repeatedly, separately, were they engaged with one another? They thought it a game. We warned them, subtly, then as open as could be. I begged her not to break the foolish decree. They thought it a game, Demetrius."

Tears began to fall from his eyes.

"The whispers rose to a level we could not allow. Umid, even I, we loved Asiya …we … loved Edjer."

Demetrius became impatient, "Speak to what you have done."

"We should have stopped them." Niobe's words paused abruptly.

"Nearly nine years to the day, a hooded messenger came through these halls amid the worst storm Perfuga had ever seen. The storms kept her walk secret. In a hood, Asiya appeared to me in this room," Niobe struggled to find the words, "She warned me of her and Edjer's misstep, an error made in which Edjer himself was not aware. She removed her hood and looked honorably upon me for direction and aid. A babe grew in her, a child made by the Prince of Death, himself," continued Niobe.

Betrayal sliced Demetrius in two. His eyes shut, but the tears found a way through. Umid spoke of a King's response.

"She had expected a helpful hand, but she betrayed me. Asiya brought a child at the point others wished to undermine my rule. Politicians would have asked for her head. Our enemies within the kingdom would have had the reason they required for Edjer's death. Niobe had no option but to speak to Jabez and I and tell us of a child that threatened the kingdom."

"*Lam yakun alhubu baynana mukhtalifan,*" whispered Demetrius. The words spoke of the past, *The love between them was no different.*

"I acted justly, Demetrius. I am a King. I think for millions, no longer just my family. I decided," declared Umid.

"You lied to her! You betrayed her! You killed her for this?! This is no act of a king," stated Demetrius. He walked near Jabez, "Master … you hold these lies from me?!"

Jabez's head sank, there was more hidden, much more.

"She was not killed," whispered Jabez.

The others, Myawi and Alcaeus, watched as the family crumbled.

"What?" asked Demetrius in horror.

"Sins of the father, sins of a mother, they fall at their child's feet," declared Umid. He had yet to turn from the door of his chambers.

Niobe began recounting the truth. Asiya had lingered back into the council room after Niobe had told her to wash in the Hall of Concubines. Niobe had promised she would find Asiya safe passage back to her lands where the baby and mother would live in secret. They had agreed to tell Edjer later.

Asiya, after her confession, had felt secure. The child inside her was not just hers, instead borne from a lineage of survival. *Love was no different, for a mother, for a lover, or for a child.* Asiya had believed the declaration. Months prior, she had refused Edjer's request to leave Perfuga for their homelands. Love of a family could not be betrayed. But Asiya had not been immune to traitorous actions.

She had returned to the Inner Council room to find Umid at the table. Next to Umid, Jabez. Immediately, Asiya had pleaded, feeling the trap laid in her midst.

No, Niobe, please, please, sister, no!

Niobe had held her sister at knifepoint, tears in her eyes as her dagger pressed against her sister's neck.

Wait, wait, Umid had shouted. A baby born of the Prince of Death was not only the heir to Perfuga, a threat, but he would be the nephew of a brother he loved more than anything.

We cannot kill her, he had ordered. The abrupt, spontaneous decision had spilled from his mouth. In the cover of the night, they had guided Asiya into the Royal Guards' dungeons.

We must not speak a word to Edjer, Niobe had warned. *We must tell him she is dead. His grief will occupy him. If he knows she lives, he will leave us no choice.*

He will kill us, Jabez had warned.

Umid had bent down to Asiya. She had sat against the walls of the dungeon. *You will not survive, Asiya. You were always warned. The baby will be born here, you will be taken care of until the child is born. I will not kill Edjer's child. Then you will die.*

For months, Asiya had sat alone with her babe in her stomach, as *The Children* divided over their hatred for Umid and Niobe, believing a sister dead. Asiya's hands had spent time brushing the lonely leaves blowing through the chilling prison. In the brightest of days, she had thought of her lover who had been only meters away. The nights had been the worst, holding a foul smell, for the sewers had ushered Perfuga's waste underneath her feet, bringing the pregnant mother to vomit.

Soon, the nights had become easier for Asiya. Alone, she had surrendered to the child in her belly. She had retold the stories to what would become the boy, Isaias.

Asiya had dangled with hunger, insanity, and yet found comfort in the stories she told. *He would live for I and Edjer,* she had thought. She had found comfort, even if Edjer would never know about his own son. That had become consolation for her. The prospect had kept her amongst the living.

Asiya had always prayed in the mornings to see the end of the day. Niobe and Jabez would bring her food in the nights to avoid being seen. Her belly grew and grew, as the rest of Asiya withered into loose skin and failing bones. She had only eaten once a day, twice if Jabez could spare a trip in the early mornings. Niobe and Jabez had expected her to die in those horrid conditions; they somewhat had hoped it to be the case.

But Asiya had endured solitude. The further into the pregnancy, the more fear she had put in them. She persevered, losing the semblance of beauty she had once held. The weight of her arms had become feathers, with the babe taking shape inside a skeleton. Niobe had stopped coming out of disgust at the dreadful sight, the daunting possibility of a birth scaring her even more. A great sin had existed in the torturous conditions, one that Niobe could not face.

But Jabez had been bold. He had monitored and fed her. He had told her stories of his dead son, the glory of parenthood as he bathed her with the warm waters from the Hall of Concubines.

Asiya had asked Jabez one day if he would bring Niobe. He had complied, as Asiya was days away from giving birth.

Niobe had not expected Asiya to have such strength in the end. She had still found her feeble, half the woman and warrior she had once been. Jabez had watched as Asiya grabbed her sister's arm for another plea: *If a child could be born from what we survived, the earth was not doomed.* Asiya had pleaded for life. *Sister, do not let the child live a life of pain. Free him, for I have seen a boy bolder than any.*

The mother had endured, as all mothers had.

The day of her delivery had been distraught, coming on the solstice of summer. The red-orange rays of the sun had flooded the cell with impunity. Steam had filled the dungeons as Asiya roared. Blood had covered her, a problematic entry into the world for young Isaias. She had pushed and pushed through the heated day and finally, forced her child out in the hot night, after half a day in delivery. The beauty of Isaias' cries had been the song Jabez fell in love with, one that had reminded him of his son's entrance.

Umid had left the castle running once hearing the news of the birth. He had held onto Asiya's meek arms as she fought. In the struggle, she had put her bloodied hands on the beige walls, leaving the stain for posterity. Niobe, her own stained hands, had been the first to hold Isaias. *A boy, it is a boy,* Niobe had screamed, laughing. The siblings had cried at the bravery, for Isaias was symbolic to them, for the lives of those who had perished on the journey to Perfuga.

Isaias, Isaias Bilal is his name. The boy of victory, staking the claim of our brothers and sisters in the new world. Asiya's words had been resounding.

Niobe had glanced at Jabez, then to her King. She had fought Umid to have the boy stay with Asiya for the day. Niobe had begged with all her might.

She had always loved her brothers and sisters deeply.

Niobe had stayed by Asiya's side throughout. The conversation between them on that day had laid the foundation for all coming calamities.

———

Thousands of days before the Ceremony.

"Asiya," said Niobe.

Asiya cradled her baby and fed him with her own breast, "I finally know," said Asiya, "...why we survived..."

Blood stained the walls, the wooden bars, the ground they sat on. The red turned black on Asiya's skin. She remained stained whilst holding her baby.

"Asiya, I need the boy."

"A moment sister, please, sit with me."

Asiya was calm, readying herself for the death she was told to come. The baby kept her alive, but she knew her time was close, as Jabez had warned, *they will kill you once the child arrives.*

Niobe lowered her head in shame. She had just witnessed the amazing birth; a hunger-stricken mother gave her all for creation, for an opportunity.

She resigned her declaration and sat with Asiya.

"Can I see your back?" asked Asiya.

Niobe hesitated, first turning, then lowering her garments. She could feel her sister's penetrating eyes dissect the scars.

"Which ones are from Edjer?"

"The long strokes." Three slashes were fresh, near her spine. Fierce scars were visible against Niobe's golden skin. Edjer's knife had gotten close to her spine. His mercy had saved her. Soon, they would fade in with the other, older, unpleasant scars.

"He loved me," began Asiya. "I wish for this child to be allowed to find that love. May no decree or law withhold him of that … fierceness of a lover. A motherless child is lost for most of their life. You will not be allowed to care for him but allow him his freedom."

Niobe nodded to her sister.

"Asiya, Umid will see him raised in the palace as an orphan. Manissa has taken your post."

"She is a fierce one … a good mother …" A tear fell from her eye.

"…he cannot kill you now. He will not." Asiya did not care to look at Niobe as she spoke. Her smile enlightened life within her pupil. The covered child felt the warmth of a mother.

"You will be exiled. Tomorrow, Jabez and I will ride with you to the Nation-States. I will give you gold, and clothes. You can never return, sister. Please."

Tears of the mother were profound as they fell onto her child. Asiya was ashamed of staining her son with dilemmas of a world unworthy of him. She closed her eyes and wiped his face. She tried to sit unphased by the news.

The whole time, Niobe had withheld the news of Edjer's exile from her.

Asiya handed the baby to Niobe, life leaving her as her arms extended. She had one request, "Protect the child. He is not just mine, Niobe. He is yours, too."

Niobe grabbed the child. Isaias did not cry in her hands, instead felt warmth, and succumbed to her confidence. Only when Niobe closed the cell on his mother did the tears begin. The loud clunk locking Asiya in forced his cries to continue until Niobe surrendered him to Manissa.

—

"Jabez, why? You keep this from me?" asked Demetrius, his voice cracking.

"Please, Demetrius. I could not even look towards the child. I watched him from the palace windows every morning. Please?"

Powerless, Demetrius froze. "And the note?" he asked.

"Semjaza wishes for the Arms of the King to meet them in the White Desert."

Demetrius stormed out as Jabez yelled his name, repeatedly, "Demetrius! Demetrius!"

"He will tell the rest," warned Umid, coming out of his trance.

"Guard!" yelled Niobe.

One of the Royal Guards ran in. Niobe gave her orders, "Escort Demetrius to the Native Quarter. Allow him to be with the Arms of the King. Listen to me! He cannot be allowed in the Hall of Concubines."

The Guard ran. Jabez shifted in his seat as the others quieted. Niobe sat in her chair. She remembered her and Jabez riding with Asiya for days. When reaching the Nation-States, she had left her sister with no words, no embrace. With a sack of gold and garments, they left Asiya in an empty field, wounded in body and spirit.

In the years to come, Asiya could never recover as her mind dulled. Asiya had tried to find her own way, but like Jabez, she had fallen into a committed life of potions and prostitution, guided by a memory of a lost son.

"What is to be done?" asked Myawi.

"Edjer has been called to the palace. I leave it to Umid," replied Niobe.

"Will the Arms of the King meet the Bear in the desert?" retorted Myawi.

Silence.

"Umid, this secret is not limited to you and the crown. Your decisions will find judgment by the people at a later time," Myawi stopped to collect the right words. "There is no path where we do not meet them in the desert. Whether the crown recognizes the legitimacy or not, our enemies hold the Heir to Perfuga hostage."

Alcaeus chuckled, coming to the same conclusion. "You should have killed the woman. Edjer must surely die."

"Umid, no!" yelled Niobe.

Umid left the steps to his chamber door and darted towards Alcaeus' seat. What laid underneath all *The Children* finally found its way to the surface of the King. Abnormal strength was displayed in how he threw the older Alcaeus out of his seat. Grabbing his advisor, he held onto him for a significant distance until Alcaeus' back crashed into the palace walls. From his waist, Umid drew the dagger of his inheritance. The sharp blade found Alcaeus' neck.

Like an animal, Umid's eyes widened. He exhaled ferociously through his mouth, nearly foaming with anger. Every fiber of muscle within him tightened. Alcaeus became acquainted with a novel fear of death.

Under the strain of his tightened lips, Umid spoke, "You fool, I hear your insults and watch the eyes of envy each day. Do not speak of matters you do not understand."

Niobe had been under a similar spell after Tafari's coronation. Her touch of Umid's shoulder was careful.

"Umid," said Niobe, placing her hand on him. He did not turn.

"You do not know what was endured by children more honorable than you and your senators, more courageous and tested than any of your kin!"

"Umid," uttered Niobe again. He ignored her.

"Do not speak until you know the love of a brother! Have you ever been present for a birth?! I saw a woman fight with the last of her wit to give birth! I saw her cry! Pray! I felt the grip of her hands — taking the place of the brother I lost because of duty!"

Umid spoke rapidly, placing the knife higher on Alcaeus' throat. His own tears fell. Blood trickled to his hands as he nicked Alcaeus' skin.

"Umid!" shouted Niobe. Finally, Umid turned to find his advisors fearfully looking at their King. He calmed his breathing and began to relax his grip. Umid was not done.

"Do not ever speak of life you do not understand," whispered Umid. He let Alcaeus go.

"Any of you speak of this, it will not only be you that finds the tip of a sword," announced Niobe.

She took the dagger from Umid as he calmed by the steps to his chambers. He sat and threw his hands into his face.

An attendant of the palace knocked and entered. She found the room in disarray, Myawi shaken, and Alcaeus bleeding.

She spoke fast, "Sire, Prince Edjer awaits in the garden."

No one moved.

Then, Niobe cleared her throat. "I will get him," she whispered.

THIRTY-NINE

21 days since the Ceremony began.

Edjer complied with his summons order. He was alarmed to hear his brothers were confined to the Compound. Whispers warned of changed circumstances.

Edjer had seen Demetrius being escorted to the Compound by Royal Guards. Demetrius refused to speak to him as they crossed paths near the palace.

But the hand signal was quick. Demetrius made sure to warn his brother as they passed. *Be careful.*

The wooden palace doors opened to a plethora of soldiers, nervous, and in full armor, watching Edjer the moment he stepped in.

Terror spread as the Prince of Death took his steps into the royal garden.

Edjer turned, finding the uneasy guards' gazes upon him.

Had the moment come? he wondered. Death would find him unafraid. His hand refused to reach for his sword.

Their eyes, terror.

Edjer walked into the castle alone. He heard recognizable footsteps. Khalil came first.

"I was told the attendants and servants have been given entry," said Edjer.

"They have locked our sisters away, Edjer," warned Khalil.

"I saw Demetrius escorted away. What has happened? Where is Umid?"

"Manissa. A child has been taken. A message came from Semjaza," replied Khalil.

Edjer was still. "What was the boy's name?"

"Isaias," replied Khalil carefully.

The name held meaning. Edjer was frozen, feeling a tingle in his fingers. A time before his journey, his father's name in North Africa had been Isaias. After a moment, he remembered the boy and his friends from the royal garden.

"You must tread lightly among them," declared Khalil.

"Your worries are wasted on me, brother."

"Please, Edjer. I am…sorry. I need your weapon. You and Umid must talk," pleaded Khalil.

Niobe walked down the steps with Royal Guards. Two trailed her, their eyes darting between the two brothers. The door to the gardens remained open, a viable escape. Khalil and Edjer did not move, watching her descend upon them in a slow, ginger manner. But she did not face them.

"The King awaits." Niobe pushed further with her orders, "Khalil, you are to return to the compound."

Khalil waited for Edjer's confirmation. Niobe's hands seemed to be interlocked behind her. It was not the case, her dagger was clenched, to act if the moment required.

"Edjer," said Khalil softly.

Niobe ignored Khalil, clearing her throat before her new orders: "Edjer, the crown desires your weapons before you see your King."

Gardeners peeked too quickly into the inner halls. Edjer watched attentively, eyeing the moving shadows near the doors of rooms around them. Hallways spoke of steps. They were surrounded.

"The darkness dances," echoed Edjer.

Edjer was slow to draw his sword. From the halls, men emerged, twitching at the release of his weapon. Royal Guards hidden in the gardens held the rear. No less than twenty soldiers surrounded Edjer. Niobe released her hand from her dagger.

"My sword...?" Edjer similarly renounced his claim to his weapon to Khalil.

Stripped of weapons, Edjer walked freely with Niobe. Edjer did not protest. Instead, he hoped for a clean death. Ascending the stairs, never did she look back at him.

Edjer finally spoke before they reached the Inner Council doors, smiling, "You fear me today. What does the King require of his brother?"

Niobe paused, then opened the door to the Inner Council room. All looked up at him, dejected. The royals were terrified, nonetheless. Jabez could not face Edjer; the aftermath of his own tears stained the cement table.

"Leave us," ordered Umid.

The others walked out. Jabez still did not face Edjer, but stopped near him, speaking, "There is courage in love. The begging of a lioness is terrifying. I have seen...survival. Forgive me boy."

The warning grounded Edjer.

Umid refused to turn. His lonely walk up the three steps was quiet. He opened the door to his chambers and waited. He left the door open.

Edjer turned to look at Niobe. She took a seat at the Inner Council table and looked at the door. Her only order was to watch. She was not to intrude under any circumstances.

Edjer took her refusal to enter as an invitation to the King's Chambers. He entered, finding his brother seated in front of an empty fireplace.

The slow creak from Edjer's footsteps brought fear into King Umid.

"Edjer, I ask you for patience, to hear my words."

Umid first removed his royal black garments. He wanted to be unclad when he confessed. He placed his weapons on the mantle behind him. Patiently, he detailed the sins of the past to Edjer.

The palace fell silent before Edjer took control. This sound was not new. Pain had its own tune for *The Children*. The news was unbearable, as had been the news of Asiya's death long ago. Asiya's survival, a son of his own, the revelations shocked Edjer. Each brutal detail was shared: her wrenching birth, the lonely sentence of solitude, the exile.

Rarely, rarely, did one lose control.

The animal within came out of Edjer. Niobe listened but would not break an order. If she intruded, it would be her death or the end of the Prince of Death. Edjer moved closer to Umid, roaring, screaming, defiling Umid's face with snot and tears. They flowed from Edjer's face, monstrously. Umid did not stall his words, nor did he hesitate. He remained composed till the end, in pain of his own.

Edjer ended his protest by screaming in his brother's ear. The veins of his neck pulsated. Edjer roared, helpless, knowing killing Umid would bring nothing.

King Umid took the verbal punishment. He awaited the return of his Prince's composure to plan for the reclamation of lost family.

FORTY

21 days since the Ceremony began.

Edjer sat in the corner of the chamber. He was voiceless, his heavy breathing spiraling out of his own control. His internal dialogue was closed. Memories, fears, all of it played in a loop in his head.

Umid was behind his desk. An uneasy stillness held the room by a thread.

Rabid anger fueled Edjer. The thought of Asiya's exile bore deep within him. A dark conclusion came plagued his mind. *She must be the prisoner.*

Edjer laid his head against the blackened walls, finding a brisk chill against his ear. The position was unfavorable, and the outcome was all but conclusive for the warrior.

Yet, his heart refused reason.

Edjer arose from the fruitless chambers. The inability to act terrified him. Requirements of the heart demanded a stand be made.

"Where do you go?" asked Umid.

Edjer left without a reply. Most soldiers were hundreds of miles away, disembarking from the previous battle with the Far

East Empire. Debyendu had been sent home, and the soldiers remaining, of the Royal Guards, who could be trusted?

Niobe watched Edjer leave. She wished to speak to him, but no words could calm the fire in his heart.

Edjer strolled out of the castle determined. He needed his brothers, the Arms of the King.

Lethargic, Umid left his chambers to meet Niobe in the council room.

"Did he speak to you?"

"No... I saw his face. He will meet Semjaza in the fields. You must stop him."

"I am a man, first, Niobe. A man cannot control his own brother."

"They will die – Umid."

A breeze blew through the room.

"Leave him."

Umid clutched his face. His rough hands were surprised to find tears of his own mixed with his brother's.

"They would follow Edjer into his rage. Our sisters would follow him."

"We have solidified our position, Niobe. As you said, we no longer have brothers and sisters."

—

The Arms of the King had been instructed. They had been given the order to prepare for battle.

The reason had been withheld.

Khalil and Demetrius kept the truth hidden from the rest. Together, they faced the fire, leaning against the mantle as the soldiers readied. Along the wooden tables, the men amassed in full gear.

"Umid has created more enemies in his accords for peace," stressed Khalil.

"We need not divide so quickly, or we allow succession of our enemies' plots," replied Demetrius.

"They have won already." He paused, "Edjer will believe she is out there with them," said Khalil.

"It is safer to believe she no longer lives."

"Brother, don't be a fool."

Both eyed the fire, wondering, hoping. *Could she live?*

The doors swung open. Their general looked different. Pain overtook his onyx skin as the bags under his eyes swelled.

Edjer hid his shaking hands from the men. His soldiers needed confidence. They rose, ready for his orders.

It was a lonely walk to the fireplace. Edjer's mind raced.

Earlier, passing the dungeons along the way, the closer he had come to his men, the more bloodshed he had imagined.

"Be seated," murmured Edjer.

Khalil and Demetrius went silent.

"Have the men been told?" asked Edjer, avoiding a stalemate. Demetrius shook his head. "I do not know where I lead the men."

"Our brothers will fight."

Khalil intruded, "If our brothers go, our sisters will follow."

Clarity came to Edjer.

"They must remain here. I worry Semjaza plans an invasion. We have only 400 Royal Guards in the Capital. Thousands still disembark from the Far East. Semjaza has the forces to storm the city before aid arrives."

Khalil's intrusion sparked their interest, "He will kill the boy if we bring others."

The boy. A son.

"We cannot allow them any more time," declared Demetrius.

"We risk the Capital, and the life of our kin if we go," retorted a calmed Khalil.

"Edjer, we cannot allow them to act with impunity?!"

"Leave him to think, Demetrius," said Khalil.

"Quiet!" ordered Edjer, loudly. His voice rang through the Compound like never before. His men turned towards him as Edjer looked to become one with the flames.

"We will meet them in the Desert," expressed Edjer.

His soldiers rose once again as he left the fire and looked to them. His words were clear, "Arm yourselves, on this day, we meet our enemies."

Khalil whispered to Demetrius after Edjer left, "Return to the castle. Deliver a message to Umid. He must see Edjer before we ride out."

"Why?"

"If we are to ride out today and live, Edjer will come for him. Umid must see him before we go..."

"You must not leave without me," stated Demetrius.

An embrace of the forearms, they tightly gripped one another in a solemn vow.

—

In the desert, the intrusion of men left the white sands stained. The sweat of impatient soldiers left a distinct sourness in the air. A fire roared above pits of rock and piles of broken branches.

Six hundred soldiers were scattered in dunes and pits. They struggled to hold their own sanity amid confusion. Memorandums had been shared regarding the next steps. A battle was to ensue with Perfugans, but rumors spread amongst the camp. It became known they were to battle the Arms of the King. Terror struck the men, even as they outnumbered the soldiers nearly ten to one.

The Prince of Death instilled the deepest of doubt in the warriors. Rumors foretold *The Children* fought with carnivorous desire for blood.

There lie few unafraid, seeking vengeance for lost kin.

Protected by their bannermen, Lomotos and Semjaza sat with Liliah and Azazel.

They were enclosed by five tents, each one of their own, while the other was for the prisoners.

"We still do not have the last piece," stressed Azazel.

"Patience, the damage has been done," reassured Semjaza, "Knowledge divides."

Semjaza punished the White Desert with a strong grip. The shapeless particles meshed with his hands.

Steps deliberately dragged outside the tent enclosure. Semjaza tensely snickered before whispering, "Lomotos."

The giant rose. He drew his sword.

"Princes, we have what you seek," stated a soldier.

One of the kidnappers held a child over his shoulder. Gagged, and hooded, the boy relaxed as he was surrendered over to another.

"Bring the boy to the fire," ordered Semjaza.

Lomotos was careful, respecting the purity of a child. The boy did not move, nor did his gaze stray. The royals found his composure amusing.

"Begin prepping the soldiers, Lomotos." The large man smiled as he left.

Semjaza removed the hood and gag. He held out a bowl of food.

Isaias' eyes adjusted to the bright reflection from the sands. He was slow to accept the provisions, taking his time to investigate.

"Eat, boy, I do not wish to poison you," affirmed Semjaza.

Isaias ate, finishing quickly.

"I am afraid it is required," said Semjaza, handing Isaias back his hood.

He ushered Isaias into a tent and sat him across another hooded prisoner. He tightened Isaias' hands to a wooden post holding the tent up, dug deep into the sand.

The tent itself was spacious, able to hold many comfortably. Lamps were placed in the corners, lighting the space. Inside, voices of the outer world were aberrant whispers at best.

Semjaza checked the locket he tied to Isaias' feet to disable any mobility. Once doing so, he fixed his posture and rose to a full standing position. The declaration Edjer had made to him became clear. *Your own cruelty is not known until the opportunity to do so is at your hand.*

Semjaza surveyed Asiya's locket before he removed both their hoods. He left before their eyes adjusted.

Isaias' eyes did not require maintenance like his mother's. His rushed meal with the royals had realigned his senses. Asiya, her repetitive blinking subdued her ability to stay attentive. Finally acclimating, she stopped moving once she caught sight of the child. A lamp near the boy illuminated his features.

Her examination of Isaias was sharp, done in an animalistic fashion, where her movements mirrored his. The hue of his large eyes, his wide shoulders, Isaias mirrored even the shape of her lover's face. *A copy, he has his loose skin, under the neck,* thought Asiya. She bit her tongue; an emotional outburst would bring initial horror to the foreign child. Asiya watched as Isaias' mind raced towards a calculation of his own. He looked at her and repelled the familiarity at first. His dreams, she was the one he had seen.

A son returned to his mother.

Asiya held her composure as best she could. Her eyes widened. Freedom was theirs for a moment, even as shackles restricted movement. She knew it was unnecessary to burden a child with her identity.

Her tears fell softly in the sand.

Bonds and shackles had always been unable to distort the time they had spent together in captivity before his birth. Isaias, eyeing her, wished to catch the tears of his mother, remembering his dreams in the fields. All his prior visions seemed to make sense in the chaos he had been thrusted into.

"Isaias?" whispered Asiya. He smiled.

"And you?" wondered the boy, holding all his questions at the tip of his tongue.

"Asiya." An unbelievable fear set in as she introduced herself to him.

"The one who tends and heals the weak."

She wished to match her son's confidence. Asiya admired his strength, the power of his awareness, but she could not match it. She was glad he could not remember the time they had spent suffering as she did.

Asiya looked at him, bewildered, wondering about the lost years after hearing him speak, what dreams he had dreamt, what time he had enjoyed.

"Who teaches you these words?"

"Headmistress Manissa."

She took a beat to smile, "A good... a good ... woman. There is power in a good mother."

"You know of Manissa?'

Meekly, the chains on her hands rattled as she brought her sleeve up. The boy could see under the shifty light, the purple flower, *Strobilanthes Dyeriana.*

"Children of nature do not veer too far..." Asiya smiled as her hands moved.

"For the mother of elements keeps a watchful eye over her kin," replied Isaias, slowly, finishing his mother's words.

FORTY-ONE

21 days since the Ceremony began.

"Where is he?!" demanded Niobe.

She came bare, without guards of her own, only Demetrius trailing her. Within hours, Perfuga's reckoning would begin.

"Quiet! He sits in the kitchens," replied Khalil.

Niobe was surprised to see her brothers eating, with a few others reading, and many asleep in the common halls. Her voice was a despised intrusion to their tranquility.

"Take me to Edjer," begged Niobe. She was powerless in the Compound.

"Demetrius, you were told to bring Umid."

"Umid is broken. I asked Jabez to plead to him and he refused."

"A King does not appear before his subjects," echoed Niobe.

"Do the games you play have no end?! You see what has been done? That child is as much our inheritance, *our* inheritance, as it is Edjer's," replied Demetrius.

"You are no queen here. Death would be yours if not the fact you are kin," shared Khalil.

"I will find the kitchens myself."

"Niobe—" began Demetrius, grabbing her hand. His grip was extraordinary. She recognized his challenge in the eyes. Demetrius, like the rest of the men, were prepared for battle.

"I will take her to him. Enough violence will be had today," surrendered Khalil.

A single candle burned in the kitchen. A plate of rice and dead game were untouched near the flame. Ale sat in a wooden mug, not a drop drunk. He was nowhere in sight.

"Where is he?"

The enclosed room was suffocating. Khalil looked through the hollow kitchen walkways. The mahogany cupboards and cabinets were open, as if a search had been conducted. Niobe stayed near his meal, leaning against the central table of the kitchens. The door swung open whilst Niobe inspected his dinner.

"You antagonize the men."

Niobe turned to Edjer, afraid for the first time since she had met him as a boy. She found his garments menacing on the day, the clear white, and the lone sword in the middle. The golden outlines against the brim of his clothes shimmered near the single flame.

"You send Demetrius to summon Umid?"

Edjer ignored her. He began his meal as Khalil walked out. They did not acknowledge one another.

"Do his bidding," commanded Edjer.

"He wishes you to wait for the soldiers retreating from the Far East. They will reach the Capital within days," She pleaded further, "You know not what awaits. Their preparation should force you to reconsider."

Edjer indulged in his ale. The prized contraband was from their homelands, for he and Asiya in their old meetings of secret.

"Does he have an order?" asked Edjer.

Defeat sieged Niobe. Umid dared not order Edjer in the face of his mistakes. He had warned Niobe against it. The Prince of Death was on a path of vengeance, and Umid wished to steer away from his wrath.

"No."

"He would benefit from our deaths. You know this... he knows this..." He paused before speaking sincerely, "I am within reach, Niobe, and I must act."

"He does not wish for your end. None do," she whispered.

"The damage is done."

Niobe walked to the kitchen door. The White Desert awaited. She hesitated before pushing the door.

"You believe her alive?" inquired Niobe, curious.

Silence.

"Her survival would only worsen the predicament," said Edjer, stern. His emotionless response triggered her departure.

He could only wish.

Khalil entered within seconds.

"You were right to take my weapon. I would have killed him," shared Edjer. He did not watch as Khalil softened, liberated from a bit of guilt.

"Are the men ready?" asked Edjer. Khalil nodded in approval.

"Eat with me," suggested Edjer, handing him a spoon. They ate from the same plate, as brothers of old.

"Do you deem me in the wrong?" wondered the Prince of Death.

"There is no action you can take in error. You can act as a soldier or a father."

Edjer abandoned pride for a moment. He was unafraid of vulnerability with Khalil.

"Self-interest is a commoner's route," said Edjer.

"What kings and soldiers have ever fought for more than self-interest?"

"What would you have me do?" begged Edjer.

"Be the man you wish to be. The soldier or the father."

"And what will you do?"

"I will follow wherever you go. A child of yours is a child of mine. Love does not discriminate."

Love does not discriminate.

He wished it did. Edjer was both a soldier and father.

FORTY-TWO

The 21st day.

Edjer watched his soldiers prepare. He stood at the threshold of the compound doors, behind the bookshelves. On the opposite side of the open doorway, Demetrius matched his brother's stance. He leaned against the open doors and together, both looked upon the men.

"Should we pray?"

"What God has watched for us, Demetrius?"

Edjer could not move his attention away from Tafari, the only one kneeling among them, searching for a God in the confusing times.

"What judge deems this path clear?"

Demetrius snickered before he spoke, "You are harsh. We have not been deprived of resources in some time, brother. We have been royals sitting in halls and chambers, refreshments provided by servants, food made from choice game. Let him be."

Edjer was cold: "Do you remember what Jabez taught us?"

Demetrius referenced one of Jabez's drunk lessons: "The night before battle, it is best to spend it with a praying man." Demetrius continued, "For it will be his last, for what Judge he believes in will honor him with a quick death. The aftermath of war is hell in itself."

Edjer's eyes could not avoid Tafari. As if he heard their words, Tafari resigned from prayer.

"The righteous soldier prays. A warrior cannot serve two masters," said Edjer.

"A warrior cannot," uttered Demetrius.

—

"The Prince of Death embarks," announced Semjaza.

Semjaza placed a scroll in his garments.

Lomotos smiled at the beginning of the end. He left to prepare his soldiers for the ensuing conclusion.

"It is time for you to return home, brother," suggested Semjaza to King Azazel.

Azazel rose and embraced Semjaza. The restoration of a proud land was near its full return. The embrace between brothers lasted an eternity. It was overwhelming for both, to be so close to retribution.

"Share my regards with Lomotos. He rushes to war."

"Our brother is eager. We will have our liberation."

A detachment of soldiers waited to take Azazel back home.

"You will end them. Be not afraid," uttered Azazel. He spoke from the top of a dune.

"I know of my task."

The Bear numbers were astronomically higher than the Arms of the King, and yet, the odds terrified Semjaza. Edjer would be no easy feat. Azazel's departure heightened the nerves of their men. Soldiers watched the king leave as their armor found their bare bodies. Reality shifted anxiety to fear.

Liliah walked to Semjaza. His glare froze on the tent holding mother and child prisoner: "It is us who must ask if you are prepared." Liliah was sharp in her critique. The plot dictated it be his hand. He had promised to deliver.

"I know no cruelty," believed Semjaza. The thoughts ran faster than the stumbling words.

"Only a cruel man could adopt such a plot, Semjaza. If you wish for liberation, it is the crude man within you that demands freedom most, before your kingdom finds its own."

"Summon Lomotos," ordered Semjaza. He removed a key from his pouch.

Liliah left him as Semjaza entered the tent alone.

Asiya's helpless scream nearly deafened him. Semjaza's hand shook as he gagged Asiya, ending her rabidness. She trembled, wishing to keep Isaias as long as possible. Her chains rattled with muffled yelling coming from her covered mouth.

Freshly healed flesh on her wrists ripped as she tussled, smudging the mark of her flower.

The boy was first. Like before, Isaias surrendered to those who controlled him. Semjaza ached to the horror of his actions. Plots and ideas were easy, but the execution, deviance was critical. He could not look at Asiya as she begged for a chance to be heard. Her broken composure frightened him.

Overthinking, Semjaza mismanaged Isaias. He got loose. A terrifying ache of worry took Semjaza as the boy ran towards the opening of the tent. Too close to the end, the open desert would prove impossible to find a little boy.

Lomotos barged in at the right moment after hearing the commotion. He was able to swoop Isaias from his feet, admiring the fight within: "I would have done the same, boy."

Asiya lost the life within her. She was freed from her chains, but Semjaza learned from his mistakes. Agonizing over his principles would leave him in failure. His words were cutthroat as he spoke to Asiya, "Do not fret like a child. Lomotos could rip him in two."

She submitted to his control.

"The soldiers, Lomotos?"

"The legion is ready."

"Let us meet your father, boy. He comes for you and your mother," teased Semjaza.

Asiya could not face Isaias. The reveal of his mother shocked the boy. He looked at her with innocent eyes. Isaias began to wonder who would come for him; what man would be brave enough to face hundreds of soldiers holding him captive.

—

Horses slowed the closer they encroached upon a hilly dune. Silence in the empty desert was menacing. He had to keep going. The horses' hooves dug deeper into the sand, alarming him that further steps atop the beasts would prove fatal.

Edjer ordered his men to disembark. Their encroachment would be on foot.

In the stillness, the soaring sunlight was an enemy to all. The Arms of the King caught sight of smoke from a large fire beyond the dune they were to climb. The sound of blazing flames could be heard, but not yet seen. Edjer knew the signal was for the Arms of the King. Before they could reach the smoke, the men faced a terrifying spectacle, a stagnant wave of clear, pure sand.

They moved forward.

Ants on an endless field, Edjer and his men climbed on all fours atop the vast dune. Edjer led, with Demetrius and Khalil at his side. The climb was brutal in its repulsion. As they penetrated the sand, they all wondered about the tamers of the flame on the other side.

Edjer finished the climb first. He did not let the anticipation take him from the duty of helping his men up. The patient pace of his brothers alerted him to the thought, *they have no clue as to what they fight for.*

The prepared baptism by fire was not the only thing meant to captivate the Arms of the King.

Across open, flat sands, Bear soldiers awaited them to finish their ascent to the battlefield. In the open terrain between the two sides, a large fire raged. Edjer's men faced over six hundred soldiers aligned atop another frozen dune of sand. The Bear Kingdom lined their soldiers side by side, astounding Edjer, and the rest of the Arms, believing within a second, their enemies would charge, and completely encircle their detachment of no more than twenty.

"Edjer…" voiced Demetrius, astonished.

Piles of stones and branches fed a fire nearly the height of two men. Its width was like that of an array of carriages, blazing in the wild sand, as the smoke flew to the sky. Perfugan flags fed the fire in the interior.

Behind the fire, emerged the objective.

Seeing the Perfugans, Semjaza appeared from behind the holistic flames. His hands grabbed the shoulders of a tearful Asiya. Next to him, Lomotos followed, his dagger firmly against Isaias' neck. They continued to walk forward to provide Edjer ample view of the stakes. Semjaza and Lomotos were careful to maintain their space, equidistant from their troops on the rear and to Edjer's men in front of them.

They dared Edjer in the sight of infinite incapability.

"Edjer," whispered Demetrius. His head lowered seeing his sister, once thought dead. All her kin were shocked to see her breathing.

Edjer, his view was split. He knew not where to place his gaze. Asiya herself weakened at the sight of him.

The love had never died.

His son witnessed the greatness of the warrior in a glimpse. The father he could only wish for, Isaias was bewildered with honor. He slowly motioned his gaze to his mother, the flower, then to his father, proud. A boy beyond his years, a smile wished to creep out at the surprise, as he watched Edjer step forward to see him more clearly. Enduring endless pain, his mother and father had returned to him.

"He will not come," said Lomotos, keeping a monotonous tone.

"Be patient," replied Semjaza.

Hundreds of Bear soldiers watched, afraid.

The Arms of the King awaited their orders, prepared for death. *The Children,* the odds did not matter to them. Asiya was alive.

"Edjer, not yet," warned Khalil, "You cannot."

Prince Edjer ignored Khalil. His feet shifted. The heart reigned over the body. The eyes of lovers were a powerful thing.

Semjaza stared at Edjer, baiting him.

His name, thought Semjaza, "Say his name."

Asiya refused. It would mean the end.

"Say his name!" yelled Semjaza. He jerked her forward, triggering a flinch in Edjer.

"Edjer, you cannot!" alerted Demetrius. He stepped closer with Edjer, as did Khalil. Their brothers followed.

"Edjer," whispered Khalil. The Prince's eyes fell onto his son. His beautiful son.

Asiya turned to the child as well.

"The boy ... Boy, say his name!!" roared Semjaza.

Lomotos pushed Isaias forward, "Speak to him, boy!"

Isaias stammered. His mind was scattered for a moment. His eyes then locked with his father's. Gratification was his already.

"Amir Almawt," said Isaias, under his breath.

"Louder, child!" screamed Semjaza.

"Amir Almawt!!" yelled Isaias, *"Fi almawt satajudini!!"* His words echoed to his father, to *The Children,* to those aware of the language, Harabic.

The Arms of the King all drew their swords in solidarity. Edjer, Khalil, and Demetrius kept theirs sheathed.

"Edjer," said Khalil, "The boy pleads to his father."

Edjer stopped, his eyes began to shed tears for his family. The words of his son spoke to the power of the lineage he and Asiya had produced. There was no pause, no hesitation.

"He is my son!" screamed Edjer, beating his chest, "He is my child!"

The Arms of the King stood together. They stepped forward.

Asiya moved forward as well, surprising Semjaza. The boy, Isaias Bilal, had spoken.

"Heed your son's words!" begged Asiya. Semjaza pulled her back, confused.

Edjer locked eyes with her. In a look, she begged him to hold. His head lowered in shame, anticipating the future he knew. There was no survival to be had.

Edjer turned to his men. He looked at the faces of his brothers. His heart sank. He finally spoke, "Go, your orders are anew." He wiped the tears from his face.

"Return to the Capital. Hold the walls if they approach. You must hold until the rest of the army returns. It is an order," said Edjer. Their hesitation pestered at his thoughts, "Go!"

His brothers, *The Children*, looked at one another, knowing what it would cost. Their feet did not move.

A boy became man as Tafari himself could not move.

"This is not a mistake you must pay for. This was a fate spoken long before you. No one will mourn for us. Return!"

The faces of his kin: the Nation-States, Africans, their gaze held strong against the telling air. Among them: Arabians, Northern and Far East refugees who met him decades ago in a treacherous time. Their feet did not shuffle to his orders. Demetrius, and Khalil, the two would not leave a brother in suffering. It was not only his kin in enemy hands.

"Boy, what did you say to him?!" shouted Semjaza. His composure withered.

"Semjaza, he will not come." Lomotos prepared for a fight.

Edjer would not. His fate was chosen to end in the sands. But Tafari, Edjer looked upon the newcomer, finding a travesty he could correct.

"Tafari, you will not be witness to the deeds of the dead today," ordered Edjer, meeting him in front of the men.

"I will fight with you. She was a mother to me," replied Tafari confidently.

"You will not. Look around. No — What is done to you is reparable. Return, now!" said Edjer, preparing for death.

"General?"

"Now," sternly replied Edjer, "Go to my sisters. Tell them what you have seen. You were meant to be better than me."

Tafari froze, looking at his general's ravenous eyes. "I see a man without flaw..." Tafari turned and ran down to the horses. He raced towards the Concubines.

"You mustn't follow me into this," announced Edjer, returning to the vanguard, eyeing the flattened sands below their dune.

"I will not leave," declared Demetrius.

Semjaza watched them stall, curious. Seconds passed, precious time. Lomotos knelt, and looked into the boy's eyes, "What did you say to him, boy?!"

Asiya took pleasure in her confession, "He has the confidence of his father."

"What did he say?" asked Lomotos, afraid, "The prince refuses confrontation."

She helplessly snickered, "He prepares ..."

"Witch, what did he say to him!?" Semjaza was at his end.

Asiya smiled at her pupil. Asiya and Isaias locked eyes in solidarity as she spoke: *"Prince of Death, in death you will find me."*

Edjer feared the aftermath of the discussion between Semjaza and Asiya. He wished to face it all alone.

"Khalil, you need not stay."

"And what would our sisters say?" said Khalil, his head held straight, facing Asiya. In the middle of the sands, the spectacle reminded him of his paintings.

"The plan does not change," hammered Lomotos.

Semjaza was visibly struck at the powerful words of a child. Would the children of the Bear speak with such veracity? He hoped, deeply, that the sacrifices made would bring about such citizens.

Semjaza pressed his knife against Asiya's neck, desiring one last charge of impatience from Edjer. The Prince of Death, unmoving, had been given orders from his son.

Semjaza hesitated. Lomotos screamed his name, "Semjaza! Now!"

Semjaza spoke to Asiya before he acted, "I will keep my promise. One will live." He was the first to slash, slicing the soft flesh of her neck. Her body fell instantly.

Lomotos, content, whispered to Isaias, "You are a brave boy." His dagger was smaller, slower. He dragged his hand across the boy's neck until Isaias fell within arm's distance of his mother.

They, together, returned to the earth, staining the floor beds with sparkling pools of the soul's fuel.

The heart of a warrior melted, as he watched. *The Children* gritted their teeth, preparing. In one accord, the endless Bear soldiers atop the dune began their massive descent into the sands. It would take time, but they would reach Edjer. The Arms of the King could only watch as their sister and child bled out beneath them.

Edjer remained on his feet, struck with a shifting terror. Grief was held at bay as the Prince of Death awaited the demise capable of returning him to his family.

"You would follow me in this?" asked Edjer, to his brothers.

Khalil and Demetrius finally unsheathed their swords, plunging their weapons deep into the sand. The others followed. Their hands remained on the grip, signaling to Edjer none would leave him in this fight. They would not leave him alone in the journey to the next life.

"Fi almawt satajudini," whispered his brothers.

Edjer finally unsheathed his sword.

FORTY-THREE

A Day of Retribution.

Friction slowed the flow to the puddles. Against purity, the red rage triumphed.

On his knees, a stained Edjer froze, surrounded. Mountains of men encircled the physical barrier his brothers had casted for him. His carnal breathing eased into routine form. The face of the Prince of Death was painted with the adhesive blood of friends and foes. Piles of bodies stacked around him, unmoving, with few hanging onto their final breaths. Their chests faintly rose to their airflow's cadence in the last moments of their lives.

Hands, limbs, scattered were the deviants of war whose lives were lost. The deaths of hundreds of men painted a human picture on a Godlike canvas.

Edjer's knees pressed deep into the powdery sand particles. His brothers had all perished in his name. It was a decisive loss, and yet Edjer had not expected his survival. The lives of each of his brothers had been taken, as they fought to their end. The Arms of the King had lived up to their expectations. The stories told would be endless. Of the six hundred men, Edjer and his fourteen brothers had taken the lives of nearly two hundred Bear soldiers.

Beside him, Demetrius and Khalil lay dead, hands on their swords.

Still, Edjer was a slave to hundreds of eyes. The Bear soldiers were terrified as he remained unmoving, prostrated up by the holistic, reddened sands.

Edjer was of an empty mind whilst the sun shone directly on him. Not even a scratch, the Prince of Death took no satisfaction in survival. Facing death, he wiped his face, finding a mix of perspiration and blood.

Around him, he saw as soldiers began to lift his men first and burn them in the fire. Then, the Bear casualties. The blood would be left for nature. Millions would tell the story of how the desert found its reddish hue within a fortnight.

Two soldiers began to execute the orders of their royals, guiding men for the last attempt to take Edjer alive.

Edjer capitulated to the first touch. He became vacant flesh at a realization. He would never hold his son in his arms.

—

A detachment of Royal Guards was arm in arm in defensive positions. In the distance, enemies holding the universal emblem of neutrality walked with a shackled prisoner.

The Prince of Death returned home.

The shackles placed on the hands and feet of the unengaged prisoner brought a cacophony of noise. Behind Edjer, a trail of blood followed, that of his brothers.

The streets were cleared in fear of a battle. Umid had put a weapon in the hand of all the capable men in the Capital. But they became surveyors of Edjer's submission. All watched as the feared man was dragged.

He marked the floors of the palace as he entered. The Bear soldiers held his weight. Their orders were plain: return him to his brother Umid. They would kill Edjer if he could not be safely delivered.

Royal Guards, swords drawn, followed the men up the stairs, through the dimmed hallways of the palace. Upon reaching the Inner Council room, a terrifying obstacle presented itself. the soldiers found reason for concern. The Concubines had their own weapons drawn, attempting to get inside the Inner Council Room.

Edjer kept sight of the ground he stained. Amongst his sisters, Tafari called out to Edjer once he saw him.

"General?!"

He did not flinch. *Would they resent me if I keep them waiting?*

"General…" whispered Tafari, terrified of the man he faced.

"Edjer," screamed one of his sisters, near the back. They all quickly turned. "Edjer!" Manissa raced towards him before Tafari withheld her from the soldiers, "Edjer! I did not know he was yours! Edjer! Let me go!"

Manissa shuddered, finally seeing her brother. The color had turned on the blood. The aesthetic created a disagreeable sight. Truth did not elude her. Her cries sank into the heart of the palace as she knew: Asiya would not return, nor would the boy she had raised from infancy. Manissa slowly crumbled as a sharp pain took her intestines, agonizing in horror.

Her sisters made a path. They were just told who the child had been by Tafari.

The Bear soldiers found the Inner Council congregated in fright. Jabez turned mute at the sight of Edjer.

Niobe knew the reckoning awaiting Perfuga once seeing her brother showered in earth and blood.

Umid stood as Edjer was paraded in. He was speechless standing still until Myawi finished dealing with the soldiers. A mix of curiosity and devastation befell Umid.

The Bear soldiers smiled, placing a scroll in Edjer's hand before leaving. Silence shrouded the room. Speaking was difficult in sight of the insentient Edjer.

"Ed—Edjer," said Umid, stuttering.

Nothing. Umid moved closer to his brother. The sound of Edjer's hands shaking against his chains was deafening. The shock was still strong.

"Edjer, what has happened?" inquired Umid, shaken at his own ability to speak. He moved in, "Come towards me, brother."

Edjer shot a glance upwards to Umid at the word, *brother*. The chains shifted from the twitch.

As if Niobe knew, she quickly darted towards Edjer.

The Prince of Death successfully took his first, but the second step, he underestimated his weight. Edjer struggled to walk on his own, his knees crumbling as if bread in milk.

Niobe caught him before the fall, marking her own black garments with the flesh of her brethren. She held onto Edjer until they followed each other down to their knees, in sight of the whole council.

"I—I did…" struggled Edjer.

"What happened?" Niobe took the scroll from Edjer's hands and placed it on the table. She did not care for it. But Umid came from the opposite side to read the message.

Edjer spaced off into the distance with his eyes. Memories. Dreams. Distortions came to him.

"Edjer! Speak to me, please, what has happened?" Fear seeped into Niobe as tears fell from her eyes. Her voice shook.

Edjer inhaled, then exhaled, a deep transaction through his nose. At its end, he turned to Niobe, eyeing her down. His pupils were wide, dilated.

"Dead—None live…" his whispers rang.

"Where are Khalil, Khalil, and Demetrius? Where are they?!"

"All dead," calmly answered Edjer. Niobe winced in pain.

Jabez sunk his face into the cement table.

Umid could not believe it. He would never be privy to the full account of the Day of Death.

Niobe remained on his knees for one last question; a desperate question she needed an answer to.

"Edjer, look at me, the boy, your son Isaias, does he live? Asiya, do they still live?"

"None...lives," Edjer doubled down.

Niobe's head lowered in defeat.

Umid was mortified by the satisfaction he had found in those words. A silence took the room before Umid spoke up, surprising even Niobe, "Myawi will take you to wash. We will discuss the matter later."

"Umid," whispered Niobe. She did not mean to speak low. Her voice was taken by remorse.

"Myawi, take him," ordered Umid.

"I would ha—," started Edjer. Panic struck the room.

Edjer remained on his knees: "He was... proud," recounting the moment Isaias realized the Prince of Death was his father.

None of the others understood.

"Myawi, help him," ordered Umid.

As they made for the doors, Umid and Niobe began to discuss.

"What of the Bear?" asked Niobe, clearing her eyes.

"Demand. Ones we must comply with." He handed her the scroll.

"Why must we comply?" asked Niobe in protest.

"'The heads of the heir and the true queen will be paraded through the Perfugan streets if you do not comply'," whispered Umid.

Edjer grimaced, hearing his brother's words.

Niobe read the message, before looking up helplessly towards Umid. Umid instead shifted his gaze towards Edjer struggling to walk out of the room.

Edjer found Tomias in the hallways, mourning with his sisters. The doors to the Inner Council shut behind him.

Unity in empathy, the women were all voiceless.

Manissa stormed from the group, drawing her weapon. She aimed straight for the council room: "They shall not live a moment longer."

Edjer's chains rattled as his meek hands grabbed Manissa's. He looked at her in silence for a moment. His grip was strong. She saw his sad eyes flutter before he spoke: "Their time has not come yet…"

Manissa retreated, slowly sheathing her weapon. All were shocked by his declaration. *Yet.*

"He's still in chains," uttered the boy who became man.

Tafari took Edjer from Myawi's hands and slowly escorted him out.

The Children, what remained, tracked Edjer with their eyes. He had been, and always would be, the Pride of the Nameless Nation in which they had been birthed as one.

A people of their own, born from one struggle.

FORTY-FOUR

28 days since the Ceremony began.

The strut of an enemy is most menacing when their steps echo in your halls.

Behind Liliah, two Bear soldiers followed. The Perfugan palace was distinctly silent.

Liliah faced the mountain of stairs with confidence. She walked freely with awareness she was beginning a noble chapter to the Bear histories.

Semjaza had desired a graceful period in which Liliah would appear to Perfuga in the name of politics. It was the final stroke of his plot.

Niobe awaited her in the council room. The doors were held open by the Royal Guards as Liliah detached from her soldiers.

Niobe stood in her presence.

Liliah's dress slithered as her steps clicked in stride towards Niobe. The chord of her tune irritated Niobe.

"Please, be seated," said Niobe.

"I hear of dead princes, my condolences."

Niobe tightened before releasing a plagiarized smile, "Thank you. The King sends apologies for his absence."

"He must mourn his Uncle," suggested Liliah. Demetrius' death had fed into the parasitical grief long plaguing Jabez. Death was on his own account. He could not mourn two sons.

"He will return to politics soon."

"Crowns can withhold you from matters of family," Liliah paused, adjusting to her seat, "It was said his Uncle was tormented by death."

Niobe did not budge.

"You called this meeting today. Do what you must."

"Loss does not feel its welcome in Perfuga. I come to only secure our demands."

"We wish to discuss one piece." Niobe found herself begging in a royal tone.

Liliah maintained a demeaning laugh across the table.

"*My dear,* this is not a negotiation."

"Then why a meeting?"

"A declaration," began Liliah, "Do not assume, in the coming times, Perfuga will see the days of its old triumph return. We force your brother's banishment. The people will follow their Prince of Death. The strongest of them will leave you. They whisper now in your brothels. 'The protector has left.' Many imagine the reasons stem from the royals they despise."

Liliah wielded the might of her position. "You cannot wish for anything. The time of a boastful Perfuga meets its end. I am here to solidify what is agreed." Liliah paused. "The Prince of Death receives his banishment well, I hear. It is said he takes up his days, alone, in the fields. He makes his way to your enemies. I am happy to hear a home will be found for the mourning prince. All your princes leave you," teased Liliah.

Niobe listened closely. She knew not of Edjer's whereabouts. He had evaded the spies trailing him.

"My dear, Semjaza warned me you would wish to see your borders remain open."

"The King is prepared to offer—"

"The Bear desires nothing!" stated Liliah, cutting Niobe off. Her voice carried to those in the halls, to Umid hiding in his chambers.

She continued, "We desire a return to balance. You steal our citizens in the name of innocence and believe no retribution is to be had?! You complied with easy requests, now you will continue. Your borders will close. The foolish debts you hold over us all will be forgiven in full. We take the westernmost walled city from you in payment for the calamity suffered in your control.

"The city profits will be divided amongst those you sought payment. The Bear are not a cruel people. What desire you may have to rebel, remember, the Prince of Death still lives. His words hold power, and the bodies of his child and lover remain in our grasp. Your people love their beloved prince. They will demand the death of their queen and king if the truth we guard in your name is revealed."

Will and spirit had broken amongst *The Children* as Tomias and the Concubines reeled from tragedy. They, too, had left the Capital.

Politicians and Senators had heard the truth through Alcaeus. Everything was falling apart. Closed borders, with debts forgiven in full, would put Perfuga's future at risk.

"Do the Perfugans agree?" asked Liliah.

"We give what you ask. The terms must be agreed to end here."

"They shall ... We will await what is to come at the hands of your people," warned Liliah.

"The people will act as their King instructs."

Liliah returned to her laughs: "You may speak plainly. Your King will either become frail or a king ruling with terror. Either direction will provide the result we desire. We know why he wishes not to show his face."

Umid held a blank look in his chambers. He sat on a stool, facing the door in patience.

"They will obey."

Liliah's chuckles transformed into a sly smile, "You foolish woman."

Niobe had had enough. She rose calmly and poured herself wine.

"You and your kin are foolish," said Niobe. She cleaned her posture, strengthening: "No matter who you think you will be, you are the one who killed a child, its mother, our brothers. You believe you killed the strongest of us?" Niobe began to laugh. "My sisters will seek their own blood account. Edjer may kill me, but he will rip your insides while you still live. You have yet to see the animal truly inside of him.

"Be aware of what you have taken. You believe yourself a devil disciplining a demon. You have yet to face a demon, *my dear*."

The chill of the day made its presence known in the flameless room.

Astonishment forced Liliah's departure, beginning to think of the Prince of Death's retribution.

FORTY-FIVE

68 days since the Ceremony began.

"It is a day of celebration for your people."

The subtle tease did not move Edjer. He sat amongst a king and a prince, in the bland dining halls of the Far East Empire.

"Umid announces he will adopt from your school on the day mourning ends for your Uncle."

Debyendu desired recognition, a response from Edjer. Fires burned, and candles brightened the black tables. In the hall, red banners with tiger sigils hung shrouding the dim room.

Messages had come in recent days from the Bear. Debts were forgotten and forgiven. Profits from the walled city would be shared amongst all kingdoms, as promised. Umid's ceremony had succeeded in accomplishing its purpose, bringing a desired peace. However, the goal had come at a greater cost for Perfuga than anticipated.

But Edjer did not care for politics. He only desired a boy's face in the bliss of the afterlife. *Would she find us there?* The food he ate turned bland amid the prisonous times befalling him.

Debyendu had pounced on the opportunity to give Edjer renewed life. He had delivered a simple letter to the banished Prince. *We would accept you.*

Edjer had nowhere else to go.

"You must have words. Grief will not find itself a leaving guest if you do not dismiss it."

"Leave him be," ordered King Akshat.

Solitude was logical for any man who had lost a son and lover. His own kin were unable to comfort this pain.

With the death of their brothers, *The Children* were lost. The finality of Asiya and Isaias had shut the prospect of life for all of them.

Edjer was now alone amongst old enemies hoping to utilize his talents.

"My sisters," whispered Edjer, "What is said?"

Debyendu's eyes lit up.

"They scatter. They follow your sister Manissa south. The scribe has taken up with them."

Terrifying times lay ahead as news of Edjer's entrance into the Far East Empire had reached Umid days prior. King Akshat had promised Edjer full citizenship, along with any rank or title he desired. He had not yet agreed.

"You wish to go to them?" asked Debyendu.

"No," retorted Edjer.

Anger had festered and colonized his dormant rage. Despite this rage, many had hoped for his status as a nomad to be at an end.

"What is your desire?" inquired Debyendu.

"Leave him be," ordered Akshat again. A stubbornness lay in King Akshat's words. Distrust was evident between Akshat and Debyendu, as the king had berated his brother for his intrusion in Semjaza's plot. Debyendu's desire for Edjer's loyalty nearly cost them profits from the walled city and an end to debts.

Edjer looked up at both men: "I resist the temptation to covet, Debyendu."

"It is our reason to live. The commoner lusts of flesh and we, the sway of commoners."

"I did not seek such things. I did not…" repeated Edjer.

"Each man seeks. We are much too tempted to avoid desire. An animal cannot resist," suggested Debyendu.

"Trouble lies in false satisfaction. A sensical dream realized is a failure itself." The Prince of Death's words rung true.

"Pessimism does not suit you."

"I have lived a life many wish to live. Your guards fear me as you do for the inconsistency of my desires."

King Akshat chuckled. Debyendu enjoyed the engagement, but Edjer's wit was terrifying, even in grief. The shell of a man remained impenetrable.

"You did not desire a son and wife?" poked Debyendu, casting a flame beneath his guest.

"A wife, at some point. But a dream realized, Debyendu, you cannot ever know who I may have become. I must settle for what I am given."

They stopped and ate in silence.

Then, Edjer looked at Debyendu. "Prince Debyendu, do not interfere."

"What…" Debyendu froze, unaware of what Edjer spoke of.

Edjer turned towards King Akshat: "King Akshat, answer truthfully. How long have you known of the existence of my son?"

King Akshat looked up at Edjer with confidence: "The Bear approached me two years ago."

"Edjer?" interrupted Debyendu.

"You disagreed with their methods?" asked Edjer, ignoring him.

"I did."

"Yet, you were paid for your silence?"

"I was returned the remains of my sister, along with promises to reap the benefits. A mercy in the eyes of the Bear," retorted King Akshat.

"What is this?" screamed Debyendu. "Guards!"

"They will not come… I have told you not to interfere…" replied Edjer.

"Why?" asked Debyendu, a question with too many layers for Edjer to answer.

He was without a kingdom, like he had been right before he first entered Perfuga. Yet, Edjer remained a Prince, entitled to Death, entitled to the blood of enemies.

"A man's child is beyond politics. The existence of his lover is beyond politics. My brothers were burned without their final rites. A line was crossed, Debyendu," declared Edjer.

"Mm," agreed the king.

Debyendu helplessly looked at Akshat before he arose with his dinner knife. From underneath his clothes, Edjer brought out the weapon, his inheritance from his people, the dagger he had stolen back from Niobe before he left.

Debyendu attempted to strike, but Edjer, in one clean slice, took his hand. Debyendu screamed in agony.

"Do not interfere, you are innocent of this."

Attempting to protect his own kin, Debyendu dove for his knife again. This time, Edjer rose and struck Debyendu, bringing the knife up along his whole spine with no remorse. Life left Debyendu immediately.

Edjer was indifferent watching Debyendu die in front of him. After a moment, he turned back to Akshat.

The king was still as a mouse, tears falling from his face, before he spoke: "Achieving your desire is like paradise. It is completed over and over in dreams, yet it is impeded upon in nightmares. The paradise you and I seek is a life beyond necessity. A commoner dreams of obedient whores, and kings, obedient commoners. But you and I, we seek those awaiting in the afterlife."

"There is no paradise to be found on this earth beyond necessity," declared Edjer, agreeing with the king.

"I knew you would come for us the moment Semjaza spoke your name...I know of your pain. Please – forgive me."

Edjer let the last tear for death fall: "Paradise was when my brothers looked out into a field of sand and saw a child of their own, not just mine. In the face of impossibility, existence. In death, you will find us together as one. It will be there I can forgive you."

That was enough for King Akshat. He closed his eyes, hearing Edjer rise and walk over to his seat.

Edjer wiped his knife before he sliced the king's neck. He waited patiently as life left Akshat. He demanded confirmation.

Outside, Tafari waited with the horses. His escape had been thought through. It was now Edjer's turn to plot.

Domination was for the kingdoms to seek, and many had thought the Prince of Death was a weapon to yield. Few had understood the man they dealt with. He now required balance.

As death had always been, Edjer was a patient man. This would be the first King of many to fall.

Prince Edjer will return...

About the Author

Daniel Mistir is a Master's Candidate, in his last year at the American Film Institute Conservatory in Los Angeles, studying Screenwriting. He is originally from Sacramento, California.

He graduated from the University of California-Davis, with a Bachelor of Science in Biomedical Engineering and a minor in African/African American Studies in 2022.

In Spring 2022, his senior year of college, he published his debut novel, *One's Posterity*. Before he returns to follow up *Pride of a Nameless Nation*, he will write his third novel, *Summer in New York*.

Made in the USA
Monee, IL
21 March 2025

14184513R00173